MY HIGHLAND ABDUCTION

SHELLEY MUNRO

MUNRO PRESS

My Highland Abduction

Print ISBN: 978-1-99-106395-3
Ebook ISBN: 978-1-99-106394-6

Cover: Kim Killion, The Killion Group, Inc.

Munro Press, New Zealand.

First Munro Press electronic publication December 2025
First Munro Press print publication December 2025

DEDICATION

For anyone who has ever felt like an outsider.

INTRODUCTION

She stole a mate. Now she'll fight for him.

Desperate and humiliated after a disastrous gathering leaves her unmated, Sienna Teague makes the worst decision of her life. She abducts a man.

Liam Brown wakes up in Cornwall with fragmented memories and a beautiful woman claiming to be his mate. Despite his confusion, he's drawn to this new life and the undeniable attraction between him and Sienna.

But before he can untangle the truth behind his head injury, Bodmin Beast hunters threaten their shifter community. When danger stalks their town, Sienna and Liam must fight as one. But the lie at the heart of their bond is a bigger threat than any beast, and when the truth comes out, it could tear them apart.

INTRODUCTION

CHAPTER 1

FAILURE HAD A DISTINCT acrid scent.

Sienna Teague inhaled it now, identifying with the misery clinging to the walls and polluting the air in Castle Glenkirk. With only three days until the end of the gathering, unmated shifters prowled the edges of the great hall with barely concealed panic—their desperation a reek only her kind would recognize.

Despite Sienna's initial high hopes, she understood the gnawing fear. Her jaw ached from clenching, yet she refused to blink away the sting in her eyes.

A hand on her shoulder made her jolt despite sensing the looming presence behind her. She turned. "Yes?"

"I hope you know CPR because..." The wolf, who she recognized from the Devon pack, took one look at her and blanched. "Never mind." He backed up hurriedly and knocked a table, but righted it before drawing attention.

Her cheeks burning, she hitched her handbag higher on her

shoulder and strode deeper into the great hall, aware of every gaze on her back. Despite her put-together appearance, no one had approached her.

Gossip. The venomous whispers had already poisoned her family's standing and now ruined her opportunity for a fresh start.

The knot in her throat grew, and she swallowed. Once. Twice.

She had a mission, and she wasn't leaving without trying every avenue.

Her family had sacrificed everything to send her to this gathering, their hopes fragile against the malicious whispers about their defective genes. No one, it seemed, wanted monstrous offspring.

Her chances had died before she arrived.

But she had to do something.

Her parents and brothers were depending on her. Surely, she'd catch a smidgen of luck soon.

Sienna drifted to the bar and waited. After pouring beers for three male shifters, the server approached her with a polite smile. She slid onto a barstool, too tired and deflated to return the smile. "A glass of the unoaked chardonnay, please." The bartender took his cue, not wasting time on chat.

She remembered the dinner where her mother had suggested this plan. No pressure, her mother had promised, but quiet hope. They needed someone to earn money. Someone whose blood might finally break the curse. She'd agreed because she loved them. Everyone saw how dire the situation had become when other shifters kept their distance, afraid the Teague bloodline might taint their own.

A lesson she'd learned from Haco, a wolf all charm and no commitment, who'd sparked the horrid gossip in Stoneford and even here.

Sienna sipped her wine, fighting the urge to take a healthy slug, swiftly followed by more glasses to dull the ache in her chest and soothe the tightness in her throat.

Two men approached, sitting on nearby barstools, and she recognized them from the group activities. Scott and Liam, with accents that sounded Australian or New Zealand.

The men were tall and lean with tanned faces, but what caught her attention was their scent—distinctly feline, like her own black leopard. Unlike the crisp tang of wolves, this was earthier, more familiar.

Three women noticed them, preened and tossed their hair, but the two males continued their discussion. The shortest of the three women frowned, her pique at being ignored amusing Sienna.

"Excuse me." The tallest of the three, a striking brunette, stepped forward.

The men ceased talking.

"Yes?" Liam replied with a touch of caution. A prominent facial scar overshadowed his striking blue-green eyes.

Scott was classically handsome, with intense green eyes and wavy black hair. He frowned and slung his arm around Liam. "Was there something you wanted?"

"You're with *him*?" one demanded, the question an accusation.

"Yes," Scott said, his gaze unwavering.

Sienna perceived tension, believing it stemmed from some shifters' rejection of same-sex pairings. These three women appeared shocked to their core. The trio conferred and sashayed purposefully toward another group of men on the far side of the massive room.

"That worked well," Liam said. "Although rumors had better not fly back to Middlemarch. We'd never hear the end of the teasing."

Scott chuckled. "Even if they did, Saber and the others wouldn't believe a word. They know we're friends and prefer women."

Sienna listened closely, drawing on her experience of blending into the background since everyone at home treated her entire family like lepers. She barely withheld a derisive snort. Her male relatives, though unconventional in appearance, possessed kindness and empathy. Beauty meant nothing if it hid cruelty or stupidity.

Her father and brothers were honest men, and she loved them. She'd readily agreed to her mother's desperate plan, fueled by months of scrimping and saving from the pottery proceeds they sold to tourists in Stoneford.

"Do you like Niall?" Liam asked.

Sienna cocked her head, intrigued. She had a fantastic memory but didn't recall a Niall.

"Suzie likes him, and that's all that matters."

"I've enjoyed the gathering, but I'll be glad to get home." Liam took a sip of his beer. "Not even the long flight fazes me. I'm ready to jump back into routine."

"I hear you. It's been a blast, but I'm eager for my comfortable bed. The excellent success rate will please the council, though."

That told Sienna something else. Unless these shifters

gossiped, Scott and Liam wouldn't have heard about her family. Neither had found a mate. Perhaps she could speak with them and ask if they'd consider her. A sigh escaped, and she drank more of the chardonnay. No, they'd ask questions, and she couldn't lie. It wouldn't be right. She ignored the flare of desperation and her sense of failure, taking another quick sip of wine. Besides, it sounded as if they were heading home after the gathering.

"Another three days," Scott said. "At least we can hang out with Niall and Suzie. The general mood and unruly behavior of the remaining shifters puts me on edge. The unpaired singles scan us like they're ordering off a menu."

Sienna's snort escaped before she could stop it. He wasn't wrong, and the bitter irony of her own situation settled over her. Even now, gazes crawled over her body and whispers passed from ear to ear—the dismissal unmistakable. Just another desperate hunter, caught in the same frantic pursuit.

Sienna savored the citrus-tartness of the French wine, watching as the two men departed. Scott seemed promising. Confident without arrogance and kind to the staff. He hadn't stared at her as if she were a curiosity or turned away in disgust. More importantly, he hadn't heard the rumors.

Her family needed someone strong and kind. Brave. Someone who could pass as a human when necessary.

A wild thought struck her. Scott didn't know about the Teague bloodline. What if...?

She exhaled and shoved the idea away, but it crept back, insistent and mouthy. Her parents had sacrificed everything. Her brothers were counting on her. What if she could convince Scott to come to Stoneford? To meet everyone and see for himself they weren't the monsters people whispered about?

But even as she rationalized, she understood she was toying with a darker, more desperate plan.

"Hello." A smooth male voice interrupted her thoughts. "I don't believe we've met."

Kevin. She'd seen him earlier, hanging with that smug pack who cackled too loudly, drank too much, and stared long enough to make her crave a shower.

"Sienna," she said. "From Cornwall."

"Kevin. From Australia." He leaned closer. "My friends dared me to talk to you. Said you were off-limits because of some curse, but I think you're gorgeous."

There it was. Not interest, but shallow thrill-seeking wrapped in false charm.

"If your friends had to dare you to approach me, you're not the man I want," she said coolly. "And while they're gossiping about my cursed bloodline, ask them how many of their daughters have jobs, or how often their mothers go without food to keep the lights on. I'm not ashamed of my family, Kevin. But you should be ashamed of your friends."

She straightened, offered a cool, polite nod, and walked away.

The snickers came, of course, and ribald laughter. But she didn't care.

Not anymore.

She climbed the stairs, Kevin's words echoing in her mind. *Off-limits. Cursed bloodline.* The casual cruelty shouldn't surprise her anymore, but it did.

She passed a trio of shifters in the corridor, who stepped

back as if she carried contagious cooties. Let them whisper. Let them recoil.

Her middle brother's offhand joke from their morning breakfast conversation returned to her—the one they'd all laughed off as absurd. *Why don't you grab one and drag him home?*

It didn't seem so ridiculous anymore.

By the time she reached her room, her mind was racing. Scott didn't know about her family's reputation. He seemed decent. And in three days, the gathering would end, and she'd return home empty-handed to face her parents' hidden disappointment.

Unless...

Game on.

CHAPTER 2

LIAM BROWN FOLDED HIS last shirt into the suitcase, eager to return home to Middlemarch. He'd enjoyed Scotland, but he missed the farm—the cattle, sheep, and dogs that depended on him. Most of all, he missed Emily's cheese scones and the familiar routine that anchored his days.

He had picked up thank-you gifts for Saber and London: a Mitchell tartan tie and a Drummond scarf. They'd been amazing when he'd arrived in Middlemarch with no references and a family who'd disowned him.

A bang on the door jerked his head upward.

"Scott, did you forget your key again?" Liam approached the door, reaching for the handle.

The door exploded inward, slamming into his shoulder and hurling him backward. His skull cracked against the wooden dresser with a sickening, branchlike snap. Pain bloomed outward in nauseating waves, and darkness rushed in at the edges of his vision.

Before he could even process what was happening, a dark-clothed figure loomed over him, their face obscured by a mask. A chemical tang hit him an instant before a cloth pressed against his nose and mouth, stealing his breath.

Liam lashed out instinctively, landing a weak punch as he kicked, twisted, and fought, his muscles screaming in protest while his attacker held fast.

"Get off me!" He tried to wrench free.

The chemical stink overwhelmed him—sharp, cloying, and wrong—burning his lungs with each breath. He turned his head, desperate for clean air, but the cloth followed. Panic surged. His arms flailed, and his movements slowed.

Liam gasped. The fumes seared his nostrils. His vision tunneled, narrowing to a pinpoint of light.

His body went slack. The world tilted, then everything went dark.

Minutes earlier...

Sienna pressed against the corridor wall, heart hammering as she listened to footsteps fade down the stairs. The crude mask itched her face, but she couldn't risk being recognized.

She'd watched Scott and Liam return from the Great Hall and noted which room they'd entered.

Now, staring down at his unconscious form, reality crashed over her. She'd done it. She'd knocked out a stranger and drugged him.

But there was no time for second thoughts. Her family's survival depended on this working, and she was so far past the point of no return.

Through the rough fabric of her mask, she studied his

face—the pronounced scar cutting across his cheek, the dark hair falling across his forehead.

Her blood turned to ice.

This wasn't Scott.

The carefully constructed plan, the desperate gamble she'd risked everything on, had failed. She'd grabbed the wrong man. Every calculation, every rationalization crumbled. Scott was the one she'd researched, the one who'd seemed approachable. Liam was just there.

But his chest rose and fell steadily, and voices echoed from the corridor outside. It was too late to fix this. Too late for anything but moving forward.

She crouched beside him and worked her arms under his shoulders, hauling him into a fireman's carry the way her father had taught her. Her legs shook under his bulk of solid muscle and dead weight.

The corridor stretched endlessly ahead. Each step sent fire through her thighs, and sweat slicked her spine. She'd mapped out her route earlier: down the servants' stairs, through the kitchens during the shift change, and out the delivery entrance where she'd left her hire car.

Her luck held. The kitchen staff was busy with dinner service, and the delivery area was empty. She bundled Liam into the trunk, her hands quivering as she slammed it shut.

With Liam safely concealed, she jogged to his room and grabbed the suitcase he'd partially packed. She tossed in his toiletry bag, an attempt to make everyone believe he'd found a mate and left.

Job done, she sneaked down the passage and out of the castle. Fortune was with her, and she didn't pass a single person.

Despite ending up with the wrong man, everything else had fallen into place. Besides, perhaps it was best she'd abducted Liam. His scars suggested he'd faced challenges with judgment and acceptance. He might understand their situation better than most.

Sienna settled in the vehicle, and only then did she allow herself a moment to let the tension drain from her shoulders.

Liam's eyes fluttered open to a blurry ceiling and the taste of copper in his mouth. His head thumped in a relentless *bang, bang, bang*, and when he struggled to sit up, nausea rolled through him in waves.

"Liam?"

A woman leaned over him. She had brown eyes and a faint splash of freckles across her nose. Something about her tugged at his memory, but everything inside him felt out of sync and disconnected.

"Water?" She helped him sit and guided a glass to his lips.

"What happened to me?" he asked, his words a hoarse whisper.

"You tripped. Outside, on the gravel. Four days ago." Her words came too quickly. Almost rehearsed.

Four days? How long had he been out? His throat burned, his muscles protested, and his sense of time had vanished completely. Had she looked after him? He remembered nothing but brief flashes. The pressure against his lips, the feel of motion. Maybe a car? Everything else was a black hole.

He blinked at her, his head throbbing a furious retort. "Tripped?"

Her words scraped across his mind, gritty and jarring. The story felt thin, like a hastily constructed lie.

"Who are you?"

She hesitated a beat too long. "Sienna. We're...mates."

This answer rang hollow to his ears.

He scanned the plain room with its wooden walls and the tiny single window, felt the lumps in the thin mattress beneath him. Not familiar. He reached for his feline, the deep, powerful hum of his inner animal that always anchored him. Nothing. A whisper of presence, dulled and barely accessible beneath the pain. The absence was terrifying. He'd never felt so disconnected, so profoundly human in his weakness.

His voice cracked. "Where am I?"

"Cornwall. My parents' cottage in Stoneford."

Cornwall? Adrenaline zapped through his veins, immediately quashed by an icy wave. "You said I tripped. Where exactly?"

"Outside, near the water barrel." She pressed her lips together. "You were out cold. I panicked and brought you here to recover."

But something in her tone didn't match her words. Too careful. Too rehearsed.

"You live here?"

"Yes, I told you. It's my family's cottage in Stoneford. You needed quiet."

The silence stretched between them. She fidgeted, brushing invisible lint from her jeans, then tried to smile. It didn't quite reach her eyes.

"I should check your bandage," she said, moving closer.

He jerked away. "Don't."

She stilled. Hurt flashed in her expression. Or was it guilt? Maybe both.

"I'll give you space," she murmured, stepping back. "But you need to eat."

He didn't answer, and she left the room.

Liam lay there, mind spinning. *Cornwall.* He had many questions. And no forthcoming answers.

Sienna leaned against the closed door, breathing hard. *Damn it.* Things hadn't unfolded as planned.

Liam instead of Scott.

Her stomach churned. He didn't remember the gathering. The head trauma or the drugs—something had wiped his memory clean. What had she been thinking? That he'd wake and agree to her plan?

"Sienna?" her mother called from the kitchen. "Is he awake?"

"Yeah."

Her mother wiped her hands on a tea towel and approached, eyes narrowed. "How bad?"

"He doesn't remember me. Or anything else, apparently."

"Amnesia isn't uncommon after head trauma."

Sienna gulped as her lies threatened to bury her.

Doubt flickered on her mother's expression. "You haven't been together long enough for trust to build between you."

Sienna's throat tightened. Trust was precisely what she'd betrayed.

The cabin must be small, since Liam could hear two women talking.

"He's lost so much weight. He can't afford to lose more," Sienna said.

"Short of taking him to the hospital, we can't do much more. None of the neighbors will help. Let's try some soup again. I know it doesn't have much flavor, but he needs liquids."

"Yes, Mama. I'll heat it now."

A spoon clinked, and Liam's tension faded. Why did he hurt everywhere? His muscles throbbed with stiffness, as if he'd lain motionless for hours.

"Oh, Sienna," a voice whispered. "Nothing goes right for us. Your papa. Your brothers and now your mate. Maybe we're cursed after all."

The voice held a deep sorrow that tugged at his emotions, and Liam ached to offer comfort. Perhaps his initial fear was unwarranted, since both women sounded concerned about his condition.

Footsteps returned, and with them, the faint scent of meat.

"Don't think like that, Mama. We've done nothing to deserve this run of bad luck. Things will improve. You'll see."

Another woman appeared—older with brown eyes like Sienna's and long black hair confined in a braid. "I'm Tamsin, Sienna's mama." Her cool hand smoothed his forehead with surprising gentleness. "At least your temperature has dropped."

She smelled of smoke and strong soap, her underlying feline essence comforting despite his confusion. The caring touch relaxed muscles he hadn't realized were tense.

"Mama, can you help Liam sit up?"

"Feeling any better?" Tamsin asked.

He shrugged, the faint movement painful enough to make him wince. "I feel like I fell off a cliff."

Tamsin patted his hand. "It could've been worse. At least you didn't break a leg or arm."

Liam glanced at Sienna. "Did I topple over a rock face? I ache all over."

"No," she said. "Just the knock to your head."

"Are you hungry?" Tamsin asked. "We have a nice hot broth for you."

"I'd prefer a steak." His voice sounded like an old, creaky door seldom used, making him wonder what had occurred. He tried to remember, but his head rebelled.

Sienna snorted, but the long silence after had him seeking their expressions.

He prodded at the past, yet nothing but white noise filled the space. Thinking hurt his head, so he allowed Tamsin to help him sit and place a lumpy pillow behind his back.

Once upright, he felt like he'd run five hundred meters at a full sprint.

"What happened? Was I in an accident?" he asked in a hoarse whisper. This was more than a mere trip.

"Stop fretting," Sienna said. "It's important to eat and rest."

"But I don't remember—"

"You hit your head." She bit her lip, hesitating at his bedside. "We were mucking around, and you tripped."

"On what?" Did that cause his epic hangover? This woman was his mate, right? But why did her voice catch when she said *tripped?* And why did she avoid his gaze?

When he'd eavesdropped on their conversation, Tamsin and Sienna had sounded worried, but he didn't recognize them.

Why didn't they seem familiar? He'd struck his head, but would a skull knock blank his mind?

Liam didn't know. But this went beyond ordinary weakness—the pain was unlike anything he'd experienced. Normally, his feline form would have kicked in by now, its rapid healing magic already knitting bone and flesh. But there was nothing. His cat wasn't responding. The truth, cold and sharp, swirled in his mind, tightening the vise around his head.

Cautiously, he prodded the most tender spot and winced, a raw gasp torn from his throat from the stabbing spike.

"Eat your soup while it's hot," Sienna said, but she watched him closely. Not concern, but calculation? "I want my mate to eat, rest, and, more importantly, recover as fast as possible. Can you hold the bowl on your own, or would you like me to feed you?"

"I can do it." His limbs refused to cooperate, shaking so hard the soup sloshed over the bowl's edge.

"Accept her help," Tamsin said. "That's what mates do."

Mates. He shook his head but stopped when burning seared his brain. Something felt off, but Tamsin was right—he had to eat.

Sienna dipped the spoon into the soup, held it to his mouth, and waited patiently for him to open.

Liam wanted to scowl, but he needed help. He swallowed the soup. It was thin but flavorful, and he didn't take long to polish off the bowl.

"Let me get you more tablets. Given how you keep grimacing, it's obvious your head is giving you trouble," Sienna said.

"Yes. I can't remember—"

"Don't worry. It's more important for you to rest and recover your strength."

"I need the bathroom."

"Of course. Let me help you up." Sienna slipped an arm around his waist as he swayed. Outside, she led him to a small wooden structure. An outhouse. He stared at the privy, something nagging at the back of his mind, but the thought slipped away before he could grasp it.

His eyes squeezed shut against the sudden brightness. He should remember, shouldn't he? Without warning, his stomach roiled, and he lurched toward the door. Tamsin, quick as a flash, opened it, but he barely made it inside before he vomited.

"Easy there," Sienna said, her voice surprisingly gentle, considering the brusque way she'd spoken earlier.

"Who are you?" he asked, the question raw. She couldn't be his mate. Every instinct screamed it, despite his confusion.

"You don't remember?"

There was a strange note in her voice—shock? Worry? Or caution? He couldn't trust his instincts, which insisted he run, yet offered no reason why. His feline was silent, his usual anchor to reality severed. This wasn't a physical weakness. It was a deeper, more insidious drain.

"Now, I'm truly worried," she said. "I wish we had the money to call a doctor, but they charge so much for house calls."

Truth, he decided, logic breaking through the haze.

"Liam, we haven't known each other long." She met his gaze, her brown eyes full of anxiety. "We were still learning about each other."

19

"You have an accent."

"So do you," she fired back.

"Where am I from?" Because try as he might, he couldn't imagine a place he called home.

"Filling in the gaps isn't a good idea. But...Australia."

Why? He needed information, but the jut of her chin told him nothing more was coming. He wiped his mouth. "I'll be okay now."

He shuffled farther into the dimly lit outhouse and shut the door, his mind a tempest of questions. His fingers trembled, but he managed. At least the place didn't smell too bad. He'd been in some outhouses...

The thought petered out before he could finish it, and a frustrated groan escaped him.

"Are you okay in there?" Sienna sounded worried again.

Liam didn't know what to think when every instinct screamed danger. If he was in trouble, he couldn't see it. The women were trying to help.

"Liam?"

"I'm fine," he said, trying to rein in his testiness. "Give me a minute." He straightened his clothes and exited. "Where do I wash my hands?"

"Over here." She rushed to his side, and he was glad of her steady support.

She directed him to a barrel with a scoop attached to the side, where he washed his hands.

Liam scanned the area as they returned inside. The cottage was small and well-kept, with bright daisies flanking the door. But when he looked at Sienna, they felt like strangers, and it was scary as fuck.

CHAPTER 3

SIENNA WAITED UNTIL LIAM fell asleep before seeking her mother's advice. A cold twist snaked through her belly while she relayed a careful version of the truth.

"I didn't intend to hurt him. How could I know he'd lose his memory or become so ill? What if he dies?"

"He won't die. Now that he's awake, he'll grow stronger." Her mother's quiet confidence helped to tamp down Sienna's fears. But as Tamsin spoke, her gaze flickered to the closed bedroom door—a subtle tightening around her lips that Sienna recognized as silent disapproval.

"We'll wait until Hedrek and the boys return from work and hold a discussion," her mother added.

Sensible though Sienna worried her audacious plan would explode with epic force.

On Monday, she'd return to her secretarial job because they desperately needed the money, and she worried about her mother's safety alone with Liam. From the little she'd learned, he seemed decent, but people hid their true selves. She'd learned this at a young age.

"I have the market tomorrow," her mother said.

"But—"

"No." Her mother cut her off. "We must carry on as normal and pray your mate recovers."

Sienna bit her lip, wanting to protest the *mate* part, but her mother was right. "The money will come in handy with an extra mouth to feed."

"I've told you before. There's nothing wrong with us. We'd live normal lives if everyone minded their own business."

"You're right," Sienna said.

"A suggestion. If your Liam is up to it, we'll take him to the market. We must integrate him in the villagers' eyes, and this trip is ideal."

"What about people gossiping? Liam might hear something he shouldn't."

"We'll do what we always do—stick our noses in the air and sashay past because we don't stoop to their level. Liam can formulate his own opinions."

"Honey, I'm home," boomed a familiar voice.

Pleasure filled her mother's face as she whirled toward the doorway with a broad grin. Seconds later, her father appeared, his unique features drawing every eye. Her mother streaked toward him with a joyful shriek, and he wrapped his brawny arms around her. They kissed as if they hadn't seen each other for months rather than three days.

"Get a room," her oldest brother, Jago, said with a grin, shaggy hair falling into his eyes.

Cadan, the middle brother, sighed, his sun-browned skin

and callused hands a testament to long hours outdoors. A crease of exasperation tugged at his brow. "Are they kissing again?"

"How did it go? Did you bring us lots of beautiful things to sell?" Sienna asked.

"We did." Kitto, the youngest, adjusted the tail of black hair at his nape, a silver hoop glinting in his ear. "These should sell well."

Jago's nose twitched, and he frowned. "Did someone visit?"

Sienna's gaze darted to the bedroom where Liam slept.

"How was the gathering?" Cadan asked, more curious than suspicious.

Quiet tension weighed on her shoulders anyway. She hesitated. Her fingers curled into fists at her sides. *Just tell them. They'll find out eventually.*

"About that."

Kitto stopped in his tracks, his cat ears pricking through his black hair. "Who are you, and why are you wearing my clothes?" He turned to Sienna, mock scandalized. "Did you and Mama adopt a stray while we were gone?"

Sienna closed her eyes briefly before rushing to Liam's side. He still looked as if a strong wind could bowl him over. She slipped her arm around his waist. "Liam, this is my father, Hedrek Teague. My brothers, Jago, Cadan, and Kitto. Everyone, this is my mate, Liam."

"He's not a healthy specimen," Cadan muttered.

"He was in an accident and has a concussion," her mother said, still in her father's embrace.

Her father gave her and Liam a long look before nodding. "Welcome to the family, son. You make sure you look after my daughter. She's my pride and joy."

"Oi," Kitto protested.

"I'm a lucky man," Liam said without hesitation.

Sienna's mouth dropped open, then firmly closed. Liam drew her closer, and she spoiled the moment by stiffening because he was essentially a stranger. She hadn't even kidnapped her preferred target.

"What's for dinner?" Cadan asked. "Jago was in charge this week and is the worst cook ever."

"Hey! I resent that," Jago said, nudging his brother with an elbow. "You're not French chef material either."

"Enough," her mother said. "Dinner won't be long. Why don't you boys wash up and set the table for me?"

"Yes, Mama," her brothers chorused and burst into action.

Sienna rolled her eyes and turned to Liam. "How are you feeling? You slept for a while."

"My skull is still tender, but I'm hungry."

"A good sign. We'll eat soon."

"Why are your brothers and father covered in fur?" He blinked as he processed his words, frowning.

Sienna scrutinized him but didn't see distaste, only curiosity.

"My father and brothers can shift to black leopards, but when they revert to their human form, they still bear some cat characteristics. Papa and Kitto keep their tails. Jago and Cadan don't. And all of them, like my father, have patches of black fur on their arms and legs, and feline ears instead of human ones." She watched his expression, wondering if he remembered his own shifter nature. If he did, perhaps the drugs she'd used were playing a bigger part in his memory loss than she'd suspected.

His frown deepened, but he nodded. "That must make their lives difficult."

"It does." She kept her answer simple when the situation was far more complex.

"Can we walk outside?"

"Let me check to see if Mama needs help first."

Her parents spoke in low voices and stopped when she poked her head into the minuscule kitchen.

"Liam wants to walk. Do you need help with anything?"

"Your father will assist me," her mother said. "Fresh air will help Liam, but don't let him overexert himself."

"I won't."

Sienna left her parents alone, aware she'd face an inquisition when Liam fell asleep tonight. She sighed. Liam would get his memory back soon. Then what?

Liam complained of nausea and dizziness and retired to bed early.

"Outside," her father suggested. "We don't want to wake the lad."

Sienna tugged her T-shirt hem straight and nodded. She and her mother had kept the conversation neutral over dinner. Her mother must've told her brothers not to interrogate her because they'd been on their best behavior. During a discussion, they'd toss questions her way like frisbees.

She followed her mother outdoors.

"Tell us everything," Papa said.

Sienna told them *almost* everything, and when she'd finished, her father sighed while her three brothers looked at her in admiration.

"Way to go, sis," Kitto said.

"Liam seems a reasonable lad. He showed respect and didn't gape or ask rude questions. He didn't display disgust. It was as if he'd seen people like us," Papa mused.

"Perhaps it's his scarred face. Maybe others have teased him or rejected him because of his appearance, so he is more circumspect," Mama said.

Papa's direct look took her aback. "Either way, he seems respectable. You don't carry his scent."

Her spine stiffened. "Liam has been unconscious and woke yesterday."

"Do you want to keep him?" Jago asked.

"We agreed to try a relationship before he injured himself."

"You don't have to do this," Mama said. "Yes, we hoped you'd find a mate, but I haven't seen any spark between you and Liam. We don't want to pressure you."

Sienna scanned her brothers' faces, then her parents'. They mightn't have wanted to burden her, but she'd still felt the silent expectation. She adored her family, and it hurt her when others shunned them. It wasn't their fault they didn't fit the typical feline mold.

"I was hoping for guidance," she said.

"Sienna, you brought this man here," Papa said gently, without blame. "You must decide whether to stay with Liam. Once you do, we will help."

There it was—unstinting love—and it made her eyes burn.

She swallowed hard and lifted her chin. "I want to keep him."

CHAPTER 4

LIAM WOKE ABRUPTLY, TRANSITIONING from sleep to full alertness in a blink. He was in a bedroom, and someone was with him. Slowly, he turned his head. Yep, a woman, although he couldn't see her face since long black hair concealed her features.

He didn't remember her or how he came to share the same bed.

He shifted his head a fraction and scanned the room. Yeah, he'd been here before, yet the place didn't seem familiar, didn't feel like home. Where the hell was he? He cast his mind back, trying to remember, but there was a yawning hole in his memory. Had he been drinking? He didn't recall...

He and Scott had been...

Scott?

Whoa. Whatever he'd done had screwed with his head. He sat up, and agony jabbed him at the temple, ricocheting back to scramble everything spinning inside his brain. His name was...

He came up blank, and panic joined the white noise in his head.

"Liam," a sleepy female murmured.

Relief struck him. *Liam.*

"Is something wrong? Is your head sore?"

Okay. His name *was* Liam, but he didn't recall hers.

"My memory." He paused. "I didn't remember my name."

"Oh. You have a concussion. You were unconscious for several days but woke up yesterday."

A flicker crossed her face—too fast to decipher. Had he upset her?

"I'm Sienna, your mate. We're at home. You fell."

His mate. He twisted this information, testing and probing for associated memories. Nothing.

"Where are we?"

"My home in Cornwall," she said. "Are you hungry?"

He paused. "Yes."

She smiled, and he stared at her, trying to remember at least one personal thing. His mate was beautiful, with long black hair tousled from sleep and deep brown eyes. Nothing about the sprinkling of freckles on her nose or the charming dimple when she full-out grinned jumped into his mind.

She was a stranger.

"We'd better fix that. I can hear my brothers, so we're the last awake." She slid out of bed and stood. She wore a thin T-shirt that fell to her knees. His mate was slender, her skin tanned as if she spent a lot of time outdoors. "Did you want to stay in bed and rest, or would you like to eat with the rest of us?"

"I am tired of being in bed."

"All right. Your clothes are in the wardrobe and the set of

drawers over there. Bottom two drawers."

She pulled on a pair of jeans, then lifted her pale blue tee over her head. A jolt went through Liam—sharp and unexpected. His body stirred with a sense of recognition, but his mind struggled to catch up. A low hum of warmth spread through him. It felt foreign, yet oddly right.

He blinked as she slipped on a navy cotton shirt, buttoning it while walking to the door. She paused, stepped back, and brushed a quick kiss across his mouth.

"See you soon. Shout if you need me."

Liam stared after her, befuddled. He had no memory of this woman—his mate—or when or how they met. And her hesitation before she'd kissed him and her expression afterward. She'd looked contrite, which made no sense. Having a mate was a joyful thing and celebrated...

Yet, he couldn't recall anything about their life together. Shrugging cautiously, he climbed off the bed and walked to the wardrobe. His clothes were on the right, while hers hung on the left. Neither of them owned much, not that this was a bad thing.

He rifled through his clothes, fingering each piece, but not one item triggered a credible flashback. He tugged on his jeans, and something crinkled in the right-hand pocket. A coffee receipt from Dunedin airport. He stared at it, and... Nothing.

Frowning and frustrated at his lack of answers, he plucked a black T-shirt from a drawer and tugged it over his head. Nothing about the clothing gave him any further information, so he finished dressing and padded from the small bedroom.

The rest of the cottage was compact, but everything was clean, and a subtle lavender fragrance filled the air. He followed the sound of feminine laughter and ended up standing in the doorway. Three large black cats zoomed around the outdoor table, having a fine old time with what looked like a game of chase.

Liam watched them before his attention turned to Sienna. "Where did they come from?"

Her brow scrunched. "Oh, Liam," she said, sounding upset. "Don't you remember? They're my brothers. You met last night."

He grimaced, some of his brain fog clearing as he thought back to the previous evening. He'd been tired. "I asked about their fur last night."

"Yes, we're feline shifters. You didn't ask questions, so I thought you understood. We can transform whenever we want. You can too." She paused, tilting her head as if considering something. "Try shifting because it might help your head."

Liam considered this. "Are you certain?"

He prodded his scattered thoughts. The big cats didn't alarm him, and that troubled him more than if they had. Normal people would run screaming, wouldn't they? Yet this felt routine. Had he always been this accepting of the impossible, or was his injured brain too scrambled to process fear?

Two cats ganged up on the largest one, who shot away with a burst of speed. No, their unexpected appearance sparked more curiosity than terror. Sienna was speaking the truth, and he understood—subconsciously, at least—the existence of feline shifters.

"How do I do it?"

She blinked, not hiding her dismay. "You visualize a black cat and hold the image in your mind's eye while willing your body to change. It can be painful. Don't panic mid-shift—you'll hurt worse than you do now."

"And to transform back?" He needed answers now. No nasty surprises. Not when he already felt like a stranger in his own skin. "Is that what happens with your brothers? They lose focus when they revert to human?"

"No." Her glare cut through him and made him blink.

He said nothing, gaze fixed on her brothers playing, the urge to run with them growing stronger. "I want to shift."

"There's no reason not to. It might speed your recovery."

"It will?" He wanted the confusion in his head gone.

"Yes, but you should—"

He pictured a glossy black leopard, the thought automatic. The shift crashed through him, shaking off the fog clouding his mind. The dull pressure behind his eyes lifted, replaced by sharp clarity. His muscles tightened, alive with new strength and control. An instant later, fabric ripped.

"—take off your clothes first," she finished, this time with a wry smile. "Stand still, and I'll free you."

He growled but stood as she plucked away the denim and the remnants of his shirt. He flexed his paws, feeling the power coursing through him. At last, he felt like himself again. Every one of his senses seemed better. He smelled smoke from the fire, the citrus-scented soap his mate had washed with, and the floral shampoo she'd used to wash her hair.

A deep, guttural roar like a saw jerked his attention to the three black leopards now observing him. He stepped forward cautiously, inhaling to imbibe their scents. These men were his brothers, and he wanted them to like him. This seemed important.

Instead of straining his brain to wonder why, he kept padding toward them. He'd almost reached them when they sprinted away.

The thrill of the chase poured through Liam, and he ran after them before the thought formed. They raced around jutting rocks and up and down a rise and jumped over a babbling brook before circling back to the cottage.

Liam loved every moment—the stretch of his muscles, the rush of blood through his veins, and the intense, rich scents of grasses, rocks, and earth. He'd done this before with other shifters. His family? He didn't know and didn't force the thought. Instead, he embraced the fun and familiar.

After their run, the three brothers shifted back to their human form.

"Breakfast time," Jago announced, glancing at his brothers first. "And you should probably shift back before Mama fusses about food going cold."

Liam pictured his human form and willed the change.

"Much better, eh?" Cadan grinned, already slinging an arm around Liam's shoulders. "Thought the shift would sort you out."

"Much." Liam stretched, more grounded and aware than he'd been since waking.

Inside, Tamsin was already setting plates around the table. "Perfect timing. How's the head, Liam?"

"Better now," he said, accepting the shirt and jeans Sienna handed him.

"Good. Fresh air and exercise usually help." Tamsin put

a plate of eggs in front of him and glanced at her sons and husband. "Are you taking him clay digging?"

"If he wants," Hedrek said. "Or he could help at the market."

"Liam, want to come with us this afternoon?" Jago asked.

Liam glanced at Sienna. "What will you do?"

"Work."

Had she told him about her job? He shifted in his seat, not liking to ask because the lack of answers battered his confidence. What if he never remembered? He ate a mouthful of egg and accepted a piece of toast from Kitto.

"I'll also help Mama sell pottery at the market," Sienna said. "Hopefully, I can take extra time for lunch."

"Can I help?" Liam asked. "I could go with you another time." He glanced at Jago and caught the tension in the male's shoulders. "If that's all right."

Hedrek gave a decisive nod. "An excellent idea. That way, Sienna won't have to ask for time off—her boss isn't always the most understanding. Later tonight, we could use your help to transport our finished products back here."

"Of course," Liam said.

"As long as Liam's headaches don't worsen," Sienna countered. "He's still healing."

"Perfect." Hedrek rose. "Come on, boys. Let's start early on glazing the pots we baked overnight."

The kitchen became a mass of activity—plates scraped, cutlery stacked in the sink, and water running as Jago and Cadan began the dishes. Kitto started clearing the table. Liam finished eating and stood to do his part.

"Tamsin, a word," Hedrek said.

She nodded and followed him outside.

"Thank you for offering to help Mama, but are you well enough?" Sienna asked while wiping the table.

"Stop babying the man," Kitto chided, waggling his brows at his sister. "He's old enough and ugly enough to pace himself. It's not like he's heading off for days of hard physical slog."

"Yeah." Cadan slung his arm around Liam's shoulders. "Your sharp tongue will send him fleeing."

Sienna paled.

"Sorry. Liam is a smart man to choose our favorite sister. He has superior taste."

"I'm your only sister," Sienna said dryly. "Stop making trouble. Honestly, you open your mouth, and crap comes out."

Liam watched the siblings bicker, envious of their close relationship. They stood up for one another, and that was a good thing. Sienna, particularly, was protective of her brothers. Liam tucked the bit of information away to add to his jigsaw puzzle of knowledge.

Later that morning, Liam joined Tamsin for the walk to the market. When they arrived, he helped unload cups, saucers, and platters from the handcart they'd pushed from the cottage.

"Please don't over-exert yourself," she begged. "I don't need another lecture from my daughter."

"She stands up for those she loves," Liam said.

Tamsin hesitated, her gaze searching his. "The locals don't respect Hedrek and my boys. Sienna—well, let's say the local lads saw one thing in her, never a partner. They were terrified a Teague would pollute their bloodlines." Her eyes shone with emotion. "I'm thankful she met someone like you who sees her as a treasure."

"Tamsin!" a sharp voice interrupted. "You're here. I gave your regular position to Alfred."

"But we're only five minutes late. We come to the market every week."

The woman shrugged helplessly, but her expression told Liam she wouldn't budge. She didn't care what Tamsin said or how much she protested.

"Where have you put us?" Liam asked.

"Over by the car park."

Tamsin bristled. "I paid for my spot last week before I packed up and left."

The woman made a tsking sound and pulled a ten-pound note from her pocket, offering it to Tamsin.

"I paid twenty-five pounds. You can't shove us to the back of the market and charge us fifteen pounds." Tamsin stuck out her chin, reminding Liam of Sienna. His mate had inherited her mother's feistiness.

"Give us a full refund, and we'll go quietly," Liam said.

"No, we won't go quietly," Tamsin snapped. "You can't treat us like this."

"You're abominations. We don't want you here."

"A refund," Liam repeated.

The woman glanced over her shoulder and saw they'd attracted an audience. "Oh, very well." She thrust money at Liam and stomped off.

Liam handed the cash to Tamsin, and the tears in her eyes alarmed him.

"What's our next move?" she whispered. "We must sell our

pottery today. It's been tough lately... I don't enjoy seeing my men go hungry."

"We'll set up where she said and figure out a plan. Don't worry—I have cash. It was in my jacket pocket. Enough to buy food to take home."

"But you and Sienna will need that money—"

"We're family," Liam said, then paused. The words had come automatically, even though he didn't remember choosing these people. Was he overcompensating, or was he naturally generous? He shook off his doubts. "We can argue later. Right now, we need a place to set up."

"All right." But the life had gone out of Tamsin. She seemed smaller. Crushed.

Liam helped her load the boxes back onto the trolley, noting the whispers and not-so-quiet laughter from those who'd witnessed the confrontation.

"Good job. We don't want them here," a woman said.

"Who is he?" another asked.

Tamsin flinched, and Liam stepped closer, wanting to protect her from the callous remarks. Once they'd finished, he wheeled the trolley toward the car park. Tamsin followed, her shoulders hunched, and her head slumped. It made him wonder how often this woman got the stuffing knocked out of her because the locals considered her family monstrosities.

"What about over there by the oak tree in the shade?"

"People like to sit there with their picnic lunches after the market finishes."

"But no signs say we can't."

Tamsin hesitated. "Sometimes, a man selling lemonade sets up there."

"We'll leave room for him, and maybe we could sell our tumblers to fill with lemonade, and both get sales."

Tamsin shrugged.

Liam unloaded the trolley again and set up the table they'd brought with them. "Do you have price tickets?"

"Yes." Tamsin showed them to Liam.

"You need to increase your prices," he said.

"It's the only way we can sell anything. We sold out last week. One man purchased the lot."

Because he was reselling them elsewhere and making a profit. The words popped into Liam's mind, catching him off guard. His memory flip-flopped like a fish out of water, and it bugged the hell out of him.

"Why don't I take care of the selling, and you do the wrapping? If that's all right with you."

"Yes."

Liam scowled, his head aching again. He couldn't tell if it was the exertion or something else. No time for self-pity. Tamsin needed help, and he wanted to do this for Sienna and her family. He pushed the pain aside and rapidly repriced the items.

Cars arrived, pulling into the car park, and many people stopped to browse the cups and other items on the table. They chattered, clearly familiar with each other.

"Where's your hubby?" a blonde asked while picking up a blue and white platter.

"Harold has an appointment to see the mayor. Some business thing," a dark-haired woman said. "I hope his mood improves. We have a Hunt Ball tonight, and it won't be any fun if he's in a grump."

"Ply him with a few drinks first," the blonde advised. "I'll take this platter, please." She handed it to Tamsin while Liam took care of the payment.

That was the start of their sales, and trade was brisk for the plates, cups, and saucers. The tumblers didn't sell as well, but if the lemonade vendor arrived, he had a plan and a proposition for the man.

"We're selling at the higher price," Tamsin whispered, sounding more animated. "We're doing better here than in the main market."

"It's because people can nip back to their cars and put away their purchases instead of carrying them around."

"Maybe," Tamsin said. "*Uh-oh.* Here comes the lemonade seller. He does not look happy."

"Don't worry. I'll deal with him. What's his name?"

"Tony," Tamsin said.

Liam steeled himself and prepared to sell his scheme. "Hello, I'm Liam. I hope you don't mind sharing your spot. They oversold the market spaces, and we had nowhere to go. I have a plan to help both of us sell more. Perhaps we could discuss it while I help you set up?"

CHAPTER 5

HER MOTHER'S SMILE WAS the brightest Sienna had seen in months.

"Best market day we've ever had," she announced, setting down a platter of chopped vegetables. "We sold everything except one chipped plate."

"Everything?" Sienna looked up from stirring a sauce.

"Every cup. Every saucer. A lovely couple from Bath bought half our stock in one go." Mama's eyes sparkled. "We can stock the pantry this week."

"Could you make small heart shapes?" Liam, who had sat quietly, spoke to her father. "In blue or blue and white. You could thread a ribbon through the top and sell them as pendants."

Sienna's mouth dropped open. A brilliant suggestion. She wanted to say so, but her brothers beat her to it.

"Yes!" Caden whooped with excitement. "Easily. They'd be quick to make."

Jago nodded. "Yeah, all we'd need is the ribbon."

"What color?" Kitto asked.

"Black might work best." Sienna turned to her mother. "Can we afford to purchase some tomorrow?"

"We can. Create a few larger hearts to attach to cards with heartfelt poems. Tourists love sweet sentiments," her mother said.

Sienna's attention shifted to Liam, and her conscience prickled before she could shut it down because he'd scrunched his brow and furtively rubbed his temples. "Liam, it's worth trying to shift. I could show you our swimming hole." Should she tell him the truth? They weren't mates, and she'd brought him here without asking his permission. The urge to scream gnawed at her, but she pushed back because this plan of hers was working.

He'd suggested a fantastic idea that might become a successful income stream and...

"Ahem!" Mama paused until everyone was silent. A soft smile formed, making her mother seem much younger. "Remember those tumblers we predicted would sell well but flopped?"

Papa sighed. "A miscalculation."

"We sold them today! Thanks to Liam's quick thinking, we struck a deal with Tony. We sold the tumblers filled with his lemonade."

Jago frowned. "But doesn't the lemonade seller set up near the car park?"

Her mother sniffed. "The woman who organizes the tables gave away our spot. But it turns out the place she put us is much better."

Sienna's chest squeezed tight, and gratitude stung her eyes. Her plan was working, and she needed to overcome her self-doubt. Liam hadn't met a mate. He'd probably be pleased if he understood what she'd done.

She resolved to become the best mate ever. Unwittingly, she'd picked the perfect shifter. If she'd followed her plan and abducted Scott, the other one...

Her cheeks heated as a profound realization struck her. Her choice of Scott was based on his ability to avoid attracting attention from nearby shifters. She'd judged Liam, with his scarred face, as inferior.

Shame had her bowing her head. She'd done a terrible thing, even if his presence was to help her family. What did she do next? A question for which she had no answer.

"Thank you, Liam," her father said.

Caden clapped Liam on the shoulder, and Sienna caught Liam's wince.

"Hey, watch it! Liam, will you try shifting again, or did you want to sleep?"

"I'll shift," he whispered.

She could practically feel his suffering. "All right. Mama, do you want us to help with the dishes?"

"No, your father and I will set everything to rights."

"What about the boys?" Sienna asked.

"We're running with you." Jago rose, jerking his head at his brothers. "Mama and Papa want private time."

"And what if Liam and I want to be alone?"

"Tough." Cadan's furry brows bobbed up and down as he tried to wink.

"They can come with us," Liam said.

41

But she and Liam needed to get acquainted. Wait. Would anyone be searching for him? Work had been busy, but she should check the internet during her lunch break. She wasn't sure what she'd do after learning more, but at least she was taking action.

"All right. Liam and I will meet you out front. And a reminder. Don't get too rough with him."

"Aw, Sienna." Caden pouted. "Where's the fun in that?" And laughing, he sprinted into the cottage to remove his clothes.

Ten minutes later, five black leopard shifters trotted from the cottage. Her brothers led the way, sprinting ahead, while she stayed by Liam's side. Her priority was his health because his injuries were her responsibility. He seemed better in the morning, but by sundown, fatigue dragged at him. She suspected the witch's drug hadn't helped, either. If not for her, he'd be home now. Was anyone waiting for him? The thought bounced back like it always did, but this time she faced it head-on. Her conscience whispered guilt; her counterargument stood firm. Liam's presence was helping them. He was giving support they desperately needed.

She let the fresh air and exercise burn away her worries, increasing her speed to match Liam's pace. They ascended a tree-clad hill, the air rich with the scent of damp earth, wildflowers, and crushed grass, before racing around the tor jutting from the ridge. As always, she paused to enjoy the village spread out below in untidy rows, the outlying farms and orchards, and the rolling hills beyond. The grass looked lush down there, and productive farms filled the valleys.

Old copper mines dotted the land around their cottage,

rendering the ground far less fruitful. To her right, she caught flashes of the sea. Sometimes, they ran as far as the cliffs and descended to a cove accessible during a low tide. Smugglers sailed along the coast, but her family steered clear of the business. Her father had declared the smugglers dangerous men. The Teagues would not align themselves with thieves and brutes, not even if they were desperate.

Her brothers disappeared down the hill, and Liam followed without hesitation. He didn't seem to have any trouble keeping up, and she mentally crossed her fingers that the exercise would help rather than set him back. And she was turning into a worrywart, but the situation ate at her because, at heart, she was an honest person.

The idea of crafting new items had excited her father and brothers. Their faces had lit up as they discussed the possibilities, and her mother's quiet satisfaction had made Sienna want to cry. She couldn't recall when her family had last shared a moment of genuine happiness.

But every kind word, each shared smile, felt tainted by her lies. She kept telling herself the outcome would justify everything, but her methods themselves were wearing her down.

The insight stopped her cold. This wasn't her. A sneak and a liar. Not who she wanted to become.

Sienna slowed to a walk, automatically scanning her surroundings as her mental gymnastics delved to the core of her problems.

A flash of light on the valley's far side snared her attention. It was on their land, and she halted, staring at the spot. The flash repeated seconds later. A set of binoculars catching the light?

Maybe. Maybe not. But whatever it was, the unexpected sight was enough for her to grunt a warning to her brothers. She crouched, slinking forward until she could see farther into the valley, and barked out another demand to hide. Her brothers melted into the cover of scrubby bushes and rocks, and Liam followed suit.

The flicker reappeared from a different position. Sienna lifted her head to sniff the air, but detected nothing unusual. While she'd been watching and waiting to learn more, Liam had joined her. She jolted and then mentally cursed because she hadn't heard his approach.

He nudged her and issued a soft, inquiring grunt. She scanned the valley, and Liam edged close enough for her to feel the heat emanating from his body. His feline scent was already familiar, his presence comforting, despite every one of her senses screaming danger.

They resided in a shifter community, but humans lived amongst them, mainly those who had taken a shifter as a mate. They held shifter secrets close and didn't speak to outsiders. But humans visited the market or purchased goods from shopkeepers. They tramped across the moor. Locals swiftly explained away any suspicious sightings with a mixture of lies and crafted half-truths. That was where the rumors of the Bodmin Moor Beast had started.

And yes, there were periodic hunts for the beast. The locals knew when to take extreme care and stay in their two-legged forms, for who knew what they'd do to any unfortunate captured beast. Mostly, there were warnings. Plenty of warnings, and maybe she was worrying about nothing, but her gut screamed otherwise.

Jago shifted and scanned their vicinity. "What's wrong? Whoa! Did you see that?"

Sienna eyed the valley slopes before shifting herself. "Someone is trespassing on our land."

"Yeah. But who?" Kitto asked.

The land was sparse, windblown moorland, except for this beautiful valley.

Sienna scowled. "Someone either doesn't know it's private land, or they've intruded on purpose."

"Any village gossip?" Kitto asked.

"Nothing unusual. The baker is having an affair, but no one is sure if it's with the launderette owner or the grocery store cashier. Locals have seen him with both. The Forbeses are having another kid, which makes seven. And the mayor keeps holding meetings and making secretive phone calls about his mall project." She didn't mention the usual whispers about her family or fresh ones about Liam. She hadn't been forthcoming, and apparently, neither had Liam nor her mother.

"Okay," Kitto said. "Let's go home now, and we'll come back before dawn to see if we can spot anything to suggest what is happening. And Sienna, you need to double down and ask questions. Someone might know something."

"Plan." Sienna shifted back to her leopard. She inhaled but still smelled nothing unusual. She glanced at Liam. He seemed calm, but there was a new, anxious edge to her brothers. The same apprehension danced in the pit of her gut. Suddenly, home wasn't the same safe harbor. Was it because she'd been away, or was it the remorse that stuck to her like a second skin?

They made their way to the cottage silently and in close

formation, using extreme caution and taking a roundabout route.

Her parents sat outside with mugs of tea, their relaxed posture vanishing the moment they spotted the group. The siblings shifted and dressed before rejoining them outside.

"What is it?" her mother asked.

Her father studied each of their faces before settling his gaze on Sienna. "What's wrong?"

"It might be nothing," Sienna said. "But I think someone was watching from across the valley. I caught the glint of light on glass."

"Binoculars?" her father asked.

Kitto pulled a band from his shirt pocket and tied back his hair. "Yeah, I saw it too."

Tension slid into her mother's slim shoulders. "Did they see you?"

"I'm not sure," Sienna said. "I saw the flash at least three times from different vantage points. We decided it was best to return and check it out early tomorrow morning."

"Village gossip?" her father asked, looking at his wife.

"Nothing unusual," she said. "Liam, did you hear anything?"

Liam grinned, the flash of humor making Sienna stare. The smile took him from faintly scary to someone more personable. A person she'd want to get to know. "The baker and his rumored affairs have tongues wagging. We served mostly humans since the shifters stayed clear. Tony told me about the baker."

Would those in the village keep such important information to themselves? Sienna considered this because many of the shifters held her father and brothers in disdain—vermin who should've been strangled at birth.

Her father sighed, the weight of intense weariness and inner conflict heavy in his exhale. "Silence might be their way of driving us out. They've tried to get rid of us before."

"They'd attack one of their own kind?" Liam asked.

"We're inferior," her father said, without inflection.

Liam patted her father's shoulder. "I get it. One look at my scar, and people jump to conclusions. Anything different makes them uneasy."

Sienna gaped at Liam. He'd spoken without hesitation, as if he'd remembered his past. Had he?

Her brothers must've thought the same.

"Dude, do you remember?" Cadan asked.

Liam's brow creased. "No."

The breath she'd held puffed from Sienna. She didn't want him with a functioning memory yet. It was too soon. The thought made her uncomfortable, but it was the truth.

"Your plan is good," their father said. "We'll return to our camp tomorrow and start making the hearts Liam suggested. We'll go earlier than usual and check for tracks or other signs of trespassers. Once we confirm a problem, we can take extra precautions."

"Tamsin and I will eavesdrop during the market and see what we can learn," Liam said. "If we're not too busy, I might introduce myself to some stallholders."

Sienna shuddered at what could go wrong. Given Liam had such a noticeable scar, everyone would assume others had rejected him. They'd think she was desperate. She opened her mouth to tell him interaction was a bad idea, but her mother shook her head. Sienna shrugged inwardly, already guessing their reactions, but so be it.

After their aborted run, Sienna's restlessness kept her moving. She put this to good use and deep-cleaned the kitchen. Liam and her brothers checked on her but soon retreated when she waved cloths at them and suggested they help. In truth, the solitary activity was exactly what she needed to stew about her situation.

Muffled laughter came from outside, and she found herself smiling. Liam didn't treat her brothers as freaks. His questions, uttered in his low, rumbly voice, drifted through the open window. He was asking about the pottery, and if there was one thing her brothers knew and loved, it was the making of ceramics.

Her father had taught them everything he'd learned, but her brothers had taken the artistry to a higher level. They were genuine artists, and she was incredibly proud of them. It was in the retail area that they'd fallen apart. This was obvious after hearing about today's market.

Her brothers and Liam fell silent, the abruptness of the action putting Sienna on alert. She straightened and hustled outside to join them.

Darkness had fallen, the light from the kitchen illuminating part of the outside area. Her parents were still sitting together, quietly talking. Or at least, they had been. Right now, they, like her brothers and Liam, were staring toward the path leading to the village.

Sienna squinted into the darkness, but her eyesight was taking time to adjust.

"It's young Jamie Pike," Jago said, his broad shoulders

relaxing a fraction.

Kitto nodded. "Yep, Jago's right."

Seconds later, the young boy burst from the darkness. His chest heaved, face flushed from running, but his darting gaze and the way he kept glancing over his shoulder hinted at more than exhaustion. His black hair stood in disarray, as if he'd been dragging his hands through it.

Liam approached slowly. "Easy there. Sienna, can you get him a glass of water?" He guided Jamie to the table where he'd been sitting with her brothers.

"Yes, of course." She hustled into the kitchen and, when she returned, set a tumbler beside the panting boy.

"Take your time." Liam shunted the drink closer. "Get your breath back."

Jamie's hand trembled when he reached for it. He drank but spilled some on his stained T-shirt.

When he almost dropped the water, Liam took it from him.

"What's wrong, lad?" her father asked.

Jamie started, and he visibly recoiled. A flash of anger struck Sienna, her instinct to slap the boy and rebuke him. She did neither because his fear wasn't his fault. Adults had spread tales about her father and brothers, portraying them as monsters.

Liam stepped forward again, and his presence diffused the tension. He crouched in front of Jamie. "Can you tell me what has upset you?"

CHAPTER 6

LIAM RESTED A HAND on the kid's shoulder, and he trembled violently at the contact. "Steady, lad. No one here will hurt you."

Jamie's gaze swerved toward Jago, Cadan, and Kitto before staring at his feet. Liam understood then, a heavy sadness mingling with frustration. These were good shifters. Decent men. They weren't to blame for their appearance.

"Are you sure?" the kid whispered, his face still pale, even though he'd recovered his breath.

"Positive. What's your name?"

"Jamie."

Liam nodded. "Jamie, my name is Liam. Has something happened in the village?"

"Hunters," the boy said, and Liam felt his blood chill. Behind him, he heard Jago's sharp intake of breath. Kitto muttered something under his breath that sounded like a curse.

"Where are they staying?" Liam kept his voice calm, but his hands clenched at his sides. "Are they human or something else?"

"Humans." Jamie's gaze darted nervously to the brothers. "Three of them at the pub. Stan works there. He helped them unload their supplies."

"Anything else?" Liam's jaw tightened. Why were they here? Were they professional hunters? Thrill-seekers? Amateur cryptid enthusiasts?

"The owner of the Cock and Bull asked Stan to spread the word about the strangers. Stan told my parents they mentioned the Bodmin Beast."

"What time did they arrive?"

"Around four."

And no one thought to warn them until now. He suppressed his anger at the villagers' superstitious fears. People treated him differently because of his scar. He...

The thought slipped away, leaving his mind blank. Liam shook off his frustration and focused on the present.

"They told the pub owner their boss collects animals." Jamie's words tumbled out faster now.

"When will they be leaving?" Liam asked.

"They said it depends on their hunt."

Liam frowned. A wealthy collector after the Bodmin Beast. That tracked. But what if that wasn't all? What if someone wanted to target the Teagues? Would another shifter stoop that low?

No, that kind of idiocy would risk the entire village.

"Is there anything else we should know?"

Jamie shook his head, fingers fiddling with the hem of his

shirt. "I thought you should receive a warning. My father will be angry if he learns I came."

Liam squeezed his shoulder. "I'm sorry you'll get in trouble."

The boy tugged at his sleeve, his gaze flicking toward Hedrek and his brothers-in-law. Ah! He'd heard stories about these men, probably exaggerated. Kitto had noticed. To his credit, Kitto remained silent, but his expression told Liam everything.

"I haven't a clue what you've heard, but we're not much different from your family. We argue sometimes, and I have to fight to get seconds at dinner. Tamsin shouts at us for tracking mud inside," Liam said.

Jamie's nose wrinkled, but his features reflected interest. "What about Sienna? Does she shout? My brother wanted to court her, and my father threw a fit." His eyes grew wide, and he slapped a hand over his mouth.

Sienna cleared her throat, breaking the silence.

Liam crossed to Sienna's side and curled his arm around her shoulders. She stiffened on first contact before she smiled—a broad one that stretched her plump pink lips. Now that his head wasn't aching as severely, he picked up on the tension between them. Maybe they'd argued? Sometimes Sienna eyed him as if he were a two-headed beast capable of snapping at any second. He shoved the thought down for later dissection and focused on Jamie.

"We shout when we're excited or angry. It's the nature of shifters," Liam said. "Do you live far from here?"

"We're your neighbors." The boy wrinkled his nose, and Liam read between the lines. His parents wished they weren't living as close to the town freaks.

"It's dangerous with hunters around. I'll walk you home," Liam said.

"I'll run," the boy said.

"And I'll run beside you," Liam said in a firm voice. "It's getting late. We'd better move before your parents miss you."

Panic marched across Jamie's face. "I'm gonna get in trouble, aren't I?"

Liam released Sienna and closed the distance between him and Jamie. "We'll discuss it while we walk."

"Liam?" Sienna said.

"Yes?"

"Take care. If you're not back in half an hour, we'll come looking for you."

Silent messages flew between them, and Liam nodded. "Let's move, Jamie."

Away from the lights of the cottage, darkness closed in, and it took a moment for his vision to become accustomed to the lack of light. The wind had picked up, whistling over the piles of rocks to his left, the mournful wail somehow familiar. For an instant, he pushed, trying to follow the wisps of shadows, then he sighed and redirected his thoughts.

Sienna jumped straight into them. She wasn't a safe topic either, since she didn't behave like a lover. Perhaps he *should* ask questions.

"You talk funny," Jamie said.

"I'm not from here." Trying to recall where only made his head thump. Sienna had told him Australia, but that struck a jarring note. Now, random images and slivers of knowledge jumbled together, leaving him unsure what was real and what was imagination.

"Where then?"

"Australia." The discordant bounce struck again, this time like a sharp dart that made him flinch. It was as if his brain was warning him not to confront the truth. Had he done something so heinous his mind couldn't cope? Did Sienna know, and that was why she was so jumpy around him? They were mates, yet they didn't touch. They shared a bed but did nothing but sleep. This wasn't the bond he wanted with a mate.

"That's far away," Jamie said, with a touch of awe. "They have kangaroos. And wombats. I watch wombat videos on social media."

"Yeah." A kangaroo, then a wombat came to mind, but neither sparked any sense of familiarity. "Tell me about the village. Is it a good place to live?"

"It's okay."

"People aren't nice to the Teagues."

"No, they want them gone. My mum said they gave away their market stall to mess with them. Everyone knows that's how they make a living."

Liam stopped walking, appalled at the locals' cruelty.

Jamie glanced back. "I don't think the same. T-that's why I sneaked out to warn them about the hunters. None of the other shifters care if something happens to the Teagues."

And they'd told their kids tall tales to scare them away.

"What about the guy who sells lemonade?" Liam asked.

"He's a human married to a shifter. The councilor's daughter."

Liam laughed because Tony hadn't complained after selling out and making more than he'd expected.

"This is my house," Jamie said.

Liam stopped beside the teen. It was like the Teagues' cottage but larger. The yard wasn't as tidy, yet these people and the other town residents judged the Teague family. One window gleamed with light while the rest of the residence lay in darkness.

"Can you sneak inside the way you left?" Liam asked in an undertone.

"As long as my brother hasn't arrived home."

Liam nodded. "Take care. We went for a run earlier and spotted someone we thought might be watching us."

Jamie stared, his mouth parting a fraction.

"Now we know to take extra precautions, so thank you. Your visit answered some of our questions."

With a quick nod, Jamie slipped into the shadows and disappeared. Liam watched for about five minutes before returning home. Once he hit the main path, he increased his pace. He'd hate any of the Teagues to come looking for him and place themselves in danger. Hunters in the area were troubling, especially since the Teague men couldn't easily hide.

Given what Jamie had said about the behind-the-scenes maneuvering, would a local shifter have arranged for hunters to base themselves in Stoneford? No, if they'd done that, they would've directed them straight to the Teagues. Heck, Liam didn't know.

Hedrek's shoulders lost their tension when Liam walked in the door.

"You've returned," Sienna said and hugged him hard.

Tamsin drew him into the kitchen, with the boys and Hedrek trailing behind. They took their seats with determined expressions, though a quiet air of resignation clung to them.

"Why do you stay here when the locals are so horrid?" Liam asked, the words bursting from him.

"Where would we go?" Hedrek asked. "We make our pottery here and stay somewhat hidden from the outside world. We'd have the same problems elsewhere, and it might be even more difficult to blend."

Liam got it. People stared at him too. But this—this wasn't living. It was merely getting by. There had to be an answer.

He shifted the conversation. "Do you think it was the hunters watching us?"

"We shouldn't jump to conclusions," Tamsin said. "For all we know, it's a competitor trying to find out where we dig our clay. Whatever we discover in the morning, we need to be careful." She scanned her husband and sons, a crease forming between her brows.

Liam's stomach twisted at the thought of other shifters treating the Teagues like lepers, when all they wanted was to live in peace. He prayed his suspicion that the locals had pointed the hunters at them was nothing more than an overactive imagination.

"I'm tired." Tamsin rose abruptly. "I'm going to bed."

Hedrek stood and slipped his arm around his wife's waist.

The boys and Sienna watched their parents disappear into their bedroom, the silence heavy with anxiety.

"Don't leave without me in the morning," Liam said. "We'll go on two feet, and if we meet anyone, let me do the talking." He didn't tell the brothers to fade into the background because they weren't novices at this.

A sudden gust of wind rattled the window, and Sienna

closed it. "I'd come with you, but I can't be late for work."

"You're better off in the village," Jago commented. "Listen for chatter."

"All right."

Liam agreed. A logical suggestion, given they needed info about the hunters. "If anything important happens, I'll walk into town to let you know."

"What time will we leave in the morning?" Kitto asked.

"Five," Jago said.

Liam extended his hand to Sienna. She blinked before grasping his fingers. Liam couldn't read her expression, and that frustrated him. What was wrong with their relationship?

"Good night," he said.

The three brothers called their responses as he led Sienna to their bedroom.

"What's wrong?" Liam asked.

"N-nothing. I guess knowing hunters are in the area has upset me."

"It's not ideal, but if we're careful, we should be okay. It's a lot of ground for three men to cover. Probably won't take them long to decide the Beast of Bodmin is tourist hype."

"I hope so," Sienna said. "But I have a bad feeling."

Yeah, he had one of those squirming around in his gut. But Sienna and her mother were worried enough without him adding to the tension.

"Is your head feeling better?" Sienna asked as he closed the bedroom door behind them.

"Yeah, shifting helped a lot."

Sienna edged away, and tension gripped his muscles. He hadn't hit her—he didn't think he'd ever struck a woman—but uncertainty gnawed at him. Anxiety swelled in his chest. Maybe it was time to press Sienna for answers. She was stunning. He wasn't. His scar made people stare and sometimes recoil. Of course, he had to consider her brothers and father. Word about them must've spread from shifter to shifter, ruining her chances of finding a mate.

"Did you choose me because of my scar?" The words fell heavy with an accusation he hadn't meant.

"No," she snapped.

"Why me, then?"

"Why were you willing to come home with me?" she countered.

They glared at each other with distrust.

"I have sketchy memories. Fragments that make no sense." He broke the silence. "But I'm not stupid. What's bothering you? And don't tell me it's your family or the hunters."

Sienna bit her lip and looked torn. "We argued—"

"It's more than that. You flinch every time I touch you. If I don't beat women, then what? We sleep in the same bed, but you'll fall out if you move farther from me. You don't wear a wedding ring." He stared at his left hand. "Neither do I. Are we married?"

She refused to meet his gaze.

"Yeah, that's what I thought. I'll sleep elsewhere."

"No." Sienna's hand shot out, gripping his forearm firmly.

Frustration settled in his chest. With no memories, he felt adrift and directionless.

"We made a last-minute pact since neither of us found mates at the gathering. I know very little about you. No, that's the truth. We'd agreed to explore a relationship, then you tripped and injured your head."

"How much of it was real?" His voice was hoarse. "The way you looked at me, the things you said—was any of it actually about me, or was I just filling a role?"

"I don't know."

Somehow, her honesty cut deeper than any lie.

"That's not good enough, Sienna. I need to know if I'm staying for people who want me here, or if I'm convenient."

"You're not convenient," she said fiercely. "You're—" She stopped, seeming to realize anything she said now might sound calculated.

"Your solution? Your backup plan?"

"You're someone who strengthens us," she said. "The way my father looks when you're around, how my brothers respond to you—that's not fake. That's not something I could manufacture."

"Why did you bring me here? Wouldn't someone at the gathering know me?"

She looked at him then, with tears in her eyes. "We urgently need help, and I thought you might be the impetus we needed to turn our luck around."

Liam gaped at her. "What if I have a mate or someone important to me? Did you consider that? Any self-respecting man would walk away right now."

"You were alone at a singles gathering and didn't wear a ring. Besides, you agreed to our pact just as I did. *Please, Liam.* We're in danger because of the hunters, and I don't trust our neighbors or anyone from the village."

Sienna wasn't wrong. Without Jamie, they wouldn't have known about the hunters, nor would they have known to limit their shifting. It might've been too late, and that brought anger. Shifters should have each other's backs.

"Why do they hate you so much?" Liam asked, putting the rest aside for now. The truth: while he wanted to learn about his past, he feared what he might find.

"Kitto got friendly with the mayor's daughter, and her parents objected. Strongly. Some locals beat up Kitto and warned him not to go near the girl again. As far as I know, he hasn't, but he refuses to discuss Jules. Since then, things have been tougher. It's a lot of aggravating microaggressions. We try to ignore them."

"And now the hunters."

"Yeah."

"What happens if the hunters come to the house or if someone informs on your family?"

Sienna gave a helpless shrug. "I don't know."

"Do your father and brothers have a hidey-hole they can retreat to while the hunters are here?"

"Yes, but long-term concealment is no way to live."

"Aren't they doing this now?" Liam asked.

"Yes, but they have a bit of freedom."

But it wasn't autonomy, and Sienna knew it. While Liam was driven to learn more about the gathering and understand the truth about himself, he couldn't leave the Teague family. He liked their calm acceptance of him and caring natures, even though it was increasingly clear Sienna was keeping secrets.

CHAPTER 7

"SIENNA, WHAT ARE YOU doing?" her mother called through the door. "You'll be late."

Sienna opened the door, still thinking about her conversation with Liam the night before. He'd guessed their entire relationship was a lie, yet he'd stayed. Even now, he was out with her brothers investigating the flash they'd seen.

"My hair wouldn't go right," she said.

Her mother's expression said she saw through the flimsy excuse. "I'm coming with you. I want to grab fresh bread and supplies. If Hedrek and the boys must retreat to their camp, they'll need stores."

Sienna picked up her bag, knowing nothing would dissuade her mother. The village wasn't the welcoming place it'd been yesterday, but they needed more information to make the best decisions for their family.

"I like Liam," Mama said after they'd locked the cottage door and started walking.

"He's a good man." Sienna meant every word, although her conscience tweaked.

"You should tell him everything you know."

Sienna didn't reply immediately. She should've known her mother would suspect there was more.

"His loved ones will be concerned about his absence."

"We talked last night. He knows—or at least suspects—that something is off. The thing is, I like him. He's kind and caring and accepts Papa and the boys without a flinch. He treats them as equals, and no one else has ever done that. I-I can't regret having him in our lives."

"That doesn't make it right," her mother said.

"You don't approve." The realization unaccountably hurt Sienna.

"It's deceit, and not the Teague way."

Sienna's eyes stung at the rebuke. "I-I know. We couldn't afford the money we spent to send me to the gathering, but I tried. The moment the Devon shifters saw me, I knew they'd start rumors. They looked at me the same way they do Papa and the boys. It was sobering. I thought I understood, but it's different when you're the one being judged." She drew a breath. "That's why it's hard to understand their positivity. But they were so excited when Liam suggested they try making hearts."

"It's your Papa. He's the steadying influence." A shadow crossed her mother's face. "But the boys are at an age when they want to take a mate. No one here will accept them. Look what happened to Kitto."

"So what do we do? Things might be even harder in a new town. At least here, we're familiar with the rules."

Her mother shrugged as they left the winding hill path and crossed the gravel road to walk along the cobblestones at the village entrance. "It's clear some people here want us gone. We can't stop them, but we can control how we respond. The less attention we draw, the better."

Her mother was a wise woman.

They reached a fork in the path and embraced.

"Have a good day, Sienna. Take care, but gather as much information as you can."

"I will. You be safe, too."

The office was busy when she arrived. Busier than normal. Sienna stowed her bag and hung her coat on a hook in the staff room before she walked to her desk.

"You're late," Molly snapped, frazzled, as the phone began ringing the second she set it down.

"I'm sorry. I'll work late to make up the time. Should I take charge of the phones?"

"Yes, please," Molly said, sounding calmer now.

Sienna took over the switchboard, answering and transferring calls across departments. Most callers wanted to speak with the mayor and complained about the hunters, though two angry men also brought up the mall project.

During her lunch break, Sienna ate her cheese sandwich before heading to the library. She didn't know his surname, which didn't help, but she had eavesdropped on his conversation with his friend. The town of Middlemarch in New Zealand was the logical starting place.

She keyed in a search and studied the results with trepidation. Middlemarch appeared to be a small farming community. She tried adding "Liam" to her search terms, then "leopard shifter," but came up empty.

Frustrated, she tried "Scott Middlemarch New Zealand" instead—maybe she could find information about Liam's friend that would lead her to him. The third result made her stomach drop.

A local newspaper photo showed a handsome man with wavy black hair—Scott—with his arm around a pretty blonde woman. The caption read: "Local farmer Scott Baxter announces engagement to Wellington teacher Harley Evans-Wilson."

Sienna studied the screen, guilt crystallizing into something sharper. If Scott had someone he loved, what about Liam? They'd been close—Liam could easily have someone waiting for him, worrying, planning a future together. She'd been so focused on her family's desperation, she'd never truly considered his life before the gathering. The thought that she might've destroyed not just his autonomy, but his happiness, settled like a stone in her chest.

On her way back to work, the streets appeared noticeably empty and lacked their usual bustle. The coffee shop, with its usual enticing coffee and pastry scents, had closed early. The locals she encountered wore grim expressions. A mother with two young children hustled them past the playground, keeping her kids close.

A tall, bulky man rounded the corner and deliberately slammed into her elbow with force. Seconds later, she struck the ground with a shocked shout. Pain shredded her knee. The man didn't stop, didn't look back, didn't say sorry.

Sienna muttered under her breath and rose. Her right knee stung, a trickle of blood sliding down her shin. She froze as the weight of a stare had her head snapping to her left. The man who'd knocked her down stood watching, gaze narrowed with predatory interest. Another man stood beside him, speaking quietly while also observing her.

The way they catalogued her every movement—the clinical detachment in their gazes—made her skin crawl. This wasn't random intimidation. They were studying her.

She limped past them, fighting the urge to look back. The pair's quiet laughter followed her, but beneath it, she caught fragments of their conversation: "...definitely responds like..." and "...should report back..."

Whatever they were looking for, she had a sinking feeling they'd tested her, and that did not bode well.

"What happened to you?" Molly asked, her gaze drawn to Sienna's knee. Like most employees, Molly was a feline shifter, and she'd smelled blood.

"A man knocked me over in the street. He came around a corner and plowed into me."

Molly's eyes narrowed. "A stranger?"

"Yes."

Molly bit back a curse, which was unusual for her. "They're causing trouble around town, hassling the local women, especially the younger, prettier ones. They got cut off at the pub last night."

That made Sienna wonder because if the hunters had been searching for shifters last night, they couldn't have also been getting tossed from the pub. "How many hunt—I mean, visitors—are in town?"

"Three booked into the local hotel. Word is they told everyone there could be more coming."

More! "How long are they staying?"

"At least a month." Molly lowered her voice. "The mayor doesn't know who is backing them. Clean up your knee before you start work again."

"Okay," Sienna said.

The mayor kept his finger on the pulse, and nothing escaped his notice. He had allowed Molly to hire her, despite the protests from the senior advisers on his team. If he knew nothing, the person responsible had been careful to remain in the shadows.

Filing and the phone engrossed her for the afternoon. At five, when she exited the side door of the council offices, she found Liam waiting for her.

"You didn't have to walk me home."

"Tamsin was worried." Liam took her arm. "Things aren't normal at present. The visitors are stirring up trouble."

"So I heard. Did Papa and the boys get away okay?"

"They left late morning and none too soon," Liam said, his tone grim. "The visitors are going house to house to ask if anyone has seen the black cat of Bodmin Moor. I saw Tony, and he told me."

"Crap," she said in an understatement. "Molly, the office manager, told me they're staying at least a month. The mayor doesn't know much and is worried."

"If they're staying a month, someone with deep pockets is financing them. It can't be cheap to employ people for the search."

"There are three men at the hotel."

"I saw two of them earlier. They're loitering and watching everyone," Liam said. "It's like they know about shifters and are waiting for someone to break."

Liam had summed up the situation concisely.

"I hate this," Sienna said. "We've never had trouble in town."

They ceased chatting when they passed one of the town's two pubs. Two strangers stood outside, talking with a group of locals and smoking. They openly watched her and Liam as they passed. It was creepy and vaguely threatening. Sienna's shoulders didn't relax until they rounded the corner and left the cobblestone path.

"How well hidden is your father's camp? If the hunters search, will they easily discover it? I asked Tamsin. She assured me they wouldn't, but what if a local informs on them?"

"They camp in a valley and are very careful when they come and go. Once they're at their camp, it would be difficult to find them. Some of their pottery competitors have tried, because the clay they use for our products is superior. No one has discovered them yet."

"What about you and Tamsin? If those men grabbed either of you and tortured you?"

Sienna gasped, shock reverberating through her. "Surely, that wouldn't happen?"

"We're best to plan for the worst."

"I don't know the location, but Mama does. We could pack up and join Papa."

"Someone would need to leave to get food," Liam said. "Also, the visitors already know the town's residents. I got the sense someone had given them a list. Tony said they were aggressive when questioning his wife."

"Who would do this? We keep to ourselves and don't cause

trouble."

"Tamsin asked the same question. We found tracks this morning when we went to the valley."

"Two or four feet?"

"Two. We were lucky to notice before any damage occurred. But as Hedrek said, it could be someone skulking around, trying to find their clay source. Not necessarily something connected to the hunters."

"Unless they're playing a long game," Sienna said.

"Possibly. I promised Hedrek I'd stay close and protect you and Tamsin. It was the only way I could get him and your brothers to stay in hiding."

They'd almost reached the cottage, and Sienna halted. "Why did you agree to stay? Why did you make your promise to Papa?"

"You're in trouble, and I want to help. The hunters' arrival could be coincidental, but I hate that no one warned your family. Perhaps they're filming a documentary, but it doesn't seem innocent. It feels planned. Deliberate."

Sienna agreed. "Are we sure they visited all the locals? They could be lying."

"We can't trust anyone," Liam said.

Sienna bit her lip. Before she could reconsider, the words spilled out, "I haven't been honest with you either. You're from New Zealand, not Australia."

His expression didn't shift.

"I'll understand if you choose to leave. Or return to Scotland. They'll assist you at the castle. At least they'll know your name." Sienna risked a glance at him.

"Is my name Liam?"

"Yes, but I don't know your surname. Abducting you was...impulsive."

"Why me?"

Sienna winced. "Um, I'd chosen your friend until I found you alone in your room. You took a tumble and struck your head when I held a drug-soaked cloth over your nose, and the rest just happened. I didn't plan it. I know that doesn't excuse what I did."

"You kidnapped me." His gaze grew stormy, his jaw turning rigid. "What about your family? Did they agree to your plan?"

Sienna took a half step back, shaking her head. "They didn't know what I did. Still don't. Ma suspects, but Papa and my brothers think we're mates."

His world tilted. *Kidnapped.* The word slammed into him, stealing his breath. She'd drugged him. Stolen his memories. Taken away his choice. Completely.

Rage roared through him—white-hot and consuming. His hands shook with the urge to act. To lash out. Damn. Someone at home was probably panicking, wondering what had happened to him. His friend from the gathering might think he was dead.

But even as the fury burned, another voice rose—quieter but insistent. *She was desperate. Her family needed help. Look at her—she's terrified you'll leave them defenseless.*

No, he wouldn't let sympathy override the magnitude of what she'd done. She'd *kidnapped* him. Made him a prisoner without bars, using his own decency against him.

Yet... Hedrek's face flashed in his mind. The old man's relief when Liam promised to protect his family. The boys' joy over something as simple as heart-shaped pottery. Tamsin's quiet gratitude.

Damn it. He wanted to stay angry. Anger was clean, simple. This tangled mix of fury, understanding, and reluctant admiration was far more complicated than he could handle right now.

"Did Tamsin approve?" he demanded.

"Ma thinks I should drive you back to the castle, but there's a problem."

He shot her a sharp look, anger tightening his muscles.

"We've spent our nest egg on supplies for Papa and the boys. It will be weeks until we have enough to hire a car and pay for the fuel to Scotland."

Liam scowled. "My promise to your father—"

"We're not helpless," Sienna snapped.

"But if those hunters turn up at the cottage, could you hold out against them? They're less likely to cause trouble if there's a male around."

Sienna spat out a quick curse, her mind racing over the whole mess. The hunters might catch wind of gossip and innuendo. It all depended on how or why they had come to Stoneford. "The entire village knows I went to the gathering. A few have asked about you, but nothing direct. Yet."

Liam's mouth twisted. "Some wouldn't have approved of you seeking a mate."

"I'm sure you've caught surreptitious glances, but I'm surprised no one has asked you why you picked a family with faulty genes."

"I've received looks, but everyone is acting standoffish. Your mother is waiting for us." He jerked his head toward the cottage doorway where her mother stood, frowning. "Before we join her, is there anything else I should know about me?"

Sienna hesitated, feeling the ground shift beneath her feet.

"Sienna, I won't be happy if I learn you're still lying to me."

She swallowed. Her plan had imploded beyond repair. No wonder Liam hated her.

"*Sienna.*"

"You and your friend talked about a place called Middlemarch. I looked it up. It's a country town."

"All right," he said and strode toward her mother.

Sienna gaped after him. That was it? Didn't he want to know more?

Her mother embraced Liam, and they entered the cottage together, leaving Sienna staring at the empty doorway. They liked him—her parents especially. Her brothers had taken to him immediately, and he seemed to enjoy their company in return.

Sienna sighed, uncertain what to do next. She'd told Liam everything. Now the question was: what did he intend to do? And why did the thought of his leaving unsettle her so much?

CHAPTER 8

"I'D LIKE TO STAY," Liam told Tamsin as she stirred a pot of soup. "At least until my memory returns." He'd spent time raging inwardly over Sienna's confession, yet surprisingly, he couldn't hate her. The woman had risked everything for her family.

"But don't you want to contact the gathering organizers? Or press charges?" Tamsin asked.

"You have enough trouble without me adding to it." He forced a laugh. "Besides, my past scares me."

Tamsin kissed his cheek. The unexpected affection filled him with warmth, and he froze, savoring the moment. "I'm afraid it's bread and soup again," she said. "I sent everything we had with Hedrek."

Sienna wandered into the kitchen, dressed in worn jeans and an oversized T-shirt. "I'll set the table."

Liam studied her openly. No, despite everything she'd done, he didn't dislike her. "I might go to the pub tonight. Found enough change in my pocket for a drink."

"Why would you do that?" Sienna asked, freezing mid-reach for the plates.

"To gather information."

"Are you not leaving?"

Sienna confused him. Most people stared at his face—the scar was a mystery to him, but the injury must've been severe if his feline couldn't heal it. Women in town had reacted with horror. Others peeked and looked away. Sienna always met his gaze, except when guilt flickered in her expression. She'd abducted him, breaking her parents' teachings. Her reasons might've been well-intentioned, but if she'd explained and requested his help, he would've politely sent her on her way.

A part of him understood her reasoning. Loyalty and love were rare—something to treasure. That was why he intended to keep his promise to Hedrek and stay. Despite her withholding some truths, he genuinely liked Sienna. A man could do a lot worse in a mate. He'd wait before delving into his past. The truth was, he was terrified of what he might find. His head ached sharply when he tried to access memories. He took this as a sign to proceed slowly with his investigation.

"It's not advisable to go to the pub alone." Tamsin rapped a wooden spoon against the side of the pot. "Take Sienna with you."

"Mama, you can't be here alone."

"I was while you were at the gathering, young lady. I'll be safe enough with locked doors."

"But what if you have visitors?" Sienna protested.

A sharp rap sounded—sudden and unexpected, as if she'd conjured it. They froze, staring at each other. Another, louder bang rattled the front door.

"I'll get it," Liam said. "Stay here." He lowered his voice. "You'll be able to hear. Just make sure they don't see you."

"It might be a neighbor," Tamsin said.

The third knock was thunderous, and Liam rapidly unfastened his shirt and the top button of his jeans. He ruffled his hair as he strode to the door. At the threshold, he paused, sniffed, and yanked it open to find two strangers. One was tall, broad-shouldered, with the stance of a soldier. His khaki pants and tan shirt reinforced the impression. The other was shorter and bulkier, dressed in a brown coat, black pants, and muddy hiking boots. Both carried light packs. No noticeable weapons, but Liam was positive they had them.

"Where's the fire?" Liam made a show of fastening his jeans and dragging a hand through his hair.

"We're with the team hunting the Beast of Bodmin. Several villagers have told us you might've seen it."

Anger pumped through Liam, but he masked it. Blaming the Teagues was pure cowardice. Rather than standing together, the locals tossed the Teagues to the wolves.

"The phantom haunting the moor?" he said with a snort. "Who spewed that rubbish? I reckon this beast is a product of too many pints at the pub. You're chasing a figment of someone's imagination."

"Our tracker arrived last night. He picked up a trail this morning," the military man said.

"What sort of trail?" Liam demanded. "We have local sheep farmers with dogs—couldn't it be them? Is your expert sure?" A tracking expert for a mythical beast? Their organization and confidence didn't match a simple legend. It was like they knew exactly what they were hunting—or at least, the *kind* of thing.

"You're not from around here," the bulkier man said, his blond brows squeezing together. "Australia?"

"Yes," Liam said without missing a beat. "Married a local girl."

"I hear it's recent."

"Correct. Which means I have better things to do than chase a mythical beast."

"Who else lives here?"

Liam didn't answer. Silence fell like a weight.

"Who is it?" Sienna called. "Get rid of them and come back to bed."

"I haven't seen the beast," Liam said. "And I'm busy. Good night." He started to close the door, but the bulkier man stuck out a foot, blocking it.

"We're offering a ten-thousand-pound reward," the tall man said.

"Whoa! Big money. Shame I can't help. We could use a windfall."

"If you hear anything useful, you can find us in town," the man said.

Liam nodded and shut the door. This time, they let it close.

He didn't move. Instead, he listened.

"Did you believe him?" one asked.

"Yeah, he looked like he'd stumbled out of bed. If that's the woman I saw yesterday, she's a looker. Can't blame him for staying in."

"Let's go. We have three more cottages to hit tonight."

Liam listened to their retreating footsteps before joining Tamsin and Sienna in the kitchen. "They've gone, but it wouldn't surprise me if they show up again, at odd times. We need to stay alert."

"At least they didn't ask about Hedrek," Tamsin said.

"They asked who else lives here," Sienna added, "but didn't push."

"No outsider has the right to question locals," Liam said. "They're not the law and have no business asking personal questions. I'd like to know who told them about the sightings, or if they're here to debunk the whole thing."

"We wouldn't have known if Jamie hadn't warned us," Sienna said. "That's what irks me the most."

"But maybe the situations are separate," Liam said. "Whoever chose not to warn you might've seen it as a chance to push you out of the village—make it impossible for you to stay. Maybe they didn't have the stomach to tell the hunters you're feline shifters."

"Perhaps you should avoid the pub tonight," Sienna said.

"I agree. We'll leave it another two nights and go as a couple. That way, we can see the reactions of locals and hunters."

"Makes sense," Tamsin said.

"This is a disaster," Sienna said. "The longer the hunters stay, the more danger everyone is in—us and the other feline locals."

"I wonder how hard it would be to learn who's funding the hunt." Liam frowned, trying to think it through, but his head throbbed. "If we knew that, it might answer some questions. Are they trying to debunk the myth, prove shifters exist, or is it really about animal collecting like they claim?"

"Good point," Sienna said. "I wonder if they've hunted elsewhere—in the UK or abroad. This group seems well-funded. The organizer has serious resources. Knowing more would help us plan."

Tamsin nodded. "Makes sense. Let's make a list of what we need to find out and tackle this methodically. We can split up, ask our questions, and compare notes later."

"Oh, I didn't think you'd attend the market," the organizer said, her tone suggesting she'd hoped they wouldn't.

"Don't trouble yourself finding us a spot," Tamsin said before the woman could offer excuses. "We're setting up by the car park again." She stalked away, leaving Liam to navigate the cart over the cobblestones.

"I'll visit the council offices to make it official," Tamsin said once they were out of earshot. "Will you set up?"

"Of course." He squeezed her shoulder. "But Tony offered to share his site permanently."

Relief flooded her face. "At least someone in this village is decent. I'll check with the council anyway."

She strode away, a woman on a mission. The Teagues had enveloped him into their family, and he'd come to appreciate their love and humor despite the obstacles they faced. And Sienna—he admired the woman who'd abducted him for her kin. She'd risked everything to help them, even when the odds were slim.

Tony had already set up his stall and was chatting with customers, who sipped lemonade.

Liam waited until he was free before approaching him. "The woman organizing the market didn't keep our stall again."

"I told you. Share my site and pay half the costs. It's a win-win for both of us. My customers loved your mugs; several have brought them today for refills."

"The foot traffic's fantastic since the council makes folks park outside the market area. I'll talk to Tamsin, but it'd be great not to worry about having a stall every market day. The organizer keeps coming up with new excuses to give our spot away."

"That woman is difficult on a good day," Tony said.

Liam unpacked their stock and sold several mugs. He made a mental note to have Hedrek design a special one, featuring a village scene and possibly the village name. Given the Bodmin Beast buzz, a design depicting a black cat might sell well. He and Tamsin had noticed the local paper headlines when they'd trundled past the bookstore.

Tamsin arrived half an hour later, fists clenched. "It feels like someone's trying to destroy us, and this woman is just another tool, using her petty power to twist the knife. The locals know we depend on this income."

"You're entitled to your frustration, but good news. Tony confirmed his offer to share his site. All we'll need to do is pay half the cost."

Tamsin brightened. "Tony, you'll let us sell from your site?"

"I will. Keep bringing your mugs, and we'll both benefit."

Tamsin beamed and extended her hand. "It's a deal. How much do we owe you?"

While Tamsin and Tony discussed business, Liam sold two more mugs and gave change.

"Have you seen the Bodmin Beast?" A teenage girl with a perky ponytail leaned across the counter.

"No, but the hunters are taking it seriously," Liam said. "Three professionals with high-tech equipment."

"I heard a billionaire is funding the whole thing," Tony added, joining the conversation. "Edwin Smith. Read it in the paper this morning."

Liam went still. *A billionaire.* That explained the professional hunters, the month-long timeline, and the sophisticated equipment. "What would a billionaire want with a myth?"

"Maybe he collects rare animals," the girl suggested. "Think about it—if the Beast is real, it would be priceless to the right buyer."

The woman beside her nodded. "Rich people collect all sorts of things. Art, artifacts, so why not legendary creatures?"

After the customers left, Liam pulled Tony aside. "This Edwin Smith—what else did the article say?"

"Just that he's funding a scientific expedition to document wildlife on Bodmin Moor. But between you and me..." Tony glanced around and lowered his voice. "Those men don't look like scientists."

Later That Night

"Edwin Smith." Liam paced the small kitchen while Sienna took notes. "We need everything we can find on him. Business interests, properties, any connection to exotic animal collecting."

"The library has internet. I can research during my lunch breaks," Sienna said.

"I'll ask around the village," Tamsin offered. "See if anyone knows more about what the paper said."

"And we need to warn the others," Liam said. "If this man collects animals, he's not here to prove or disprove a myth. He's here to capture one."

Sienna tapped her pen on her notepad. "How do we warn Papa without leading the hunters straight to them?"

Liam's jaw tightened. "Carefully. If Smith's people are half as professional as they seem, they'll be watching us."

CHAPTER 9

THE KNOCK AT THE door last night had rattled them, leaving everyone jumpy, ears tuned for any unusual sound. Still, Liam's quick thinking—rumpled hair, unbuttoned shirt, the illusion of interrupted intimacy—had been convincing enough to send the hunters away. Sienna couldn't stop thinking about how easily he'd played the role of her lover. How natural it had looked when it was anything but.

"I keep expecting another rude interruption," she said, focusing on drying dishes. "That was good acting last night."

"Was it?" His voice was closer than she'd expected.

She turned to find him watching her, his expression unreadable.

"This isn't working."

Sienna returned to her task. "What isn't?"

"This. Us. Whatever this polite dance is supposed to be." He gestured between them. "Your mother thinks we're mates, but we act like strangers forced to share a house."

Her hand trembled as she reached for the last soup bowl, and she tried to ignore the sudden spike in her pulse. This was getting harder by the minute. Every time he spoke in the sexy accent of his...

"We need to talk about the sleeping arrangements."

"I—why?" She wasn't comfortable sharing a bed, not after what she'd done.

"You're the one who abducted me. Isn't seduction the next step?"

"You discovered I snatched you from everything you know. Aren't you supposed to flee the lady kidnapper?"

His gaze stayed sharp, but a flicker of wry amusement—or maybe resignation—crossed his face. "A promise means something to me. Your father worries when he's away, especially with things getting tense in the village. He and your brothers wouldn't have left if I wasn't here."

"I can't believe he trusts you." She paused, biting her lip to rein in the resentment. She understood her father's concern, but he barely knew Liam.

"And I won't betray him. I assume others have."

He grinned, and her heart skipped a beat. Gorgeous. His eyes reminded her of a stormy sea today, more blue than green. They lit up when he smiled, and the scar only made him more distinctive. It didn't repulse her, unlike the crude comment she'd overheard at the library. Some local shifters whispered she'd mated a flawed man because she couldn't do better.

They knew nothing. Not a damn thing.

"Thank you. Mama mentioned you're running low on stock. If we have nothing to sell..."

"One of us needs to visit the camp and collect more. Tamsin

and I discussed it during the walk back from the village. I offered to go."

"Why can't I?" Sienna bristled. It felt like he was pushing her out, which was ridiculous. She was the one who'd dragged him into this mess.

"Tamsin wanted to go too, but we risk meeting the hunters. The less interest they show in us, the better." He paused. "Can you research this so-called billionaire tomorrow?"

"I will. Molly at work might have some useful info too."

A thump at the front door made them whirl. Another thump set Liam in motion. Tamsin appeared in the corridor, her hair mussed like she'd been sleeping. A sharp pang of guilt prickled in Sienna. Liam's takeover irritated her, but the forced distance always ate at Tamsin. Their parents deserved peace. Safety.

"Hunters again?" Sienna whispered.

Liam didn't think so—he recognized the scent. He opened the door, and a black leopard slipped inside. Liam shut it quickly after him.

Sienna's worry increased tenfold. "Jago, what's wrong?"

He let out a low bark, and she finally noticed the black pack he carried. Liam rapidly unstrapped it, and Jago shifted. Her mother handed him a pair of sweatpants, and he pulled them on.

"Jago, has something happened?" her mother asked, her voice tight with fatigue and anxiety.

A hollow ache settled inside Sienna. She should've noticed how much her mother was struggling. Consumed by the secret and Liam, she'd been blind. The man unsettled her, yes, but this failure was hers alone.

Jago flashed a smile. "Everything's fine, and work is going well. We haven't seen hunters near us—at least, not until tonight. I had to hide in the bushes while they were traipsing around the moor. Luckily, one of them tripped, and I heard before they spotted me."

"They visited last night, offering a reward for information leading to the beast's capture," Liam said.

"It's close to full moon," her mother snapped. "Why risk coming home now when visibility is excellent?"

"We needed to check if our work is suitable for sale. Someone had to come, and since I'm the oldest, I volunteered. Besides, Papa was worried about you."

"You've stayed away much longer before," Sienna said.

Jago shrugged. "We don't know what's happening, and besides work, life at the camp is pretty monotonous."

Sienna opened her mouth, ready to blast her brother, but her mother's grip on her forearm stopped the words trembling on her tongue.

"What did you bring us?" her mother asked. "Are you hungry? Would you like soup?"

"Yes, please. In a moment. Look at what we've made. We think Kitto did an excellent job on the painting, but we wanted to check before making more."

Jago opened the pack and slipped out a cloth-wrapped parcel.

The hearts came in two sizes. Kitto had painted some in blue and white, echoing their traditional pottery, and others in bright colors with flowers and local landmarks.

"They're perfect," Liam said. "All they need is a ribbon so ladies can wear them around their necks."

"We made two special ones," Jago said, handing a smaller package to Sienna and another to their mother.

Sienna unwrapped the fabric and stared at the heart. White and blue with small starbursts in a darker blue—it was beautiful. An understatement. It was a masterpiece.

Her mother's heart was soft amber, decorated with two intertwined hearts.

"Papa made it for you. What do you think? Oh—we made hearts in three different sizes as keepsakes." Jago handed those over for inspection.

"Brilliant job," Liam said with a grin. "You've nailed it. These will sell very well."

"Really?" Jago's cheekbones held a trace of pink, while his mouth stretched in a smile.

Jago was basking in Liam's approval, a reminder to Sienna of how isolated her father and brothers were by the locals' outright rejection. Many men would've grown bitter, but her father never had, and somehow, he'd taught her brothers the same resilience.

"Yeah," Liam said. "The hearts must be fiddly to make. How is production? Your mother and I are nearly out of stock. We were trying to work out how to contact you to get more product."

"The hearts are quicker to produce, but decorating them takes Kitto extra time. Tomorrow, we'll make more drinking cups. Probably platters, too. We've already made more hearts to keep Kitto busy." He frowned. "We're going to need more paint."

"I can work as a go-between. Give me a list of supplies, and we'll get them," Liam said.

"I can help," Sienna protested.

"We want to keep a low profile, and leaving Tamsin alone isn't ideal. She's not doing well without Hedrek," Liam murmured.

Both siblings glanced at their mother, sharing a troubled look. Tamsin had been fine during the market and the walk home, but now the strain was clear. Understandable—between the hunters and the fear of exposure, it had to be taking a toll. Sienna hadn't stopped to consider how strong her mother had to be or how cruelly the locals treated her.

She nodded, chastened. Liam was right, and none of them had seen it. "If you're certain."

"I am. Jago, grab something to eat and rest for an hour. Spend time with your mother. Sienna and I will go for a walk and suss out what the hunters are doing now."

Sienna let Liam usher her outside, her senses delighting in his nearness. She wasn't sure what had come over her lately. She couldn't stop thinking about him, imagining his touch. And now, he wanted them to keep sharing a bed. Not great for her sanity.

"Where are we going?"

Liam drew her close, resting a hand on her lower back. "Let's walk beyond the village. We'll play the courting couple, so don't act surprised if I grab and steal a kiss."

Sienna blinked once. Twice. She swallowed hard to regain her equilibrium. His touch did strange things to her knees, and the slow, rumbly voice and enticing accent whispering in her ear didn't help.

"Do you think we'll see them?"

"Possibly not," he murmured, "but we'll hear them. They're unfamiliar with the terrain and stumble around more than shifters."

Liam led her along the dirt path, keeping her close. "Who lives there?"

"The Carters. An elderly mother and her daughter. We don't see them often because there's another path to the village near their cottage. It's the original track, but during severe storms, the river overflows, making the bridge impassable. That's why locals built a second path."

A faint flicker of light was visible behind the shrouded windows, but no one was visible as they strolled past.

"We could sit on the bench seat farther along the path," she suggested.

"Good plan. We'll sit and listen."

They'd barely sat when masculine voices drifted closer. Liam cocked his head, listening intently, and she did the same.

"This is a waste of time," one man grumbled.

"He's paying us, so we'll follow instructions."

Another asked, "Do you really think a leopard is loose around here, or are we chasing ghosts?"

Three men.

Only two had come to their door.

"It's them," Liam whispered in her ear.

Then, louder: "Hello."

The men fell silent, then appeared on the path seconds later. Two black-haired men with beards and a squat, bald man.

"What are you doing here?" the squat man asked.

His demand irritated Sienna. "How is that your business?"

"I'm the one asking the questions," he shot back.

Sienna glared as he shone a torch in her face.

"We live with family and wanted privacy since we're newlyweds," Liam said, showing more patience. "I'm sure you can understand our need to be alone."

The man released a coarse laugh. Sienna bristled inside but maintained a smile and fluttered her eyelashes. "Are you boys patrolling all night looking for the beast? Staying awake must be tough."

"We're getting paid," one bearded man said. "Money makes it easier."

Sienna frowned. "How do you search in the dark? Isn't the beast meant to be black?"

"We have special gear," he said. "Including night-vision goggles. If the beast exists, we'll find it."

"Plus, we have coffee to keep us awake." The squat man patted his hip where a slimline flask poked from his jeans pocket.

"Wow." Sienna giggled, feeling Liam's hand tighten on her hip. He stayed quiet, so she focused on what info they could gather. Jago and Liam had to avoid the hunters.

"It sounds like lots of lost sleep."

One bearded man shrugged. "I'll keep going for as long as I get paid. Beats working at the local cannery factory."

Exactly what Sienna feared—the time these men were willing to invest. Did they truly suspect shifters in the area, or were they chasing rumors? Staying hidden wasn't easy in the modern world, and accidents happened, especially with younger shifters.

What worried Sienna more was the hunters' capture of her father or brothers. Fear rippled through her belly, a sudden cold chill bringing a shiver.

"Thank you for checking on us," Liam said, "but as you can see, we're fine."

"Some of the men are jumpy, so it's probably best to skip the romantic walks for now," the squat man said. It didn't sound like a suggestion.

Their presence would make her family's life difficult, and getting the products to the market would require extra effort. Her shoulders slumped, and she burrowed closer to Liam. His arm tightened around her, his quick squeeze giving her a shot of encouragement. But at least a month of this. Their backer must have deep pockets.

The men called goodbye and moved purposefully along the track. Sienna waited until their footsteps faded.

"This is bad. The longer we must conceal Papa and my brothers, the higher the risk to all of us."

"Yeah, if they catch us wandering at night, they're gonna ask questions," Liam said.

"It's none of their business what we do, day or night. Yet they're watching everyone like we're criminals. It's not right. They have no legal power over us."

"What does the mayor say?"

Sienna snorted. "The mayor doesn't talk to a lowly person like me."

"Fair enough. So why don't Tamsin and I ask questions? Stir the rumor mill. Maybe we'll get a better sense of what is going on, and why the hunters behave as if they're in charge."

"Excellent idea." Liam impressed her. He was smart, and she liked him way more than she was comfortable with. Forcing her thoughts away from how decadent it felt to sit this close to him, she added, "I'll do the same. If nothing else, it might get the other villagers asking questions. The longer the hunters hang around, the more dangerous it gets for every shifter."

"Are you positive your father and brothers are safe in their current hiding place? What if the hunters pick up a trail, especially since we need to get their products?"

"Papa says it is safe, but I worry. Mama does too, but what's the alternative? We can't move elsewhere." This was why Sienna had taken a risk and attended the gathering. She inhaled before saying, "Liam, I'm scared for the future. That's why I gave in to desperation and dragged you into this."

Why was he still staying with them? He had his excuses, sure—but if she were in his shoes, she'd be furious, desperate for the answers she couldn't remember. She'd have marched to Scotland and pounded on the castle gates, demanding the truth.

To her frustration, he didn't say a word, just nodded.

"Do you have suggestions?" she asked.

"Not at present. It's difficult when I can't access my memory and experiences."

Sienna pressed her lips together. He blamed her—of course he did. On the heels of this thought, another heavier one came. It *was* her fault he'd hit his head and lost part of his past. She should've researched those drugs before using them and suspected they were behind his lingering struggles. Despite that, he was coping better than she would in his place.

"Papa and Mama haven't come up with any alternatives, and they've tried." Tears filled her eyes, and she swiped them away. She worried about her brothers' futures. How could they meet mates? The village residents certainly weren't helping.

Liam lifted his hand and gently cupped her chin. With slight pressure, he signaled he wanted her to look at him.

Sienna struggled for an instant before giving in to his silent demand.

"Aw, sweetheart. Somewhere, there will be an answer. We'll find it."

Sienna gulped on seeing the caring in his expression. She didn't deserve it—not after ruining his life and destroying his trust.

CHAPTER 10

LIAM LED SIENNA BACK to the cottage. He'd discovered he enjoyed holding her hand, enjoyed having her close. They'd share a bed tonight, no matter how late he arrived home after helping Jago. He wasn't certain why, but his feline half stirred in agitation when they were apart, so he'd go with the flow and figure out everything later.

Yes, he was furious at her manipulation, but the concussion had been an accident—he believed this. He'd seen how the villagers recoiled at his scarred face, and their reactions stirred sympathy for Sienna's father and brothers. More than that, they made him want to stay, to help, instead of chasing a past that felt terrifyingly blank. And if he was honest, being near Sienna seemed right.

"How will you and Jago get past the hunters?" Sienna asked, dragging his thoughts back to their immediate problems.

"If we leave home around one or two in the morning, chances are they'll be tired of patrolling in the dark. We'll go in our human forms and keep our fingers crossed."

"Might work," she muttered. "And if either or both of you get captured?"

"You, Tamsin, Hedrek, and the boys will need to devise a plan to rescue us." Liam forced a teasing note into his voice.

"This isn't funny."

"Believe me, I know."

The thump in his head intensified, and he barely resisted rubbing the sore spot. His headaches never disappeared—just ebbed and surged without warning. Fatigue, maybe. Who knew? What if his memories never returned?

Oddly, he could live with that. He liked the Teagues—their closeness, the way they looked out for each other. Even without his past, he doubted he'd had a family who cared like that. He frowned, uncertain if it was the truth or a defense against the sting of rejection.

"Hunters ahead."

Liam cocked his head and heard their animated discussion. "Something has happened."

"Yeah. If we can see which direction they go, you and Jago can sneak out earlier than planned."

Without words, they hastened their steps, trying to get closer to make sense of what was happening.

One man noticed them and nudged the tall dark-haired man next to him.

"What are you doing?" a tall, wiry man with a black beard and military bearing demanded.

"Walking home," Liam said. "Our cottage is off this path."

"Get on with it then and don't wander at night. It's not safe."

"Because they might shoot us," Sienna muttered.

Liam looped an arm around her, keeping her close, and he heard Sienna's breath hitch. Even through the fabric of her shirt, her warmth seeped into his palm. When she unconsciously leaned into him, something primal stirred in his chest—not just attraction, but possession. *Mine*, his feline whispered. The thought should have alarmed him. Instead, it felt like the first true thing he'd known since waking in the cottage.

Liam tightened his grip on her hand in silent warning. He tugged her past the men and along the path.

"Who died and made him boss?" she demanded.

"It's best if we keep up our newlywed cover."

As they turned off the path toward the cottage, the men loped past, their radios squawking. They disappeared around the corner.

"I'll follow for a bit to work out their direction. Tell Jago to get ready—we'll leave early while they're distracted."

"Take care. You don't want them to spot you."

Liam nodded and slipped into the shadows, following the men. It was easy enough since they were in a hurry and not checking behind them. The group seemed headed for the opposite end of town. Excellent. Liam skulked in the gloom until he confirmed his suspicions.

His low-grade headache had bloomed into something sharper, and he considered shifting. No—too risky.

Once clear of the village, safely out of sight of any hunters, Liam drew a deep breath, trying to steady himself. The pain only intensified, his vision swimming.

He slammed his eyes shut, but the darkness burst into

color—purple, green, flashes of orange.

His heart pounded, slamming against his breastbone as if it was trying to claw free. His knees buckled, and he collapsed to the ground—just as a cat's snarl echoed around him.

Hell!

Had he made the sound?

He slapped his hand against his mouth to hold the cries inside and tried to focus. Nothing but a moan squeezed past his lips. The feline cry repeated, this time a clear distress call he could hear above the thundering of his pulse. Liam attempted to stand, and on his second attempt, managed it. A faint sound from behind had him stiffening, but the familiar scent washing over him brought instant comfort.

"What's happening?" Sienna clutched his shoulders, her fingers digging into his flesh painfully, yet somehow centering him. Her hand slid beneath his T-shirt to rest on his belly, skin against skin, and the relief was immediate.

"Better," he managed, leaning into her touch without thinking.

"The headaches are getting worse, aren't they?" Her voice was thick with guilt.

He wanted to lie to spare her, but found he couldn't. "When I get tired."

His head still ached, but his awareness sharpened.

A man shouted, his voice tight with excitement. "Go that way. Head off the creature. Can you see it with the night vision glasses?"

"Who the heck was stupid enough to shift to feline with the hunters around? Did you see anything?" Sienna moved closer so he could hear her easily.

The war raging in his mind and body righted itself even more, enough for him to think.

"Hurry! Cut it off, dammit!" a second man roared.

"They haven't caught anyone yet. We have to help," Sienna said urgently.

Liam grasped her hand, using her strength to support his shaky limbs. Once confident of his balance, he released his grip. "I'll shift and distract them. If half of them chase me, we'll increase his chances of escape."

"No! You don't look well, and I can tell your head is hurting again. You're rubbing your temple."

"It's better after I shift. Here, take my clothes. You go with Jago, and I'll catch up with you. Don't let them see you."

Sienna hesitated, her beautiful face full of conflict. She didn't want to leave him, but saw the wisdom of his suggestion.

"Make sure they don't capture you because it will displease me." Her fierce words and matching expression surprised him. But it shouldn't have, given she haunted his thoughts so often. Aware of the passing time, he jerked off his boots and stripped. He thrust his garments at her and let his shift take him.

The pain in his head decreased, and his breathing became easier. After scenting the air, he slipped into the shadows, ready to help whichever shifter had run headlong into danger.

He glanced back once to ensure Sienna had gone, relaxing when he couldn't see her. Keeping to the shadows, he slipped forward, senses alert for the hunters' positions and the unlucky feline. If he were them, he'd have dart guns. He'd need to take care and remove them one by one. They'd seen three men, and hopefully no one else had arrived to bolster their numbers.

Liam crept closer to a man shouting orders into a radio. "Shoot it with the dart gun."

"Got him!" another voice shouted.

Crap, he had to move fast. Once they got their hands on one, a rescue would be difficult. What the hell had the feline been thinking?

He sprang at the speaker, catching him off guard. The wiry hunter hit the ground hard, shouting in astonishment as his glasses flew into the undergrowth. Liam shifted and, with a silent apology, struck. The blow dropped him instantly. Liam shifted again, feeling better than he had all day. His transformation eased his suffering—at least for now. On the move once more, he skulked through the shadows, stalking his next target.

He took out the hunter before the third man spotted him. For a long moment, they locked gazes. The man lifted his dart gun but fired wildly in shock or excitement—Liam wasn't sure which. Liam didn't hesitate because speed was of the essence. They'd downed the shifter but hadn't contained him yet. He retreated, circling to come in at a different angle and scoop up their prize.

Liam took a risk and shifted. He scooped up the darted animal and silently withdrew, hoping the panicked hunter wouldn't see him again.

The reek of alcohol filled his nostrils. A shifter could drink a large quantity of alcohol and not feel the effects, but perhaps booze explained this debacle. Liam angled toward the neighbor's property since it was closer, and the leopard he'd hauled over his shoulder was damn heavy.

A soft rustle to his right sent Liam rigid with alarm.

"Over here," a quiet voice said.

It was Jamie.

"Ma sent me to follow him to ensure he didn't do anything dumb."

Liam wondered what qualified as *dumb,* considering this idiot had made life difficult for every shifter in the village. The hunters had seen him in his leopard form, and now they wouldn't stop until they captured one. With the billionaire's money behind them, Liam figured they had time on their side.

"Which way?" Liam asked.

"There's a nearby cave," Jamie whispered. "Dad goes there whenever he and Ma fight."

"Show me."

Jamie cocked his head, listening before setting off at a brisk pace. Liam followed, and to his relief, gradually, the kerfuffle faded. He relaxed until Jamie froze.

Liam heard it too—a hunter talking on a phone or radio, attempting to contact his colleagues. He set the shifter down in the shadows, and he and Jamie squeezed back into the darkness as the man moved closer. There *were* more hunters now.

"We've seen one," a male voice squawked on the radio.

"On our way," the bulky hunter shouted, heading in their direction. Excitement radiated from him as he hastened his pace, jogging past and vanishing into the night.

Liam and Jaime waited until he was out of earshot before Jaime led the way to the cave. By the time they reached the dank entrance, Liam's muscles trembled, every fiber screaming with fatigue. He fought the quiver in his arms as he lowered the bulky cat to the ground. The cat twitched, eyes flickering before squeezing shut.

"Dad," Jamie said, his voice harsh. "You almost got caught."

The leopard let out a testy grunt and staggered to its feet, swaying unsteadily.

"What did he drink? How much?" Liam asked.

"Homemade grog. It's potent, and Dad and his friends like it because it gives them a buzz."

Anger pumped through Liam, throbbing in time with the pressure in his head. "Do you realize you've placed an entire village of shifters in danger? Not one of them is safe. They saw you in your leopard form. Now, they won't leave until they capture one." Liam bit off the words, not bothering to hold back his fury.

"Dad, you've screwed up bad this time."

The leopard snarled at Jamie and took a step toward him. The teenager didn't flinch, and Liam sensed Jamie had reached his limit.

"Go back to your smuggler friends," Jamie spat. "Make your money, but at least give some to Ma. Don't drink it all."

The leopard shifted, and the man would've struck his son if Liam hadn't stepped between them.

"I'm tired of you hitting me," Jamie bit out. "I'm done. No matter what I say to Ma, she won't leave you, but I can and will. You're not dragging me down to your level. I refuse to join the smugglers. I aim to make something of my life."

"Bah! You won't last a week on your own," the man said, his broken front tooth flashing.

The reek of alcohol was strong enough to make Liam reel.

"Maybe, but I'll have my pride." Jamie gave his father one last long look, his jaw clenched tight—disillusionment and distress warring in his features. He stumbled as he exited the dank cave.

Liam didn't see an ounce of regret or love for his son. The feline shifter didn't care. Somewhere in the dark recesses of Liam's mind, an image of an older man formed. He froze, not wanting to push at something that might crumble into dust if he gave it too much attention. Then he shook himself. He couldn't let Jamie leave alone. He was a kid and needed help, especially with hunters roaming the moors.

If they spotted Jamie, they'd ask questions, even though they had no business interrogating anyone.

"Jamie, wait," Liam said.

The teen's shoulders tensed, but he slowed his steps until he and Liam walked side by side.

"What's your next move?" Every instinct told Liam to let the teen figure out his future instead of trying to dictate it. Everything about this situation seemed eerily familiar, and he couldn't explain why.

"I had a little money saved from working at the market, but I gave it to Ma to buy food. Dad stole it and spent it on booze. Ma took Dad's side." A fat tear slid down the teen's face.

"Stay with us. Hedrek and the boys aren't at home, so we have room."

"But I can't pay."

"Payment isn't necessary." Although it wasn't his home, he instinctively understood Tamsin wouldn't turn Jamie away.

"Thanks. I'll find a way to pay for my board. Chop wood or do dishes."

Liam placed a companionable arm around Jamie's shoulders and briefly squeezed the teen to his side. By common assent, they didn't speak again until they reached the path leading to

Tamsin and Hedrek's cottage. Luckily, they didn't see or hear any of the hunters.

"Tamsin, it's me," Liam said after tapping on the front door.

The door flew open to reveal Sienna and Tamsin, who both appeared anxious.

"Thank goodness you're back," Sienna said, and the relief in her voice did something to his heart.

She took one look at Jamie and drew him inside with a reassuring smile. She and Tamsin fussed over the teen, offering comfort. Liam watched her with growing wonder. This woman, who'd kidnapped him out of desperation, was the same one who'd open her home to a troubled teenager without hesitation. The contradiction should have bothered him. Instead, it made him want to understand her more.

"You're staring," she murmured.

"You took in Jamie without question."

"He's as pale as my white tee. Obviously, he needs help."

"Like your family needed help when you came to that gathering." Pieces were clicking together. "You never take the easy path."

Her gaze was direct and held a hint of surprise. "Sometimes the right path isn't straightforward."

"No," he agreed. "It isn't."

Jago poked his head around the corner of the doorway, his expression tense until he spotted Liam. "What happened? We couldn't leave without knowing."

"My father," Jamie replied before Liam could explain. "He got drunk and shifted after he and Ma had a fight."

Tamsin and Sienna gaped at Jamie.

"The hunters spotted him." Jamie answered their unasked

question. "Liam helped me get him into hiding."

"I told Jamie he could stay with us," Liam said.

"Of course he can," Tamsin said, as Liam had hoped she would.

Tears welled in the teen's eyes at their calm acceptance, and a twang of familiarity played through Liam's mind. Jamie's situation resonated with him. He didn't push the memory—forcing it only made the pounding in his head worse.

"What will we do about our pottery supplies?" Worry sank into Jago's forehead. "Is it safe to go out tonight?"

"The hunters were searching nearer our house and toward the village," Jamie offered.

"We should go soon," Liam said. "Let's not give them a chance to reorganize."

"Jago and I were going to leave, but Ma suggested we wait for you," Sienna said.

"You have work tomorrow," Tamsin said. "We can't afford for you to lose your job."

"I can help," Jamie said. "Whatever you need."

"How do we know we can trust you?" Jago asked.

"Jago!" Tamsin turned a glare on her son. "Jamie warned us about the hunters. He risked a lot to help us."

"Yes, Ma," Jago said with a twitch of his nose.

"If Jamie will help, we can bring back more supplies," Liam said. "And it will mean Jago won't need to make a dangerous return trip."

"It's a small way to repay you," Jamie said, his expression earnest. "I'd never betray you." He turned to Tamsin. "You gave me a jam sandwich when I know you didn't have much.

I hadn't eaten for a long time, and I've never forgotten that. That's why I came to warn you. You and your family don't deserve the way the locals treat you. You treat everyone with respect. I-I admire that."

Tamsin hugged him. "You're welcome, Jamie."

"We'd appreciate the help," Jago said.

"We should go before the hunters regroup. Half of them didn't believe the beast existed," Liam said. "Now, several hunters have seen a leopard. They'll double down and get more aggressive."

"It won't be safe for anyone," Sienna said.

An understatement, although Liam didn't voice his concerns. They needed a plan to leave Stoneford, but where could they go? Hedrek and his sons would face scrutiny no matter where they settled. He was at a loss, and unfortunately, his memory, or lack thereof, didn't aid him in devising a plan.

Yeah, now that the hunters had a positive sighting, they'd report to their boss. A billionaire could throw more money and men at the problem.

With proof of a leopard in the vicinity, everyone was in danger.

CHAPTER 11

JAGO SET A RAPID pace through the dark landscape. Jamie followed closely while Liam lagged, slowed by the pounding in his skull. The pain made him clumsy and foggy. How much longer could this go on? Sienna had said he'd hit his head on a chest of drawers, but something didn't fit. She'd used drugs to knock him out. Could that be the issue? Surely the headaches shouldn't still be this bad. If he could trust them, he'd see the local feline doctor for advice.

Despite their haste, they listened for hunters, kept to the shadows, and took care with their foot placement. Up ahead, Jago froze, and he and Jamie followed suit. Voices became audible, coming from in front of them. Jago dove into the undergrowth, blending with the deep shadows. Jamie slipped behind a scraggly bush. Liam frantically searched for a hiding place, but his only option was to go up. He swung into the tree branches and winced at the rustle of the sparse leaves.

Three hunters marched along the path seconds later.

"Did you hear that?" the one walking in the lead demanded. He paused, his gaze shooting from side to side.

An eerie, piercing shriek cut through the night, and Liam flinched, almost losing his grip on the branch.

"That sounds like a fox," the man at the rear said, yawning. "I saw one earlier."

And thank goodness for the sighting. Liam peered down at them and wished they'd leave. If they glanced up, they'd see him.

Finally, the trio moved on, but Liam didn't risk drawing attention with a premature descent. He remained still, barely breathing, until he could no longer hear them. Then he climbed down and joined Jago and Jamie.

"They must've lost the trail," Jago said.

"They sound tired," Liam said, exhausted himself. "Perhaps they'll call it a night."

"I hope they don't bring in more hunters," Jamie said. "I'd hire more manpower if I were in charge."

Jamie was right. Liam and Jago exchanged a glance, recognizing this truth. They needed to find a solution to their problem soon, or none of them would survive. The person who'd encouraged the hunters to stay in the village had created a significant problem. They might have considered eliminating the Teagues, but they had simultaneously brought suffering to the other villagers.

Jago led the way again, quickening his pace over the rocky ground. Sharp stabs of pain lanced behind Liam's eyes, the discomfort worsening until he had to pause. His breath came in harsh gasps, and a sudden wave of nausea caught him off guard. Liam vomited at the side of the dirt track, his stomach churning as he struggled to stay upright.

A gentle hand touched his shoulder, and once he was confident he wouldn't barf again, he glanced up, the sour taste still coating his tongue. Colors flashed in his vision—oddly familiar. He'd experienced this before. But when? The answer hovered out of reach, buried beneath a haze that clouded his mind and churned his gut. He gave up chasing the fragments of his past and focused on breathing.

"Liam," Jago said. "It's not far. About fifteen minutes. Can you make it?"

Liam wasn't sure he could manage a hundred meters, let alone fifteen minutes of walking. But he gave a grunt of agreement and pushed himself upright, wavering. Without Jago and Jamie steadying him, he would've face-planted in the dirt.

He must've blacked out because when he came to, he found himself in a makeshift hut made of rocks. It was pitch black, apart from the light of a partially shaded lamp, and a drummer reverberated offbeat in his skull.

"Liam!"

The splitting headache he'd had for days was now a dull, erratic rhythm at his temples, but something else was wrong. The fog in his mind was lifting, and with it came a flood of images that hit him low and hard, leaving him queasy.

Scott. The castle. The gathering. The bar where they'd talked about...

"Middlemarch," he whispered, the word feeling like home on his tongue in a way Australia never had.

"Liam, are you feeling okay?"

He looked up at the concerned faces surrounding him, and

for the first time in days, they came into sharp focus. Not kin by blood or truth, but strangers bound to him by circumstance and secrets.

"I remember," he said, his voice hoarse. "The gathering. Scotland. My friend Scott." He rubbed the side of his forehead, where a dull throb persisted. "Your sister didn't just find me after I fell. Something's missing. How did she get me here?"

The silence stretched, heavy with confusion.

"She told you we were mates. But we'd never met before that night."

Hedrek's shoulders sagged. "Lad, I—"

"She kidnapped me." The words slipped out flat, but beneath the calm, a storm brewed—anger, pain, and a raw sense of loss.

Silence hung thick for a moment, then tension rippled through the hut like a sudden chill.

He should be furious, demanding they take him to the nearest police station. Instead, he found himself studying Hedrek's weathered face, the worn features stirring painful recollections of his own father's death, and how his mother and brothers had turned against him.

These people had wrapped him in warmth and acceptance. Even built on lies, it was more family than he'd ever known.

Not that it made things right.

Hedrek brushed his hand over his face, the rasp of stubble rough in the silence. "I suspected something was afoot, but you were helping us, and selfishly, I wanted to hold on to the positive changes you brought. I'm not blind. Neither are the boys. Tamsin and Sienna bear the taunts and shunning from the locals. We're failing them, but I'm struggling to find a solution. Now, Sienna... I'm sorry. Is there any way we can make this right?"

Sincerity shimmered through his words, and Liam's anger softened.

"What will you do?" Jago asked. "Sienna shouldn't have done what she did. She's our sister, and we love her." The unspoken message was clear—they stood by her, no matter what.

Loyalty. Liam understood it well, having found it in Middlemarch with Saber and London. They'd given him opportunities, and Saber had helped him find a job and a place to live. He'd made friends there, and through them, he grasped the meaning of trust and allegiance. Something his own family had never shown him.

"My friends will be concerned about me," Liam said. "There's so much I don't remember." The thought struck straight to the gut. Were these even all his memories? What if there were still gaps?

"Lad, I'm sorry, but that's the least of our problems," Hedrek said. "Jamie told us what happened tonight. This will make things a mite difficult for everyone. We're in danger—every single village resident with feline blood."

"As long as people don't start pointing the finger at others," Kitto said.

"Already happening." Jamie scowled. "They knew the hunters were coming and still didn't tell you. That's messed up, especially when you shift lots and are more likely to get caught."

Despite trying, Liam couldn't think of a solution. "How

long can you stay here without needing supplies?"

Hedrek paced the cramped hut. "Three weeks. We'll fish, trap rabbits—whatever we can catch. The meals won't be fancy, but we'll make do. I'd rather not leave Tamsin and Sienna on their own for too long."

Liam nodded and instantly regretted it. He froze, waiting for the knife-like stab to ease at the base of his skull. "Sienna told me a little about what happened. But not everything."

"She told you?" Hedrek blinked. "But you stayed."

"I wanted to help. You lot grow on a person."

"Aw, he likes us," Jago said.

Liam brushed this aside. "We need to leave the area."

"How?" Hedrek didn't bother to hide his frustration. "We're barely managing now."

True. Tamsin and Sienna struggled to stay within budget and keep everyone fed and clothed. "I wonder what Sienna did with my wallet and phone. I could call for help."

Calan tilted his head. "Call someone in Australia?"

"New Zealand. I live in a country town in the South Island," Liam said. "I work as a farmhand." He wasn't sure how long help would take, or if the Feline Council would even assist outsiders.

"What about Sienna?" Hedrek asked.

Sienna had put his job in jeopardy. The farm where he worked was a busy one, and Ted, his boss, was pragmatic. He'd hold Liam's job temporarily. "I don't know," Liam said, wanting honesty.

Hedrek released a harsh sigh. "I understand. Sienna committed a crime."

But that was the thing—was he angry? Hell, yes. But after

living with the Teagues and seeing how hard they worked to survive, he got it. And that understanding made his feelings as tangled as the village's problems.

Instead of dwelling on Sienna—infuriating, complicated, and far too attractive—Liam forced his focus back to the real issue: finding a solution.

"I'll ask Sienna what happened to my stuff once we get home." His thoughts stuttered because he'd called the Teague house home. They were genuine, and he liked them. Admired them. And Sienna, while she'd kidnapped him, hadn't used her body to trap him into closer ties. Yes, they'd slept in the same bed and shared a kiss, but she hadn't let him take things further. He could walk away, and no one could call him out. No consequences.

Just what every single man wanted.

Jago tapped his arm. "Liam? You keep zoning out on us."

"Sorry." Liam scraped his hands across his face and tried to focus. "If we could get my wallet, I could use my credit card for vehicle hire."

"Me too?" Jamie asked.

"If that's what you want, lad," Hedrek said without hesitation.

"We need to earn as much money as we can," Liam said, thinking aloud. "If the hunters stick around, leaving could get tricky. They might block roads or step things up, acting like they've got the law behind them. Now that they've seen a big cat, they'll double down on catching the Beast of Bodmin."

"Makes sense," Jago said. "What'll bring in the most profit?"

"You should make more of the hearts—they're easy to transport," Liam said. "And I think mugs with a Beast logo

110

would sell well."

The Teague men gaped at him before Callan burst out laughing.

"Really?" Hedrek asked.

"Yeah. The deal with the lemonade seller works well, and we're low on mugs. I think Beast of Bodmin ones would sell fast."

Hedrek tapped his chin. "How many should we make?"

"Fifty to a hundred," Liam said. "More if possible."

"You won't be able to carry them," Hedrek said.

"I'll make as many trips as it takes," Liam said. "Just focus on the hearts and mugs. Jamie and I can carry back whatever fits."

Hedrek moved to the doorway and studied the horizon. "Rain's coming. Stay until tonight. It'll ease off to a drizzle, and if we're lucky, it might keep the hunters inside. Now—are either of you any good at drawing?"

"Not me." Liam grimaced. "I can't even manage a stick figure."

"I can," Jamie said.

"Excellent. Help Kitto. Liam, you look like you need a break."

"My brain feels like it's on fire."

"Not surprised. Jago said you hit a rock—there's a decent lump on your temple. If you can't sleep, come sit with me while I work on the mugs," Hedrek said.

"Um, I have an idea," Jamie said. "It's not legal, but it might work."

Hedrek's brows rose. "Breaking the law is never a good idea."

"Let's listen to Jamie's idea," Liam said, his vision wavering.

"The smugglers," Jamie said. "If we pay them, they might drop us off further up the coast. From another town, it'd be easier to grab a van."

Hedrek tilted his head, his feline features tightening in thought. Liam waited for him to speak, considering it a solid plan—if they could rely on the smugglers.

"Jamie, lad, that could do the trick. Think they're trustworthy?"

"No," Jamie said without hesitation, "but they might do it for the money."

"How much would they charge? And who would we approach?" Liam asked, trying to think past the throb in his brain.

"If they catch on you're desperate, they'll jack up the price. They'll want to know why you're trying to bail."

"Let's keep this idea for later. We need to make money first, whether we pay them to take us up the coast or walk to get a van," Liam said.

"There's another way to make cash," Jamie said. "One of their ships got hit by a freak wave and lost four crew. That's what I argued with my dad about. He's on that crew and wants me to join the smugglers. The pay's good—as long as you don't get caught."

"But you don't want to join, right?" Liam asked.

"No way. But I'd do it for a bit if it helped me get out. My dad drinks way too much. Mum loves him but never calls him out."

"I'm sorry, lad," Hedrek said. "It's a decision you should never have to make. It's not right."

Jamie shrugged, but Liam saw the emotion flashing across his face. "I like your family," he said, the straightforward honesty striking deep.

Hedrek straightened his shoulders, his pride clear. "Thank you, Jamie, lad."

"We'd better get to work," Jago said.

The boys settled at their stations while Jamie worked with Kitto.

Liam tried to stand and swayed. "Hedrek, I need to shift. It might help my head."

"You do that, lad, and thank you. Sienna may not have done right by you, but having you here gave us the push we needed. We were stuck, unsure how to move forward. I'm grateful for your help and will do everything I can to support you in return."

"It's unnecessary."

"I know," Hedrek said. "Just like you could've walked away once you discovered what my daughter did. Shift, lad. We all need to be at our best if this plan is going to work."

Liam wobbled as he tried to shrug off his shirt. In the end, Hedrek helped him undress and held him steady, worry etched into his face.

"I don't like this, lad. We should get a doctor to look at you." He bit his lip because the local feline doctor might refuse to treat Liam.

"I'll be fine once I shift." Liam pushed himself to focus and pictured his leopard. Quick, stabbing shocks speared him, but he held firm, and gradually, his shift began. It was slow, and worry flooded him, but pulling out of his shift halfway through would cause bigger problems.

By the time he sank onto the hut's earthen floor, Liam was panting, his sides heaving. He closed his eyes and drew slow, steady breaths to keep panic at bay. Exhaustion pulled him under, and he let himself drift toward sleep. He'd rest while Hedrek and the boys handled things, and when he woke, he'd take the hearts and mugs home to Sienna.

CHAPTER 12

LIAM AND JAMIE HADN'T come back. Sienna gave up the pretense of sleep and slipped into her clothes with trembling hands. In the dim kitchen light, she poured a glass of water and sat, silence pressing down around her. After a long moment, she pulled out the ribbon she'd bought for the pottery hearts and tried to busy herself.

Outside, birds chirped in a morning chorus, but instead of comfort, the sound only deepened her worry. Had the hunters intercepted them on their journey there or on the way back?

Her mother entered the kitchen. "Oh, I thought you'd still be asleep."

"Liam hasn't returned," Sienna said, not bothering to hide her unease.

"Don't jump to conclusions. There could be plenty of reasons they're not back yet. Get dressed for work, and I'll make us some eggs on toast."

Sienna nodded, unappeased. Tensions were rising in the

village, and danger lurked everywhere. But her mother was correct. She could only control her actions, and maybe there was a good reason Liam hadn't returned. Still, she worried about him. She liked the man. A lot. He treated everyone with respect, which had won her over from the start.

Sienna dressed in a plain black skirt and a white blouse. She screwed her hair up into a clip and joined her mother.

"Have you got enough things to sell at the market today?" she asked.

"Yes, but I rely on Liam's help. I feel safer with him around."

"Me too," Sienna said. "We can leave early, and I can help you set up."

"I'd appreciate the help." Her mother chewed her bottom lip, and Sienna could see the stress in her expression. This wasn't easy for any of them, and the thought that some neighbors wanted them gone so badly they'd put everyone at risk didn't sit well with Sienna. Liam was right. They needed to get out before the situation exploded with them caught in the middle.

"We'll head off once we've eaten," Sienna said.

"I hope we don't run out of items to sell."

Sienna snorted. "We used to worry about selling enough to fill the pantry. Keeping up the stock is a better problem. What are you doing with the plain hearts?"

"I have cards with inspirational sayings, and I'll attach them. I'll also offer some for sale with no additions. It will be a test to learn which one is more popular."

Sienna smiled at her mother's enthusiasm. Liam's idea had them all excited. Her joy fled when she remembered Liam's prolonged absence.

"If the hunters have done anything to Liam and Jamie, we'll hear about it in the village," her mother said. "You're worried, and so am I. I keep thinking about Hedrek and the boys. None of us is safe. Right now, our priority is to carry on and earn as much as we can. Liam's right—we need to leave Stoneford and find a safer place."

Sienna nodded, understanding that the person behind the hunt wouldn't stop until he or she got what they wanted. Her mother set a plate before her. Eating was the least of her concerns, with her stomach tied in knots. But the last thing they wanted was for anyone to get sick, adding another burden to their already overwhelming difficulties.

She ate on automatic while her mind raced ahead. "How long will you be at the market?"

"I'll stay while I have items to sell or until everyone leaves the car park."

"I'll stop by during my lunch break before I head to the library to research Edwin Smith." Sienna ate the last bite of eggs and stood, taking her dirty dishes to the sink. "Are you ready to leave, or should I help you load the trolley?"

Her mother shoved her half-eaten breakfast away. "I've packed everything, but I can't eat when I'm anxious."

"Let's go then."

They set a brisk pace on the walk into Stoneford, not passing anyone. Birds chirped from the thickets, but the lack of noise from the carpenter's shop concerned Sienna. Normally, the place bustled with activity.

"It's too quiet," her mother whispered.

Sienna understood why her mother had lowered her voice. The stillness was eerie and slightly disturbing. "Are they holding the market today?"

"They will because many of the vendors rely on the income."

Her mother proved correct, and as they entered the village center, locals were busy setting up their stalls. The absence of the usual loud chatter and banter felt eerie, but grim faces told the story. Unease settled over the group, fueled by the news that the hunters had seen a leopard.

"The mayor told us to cooperate with them," a woman said to her neighbor as they walked past.

"That's true. He vouched for them, but they don't have true authority here."

Sienna slowed her steps to hear the reply.

"It's easier to go along with them, rather than attract their attention to my family," the woman said.

Yes, everyone, including her, was wondering what would come next. The leopard had slipped away, but the hunters had overstepped, barking orders at everyone like they owned the place. Life here was about to get unbearable, especially if the person in charge threw more money at them to ramp up the hunt.

"This is the site?" Sienna asked after her mother pushed the trolley past the rows of market stalls where the stallholders avoided eye contact, toward the distant car park. "I know you said it was by the car park, but this is so out of the way, you're lucky to get any foot traffic."

"I worried at first, but we get more pedestrians here than at our previous spot."

Given their position, Sienna couldn't believe that. She checked her watch. With so many shops still closed, she'd thought it was much earlier than eight. Where was everyone? The lemonade seller arrived, calling out a cheery good morning.

"Is Liam not here today?" Tony asked. "I've implemented his ideas, and I'm eager to learn whether they improve sales."

Sienna glanced askance at her mother, but Tamsin shrugged.

"Liam is helping my husband with the production side today," Tamsin said. "Hopefully, he'll be by later."

Tony jerked his head to the right. "Looks like our customers are starting early. Lucky for us, we're here. Early bird and the juicy worm."

Sienna helped her mother set up the folding table and display their stock. "How much are you charging for the hearts?"

"Liam and I didn't discuss the pricing," her mother said. "Twenty dollars?"

"We need money," Sienna said. "Which means maximizing prices. What price do you have on the mugs?"

"We were selling them for ten pounds, but Liam doubled the price, and they sold better."

"All right. Let's try forty pounds for the painted hearts on ribbons. The loose hearts, perhaps thirty? And the ones with your cards, say thirty-five."

"Seems expensive," Tamsin said, doubt in the line of her slumped shoulders.

"Let's ask for a second opinion," Sienna said. "Excuse me, Tony, do you think we could sell these for forty pounds each?"

Tony studied the hearts closely. "Yes. Who did the artwork? It's beautiful. In fact, could I have the one with pink roses instead of you paying me for your share of the site this week?

It's my wife's birthday on Thursday, and I think she'd love it."

"Done." Sienna grinned, plucking the heart from the black velvet where they'd nestled each item for display. She packed it in a velvet pouch she'd helped her mother make yesterday. "I hope your wife enjoys the gift."

"I'm taking her out to dinner at her favorite restaurant," Tony said.

"Wish her a happy birthday from us." Sienna glanced at her watch. "I'd better go, or I'll be late. Will you be okay?"

Tamsin kissed her on the cheek and shooed her away. Two women paused by their stall, their attention immediately claimed by the heart display. Sienna would've liked to linger to see if they purchased one, but aware she couldn't afford to lose her job, she rushed away.

"You're late," Molly snapped when Sienna sat behind her desk. Both phones rang, and the public waiting room looked packed to capacity.

"No, I'm right on time," Sienna said evenly. "Should I take over for you now? And is there anything urgent I can help you with?"

Molly lowered her voice. "Sorry, it's the hunters. Three more showed up, and everyone's on edge. Handle the calls for now, will you? And if you get a quiet moment, a cup of tea would be amazing."

"I'll do the tea first," Sienna said, bustling to the kitchen to make a large pot. The others would undoubtedly enjoy tea and biscuits. With refreshments distributed to the rest of the staff, Sienna concentrated on answering the phone and filing between calls. Meanwhile, she kept her ears open to gauge the mood and to learn if anyone mentioned Liam or Jamie.

All she learned was that the hunters' presence had scared locals, and more than one glared at her as if she were to blame, which was ludicrous. Toward the afternoon, three hunters appeared in the waiting room. They were big men and wore black, which gave them a menacing air.

Molly hustled over to them. "Can I help?"

"We're here to see the mayor," one said. His brown gaze was piercing, his attitude one of confidence, and Sienna bet he missed nothing.

"The mayor is in a meeting with the bank manager," Molly said, her voice level but her cheeks paler than earlier.

"I don't care. He gave us assurances and hasn't upheld his end of the bargain," the man said. "Either the mayor sees us now, or we interrupt his meeting."

Was the mayor behind this? But he'd let Molly employ her, which Sienna took as a sign he was sympathetic to their plight.

"The mayor?" the hunter snapped, pulling Sienna from her racing thoughts. She flicked her gaze over the determined hunters and busied herself filing until she discovered one leering at her.

Molly said something Sienna couldn't hear before hustling to the mayor's office. It was apparent she'd expected the hunters to wait, but the leader trailed her, and after one final insulting smirk in Sienna's direction, the hunter's friends followed.

"Don't bother introducing us, sweetheart," the hunter told Molly. He muscled her aside and strode into the mayor's domain.

"Hello, mayor," he boomed. "We need a discussion."

The other two hunters entered the office, and a red-faced

bank manager exited a moment later. The office door shut after him with a definitive click.

"I'm so sorry," Molly said to the furious man. "Should I reschedule your meeting?"

The man tugged at the hem of his black jacket even as he sniffed. "The mayor wanted my help. He was asking *me* for a favor. I told him I couldn't help him because it was too late. The vultures are already circling. He should've listened to me when I warned him about that mall project." And with those strident words, he marched from the office, his shoulders straight and his head held high.

Molly sighed and sent Sienna a wan smile. "I can tell this will be a trying day. Perhaps I could have another cup of tea to bolster my fortitude."

Sienna nodded, weighing the man's words. What favor did he mean? Was the mayor using these men—or being used himself? Mama had mentioned talks about the mall build circulating at the market. "Of course. I'll get tea for you now."

Shouting boomed from the mayor's office without warning.

"Oh, dear," Molly said. "I told Cormoran these men would be an issue." She fumbled in her desk drawer and pulled out a mini liquor bottle. "For my tea."

Sienna bit her lip, trying not to laugh because this wasn't a comical situation. Each of them was at risk, and things were about to become worse.

Chapter 13

The damning knowledge sat in Sienna's stomach like a stone. All morning, she'd watched Molly bustling around the office and dealing with visitors, completely unaware that their boss had sold out half the village.

Cormoran. The man her mother had once considered marrying. He'd turned the rejection into a decades-long feud.

Every time the mayor's door opened, Sienna's pulse spiked. Every time he smiled at her—that same polite, distant smile he'd worn for years—she wanted to scream. How long had he plotted this? Had he been waiting for the right moment ever since her mother chose Hedrek?

"Sienna, could you file these for me?" Molly handed her a stack of permits, oblivious to the cold, heavy pressure settling in Sienna's chest.

She nodded, her throat too tight to speak. A tremor shook her hands as she sorted the papers. Property surveys. Building permits. A thick folder marked *Teague, H.—Pottery Operation.*

Her father's business license. Filed where the mayor could easily find it. Where he could give it to anyone who asked the right questions.

And then there was what she'd overheard. Edwin Smith's name.

"Your debts don't disappear just because you're having second thoughts, Cormoran." The mayor had answered—calm, measured, not shouting. That was the worst part.

The hunter hadn't used the same restraint. "Smith bought your markers fair and square. You deliver his beast, or he calls them in."

The hunters' confident voices echoed from his office, and now she understood why they sounded so sure of themselves. They weren't visitors; they'd been invited.

Locals bombarded the mayor's office with phone calls and in-person meetings, and Molly kept Sienna busy for the entire day. She hadn't had time to check on her mother, and apprehension nudged at her. She practically ran home, while telling herself that if her mother had suffered problems, she would've heard by now.

Sienna came to an abrupt halt in the kitchen doorway, startled to find Mama humming as she chopped onions and cabbage.

Her mother turned with a grin Sienna hadn't seen in weeks. "The hearts sold out. All of them."

"That's wonderful! But what about tomorrow?"

"They delivered while we were gone." Her mother gestured toward the two boxes on the bed. "Hearts and tumblers. Look at these."

Sienna picked up a tumbler painted with a snarling leopard.

Each one was different, but all featured cats. "These are brilliant. The village is crawling with beast hunters—tourists will snap these up."

"The boys have outdone themselves. And Kitto didn't paint all the hearts. You can see the different styles." Her mother showed her an elegant lady in a garden, then a heart with a fierce cat's head.

"They're running low on supplies," Sienna noted, spotting the scrawled list. "Paint and brushes. We'll need more ribbon, too."

"I'll get everything after tomorrow's market." Her mother's enthusiasm was infectious. "We might actually have enough to leave soon."

They might also have to flee before being fully prepared.

"Okay," Sienna said. "What if we stocked up on hearts and sold them in markets on the way north?"

"Excellent idea. I'll leave a note to ask Hedrek and the boys to concentrate on the hearts."

"It will be dark soon. We should have dinner and get to work preparing the hearts for market."

A cheerful whistle had their heads jerking toward the sound.

Jamie strode out of the gloom, carrying a box and a large backpack. Sienna's breath caught, and her gaze darted past the teen, but disappointment struck. Liam hadn't come.

"Jamie, you've been busy," her mother said. "Are you hungry? We're about to have dinner."

"Starving," he said with gusto. "I brought more hearts and tumblers. They told me to stay the night and return with supplies in daylight. Hedrek said I should help you at the market, then bring the rest back afterward. Do you like the hearts? Kitto and I made them."

"They're fantastic," Sienna said. "I thought Liam might've come with you."

Jamie's smile fell away. "Liam hasn't been well. Hedrek said it was better for him to rest."

"What's wrong with him?" Sienna demanded.

"His memory is back, but he's still having problems. Hedrek said the knocks on his head were taking a toll, and he needed quiet and rest."

"No." Sienna clapped her hand to her mouth. "I should go to him."

"No," Jamie said.

"No," her mother said at the same time.

"But—"

"You need to stay here and continue working. You're our eyes and ears."

"Mama, I meant to tell you, but you distracted me. The mayor is the one who called the hunters. I learned that today."

"The mayor?" her mother asked, her tone bewildered. "We were friends when I was your age. After I met your father, he and his family refused to speak to me. Are you certain?"

"Yes. I overheard quite a bit about Edwin Smith. The mayor knows him."

"At least Cormoran didn't point the hunters directly at us."

"The bank manager also met with the mayor. Have we heard whispers of financial problems?"

"I heard rumors maybe three or four months ago, but I didn't believe them. Cormoran's family has always had money."

"But what if he has spent it? He doesn't have a gambling

problem, does he?"

Her mother scowled. "Cormoran has always pushed to get ahead."

Jamie's gurgling stomach interrupted the conversation. His cheeks turned pink. "Sorry."

"Nothing to be sorry about," her mother said. "You're a growing lad. We'll eat, and you can help us prepare the hearts for sale. We want to be inside before the hunters do their rounds."

"Did you see any while you were walking here?" Sienna asked.

"No, but they'll be everywhere tonight."

"I saw one in the village, but he kept to himself," her mother said. "Also, two passed me when I was walking home. They looked tired and dusty as if they'd been out all night."

"We'll have to get used to them being around. From what I overheard, they're not leaving soon. They're furious with the mayor, but I didn't understand why. Molly told me he was in London and only arrived home this morning," Sienna said. "Perhaps he's distancing himself and pretending none of this is his fault. It could be guilt."

Her mother tut-tutted. "It's a terrible thing he's done—if he's responsible for the hunters. Some of the older residents enjoy shifting whenever the whim takes them. This enforced time in two legs might affect their mental health. Surely the mayor knows this."

Sienna snorted. "Mama, you see the good in everyone."

127

The throbbing in his skull shifted, and suddenly he was fourteen again, lying in twisted metal, his father's voice cutting through the chaos. "I'm proud of you, son. Always remember that."

Liam's breath caught. He'd buried that memory so deep he'd forgotten his father's last words weren't about blame—they were about love.

"Lad, is there something wrong?" Hedrek edged closer, and when Liam didn't react to his sudden appearance, he sat nearby. "Something on your mind?"

"Sienna." Liam had to talk to someone because he was confused. He hated the uncertainty. Or maybe that was the recent jolt to his head, still causing problems.

"Ah," Hedrek said after a pause in which he scanned Liam's expression. "You like her, and you're not sure what to do with this when she essentially upended your life."

"Yes," Liam said, glad he didn't have to put his tumultuous feelings into words.

"Only you can decide. You're still with us, which tells me you're torn."

"My friends will be worried."

"We don't have a phone, but someone in the village might lend you one. Sienna uses the internet at the library if we need to look up anything. Could you contact your friends from there?"

An excellent solution, but they'd want to help him, and he hated to drag them into danger. "Yes, I could."

"And?" Hedrek asked.

Liam shrugged, thinking about his friends. Not only would they worry, but they'd be searching for him. But they'd also understand once he explained. His friends would support him one hundred percent. It was this certainty that relieved the stress in his shoulders.

"What about your kin, lad? Won't they be worried?"

And just like that, the tension returned, sending a chill down his spine. His mother and brothers hated him and hadn't spoken to him in years. Not since…

"My family holds me responsible for my father's death." The words tore out of him. "My mother won't speak to me. After all these years, they still think I'm a murderer."

Hedrek rubbed his chin, his gaze thoughtful. "And what do you think?"

"I think…" Liam's voice cracked. "My father died telling me he loved me, and I've been too afraid to remember it."

Hedrek lingered in silence, then gripped Liam's shoulder in quiet resolve. "Listen to me, lad. A father doesn't lie with his last words. He spoke the truth. The rest of them let their grief turn into cowardice."

The immense sadness in Hedrek's voice told Liam he meant every word. This man was genuine and a gentleman through and through. The Teagues didn't deserve the hate leveled at them. It was time for honesty from his side. At least as much as he could give.

"Your family stands by each other no matter what. Mine threw me away the moment things got difficult. That's why I can't walk away from Sienna. From all of you. You've made me feel like I belong somewhere."

Hedrek squeezed his shoulder, and this physical contact, along with Hedrek's sympathetic face, had Liam wanting to blubber. He coughed to clear his throat and changed the subject.

"As soon as I'm able, I'll help Jamie take a load of items back to the cottage. The people at the castle are shifters, and they might help. If they won't, we should be able to hide out in Scotland."

"Lad, we won't have the clay to make our goods. The clay here is high quality."

"I understand, but it's dangerous staying in Stoneford. I'd hate the hunters to capture any of you. This situation won't end well."

Hedrek issued a deep sigh that seemed to come from the pit of his stomach. "You're right, of course, but change is difficult, and this place is my home. I know nothing else."

"I might have an idea," he said. "We should leave as soon as we can afford to hire a vehicle, but while we're waiting, I'll contact home."

He didn't mention his whirling thoughts yet—he wasn't sure if his friends would help, or if the Teagues would even want to leave Cornwall.

"You think those hearts will sell well?" Hedrek asked.

"I do, but Jamie will tell us how the initial sales went. Once we hear a yes or no, we can adapt."

Hedrek sighed again, and Liam realized he wasn't as calm as he seemed. This was hard for him. He was worried about his wife and daughter.

"The hearts are easy to make, and the boys enjoy the change. Kitto especially—he loves painting, and this pushes him creatively. But me, I prefer making platters the way my father taught me. There's real satisfaction in shaping the clay. This new direction...it might not be right for us."

Hedrek fell silent, and Liam understood—the weight the shifter carried, the stress woven into every decision. He understood how unforgiving the world could be toward those who were different, and that Hedrek and his sons were fighting a losing battle.

A pulse had him rubbing his temple. He'd experienced this before... The thought made him frown and prompted him to recall his injuries. Yeah, he'd also had a knock on the head that time but had blocked it out because he hadn't remembered until now. Hell. That day so long ago replayed through his mind, and he winced when he reached the moment of impact, the bawl of the cow, the car, then the crushing silence.

A phantom chill ran down his spine, leaving him momentarily breathless. *He hadn't realized how much of himself had been locked away, even before Sienna.*

"How did I not remember?" Liam muttered, his father's words of love crystal clear in his mind.

"Lad?"

"Um, something I haven't thought about for a long time," Liam said. "I'd forgotten. My family blames me for my father's death. But it *was* an accident."

Hedrek placed his hand on Liam's arm again. "How old were you?"

"Fourteen. They sent me to live with my uncle. My father's brother held me responsible, too, but he told me he'd see that I reached adulthood. He owed it to my father. On the day of my eighteenth birthday, he forced me to leave. I haven't seen or talked to any of them since."

Hedrek snorted. "You are an honorable man and exactly the sort of mate I'd wish for my daughter. Sienna might not have approached you correctly, but I couldn't ask for a better son-in-law. I hope you and Sienna can reconcile, but I don't want to pressure either of you. This is one problem you must solve together."

"Thank you," Liam said, wanting to sob at the simple acceptance. The only other person to show him this level of support was Saber. And his father. He'd been proud of Liam and had told him so.

Liam had survived the accident because of his feline genes, which were passed down to him by his mother. His father had been human and more fragile, especially when the other vehicle had hit their car because of low visibility.

They'd hit an animal. He hadn't remembered that, and no one else had mentioned the cow because it had run off after the collision. Liam rubbed his temple again and realized his head wasn't as sore as earlier. Liam didn't know if it was because he'd remembered minor details of the accident he hadn't before, or if his feline was helping him to heal. He yawned, and Hedrek noticed.

"Try to sleep, lad. The boys and I will work a little later to get a head start on our work for tomorrow. Sleep tight."

"Thanks, Hedrek.

Hedrek patted his shoulder. "Thank you, lad. Thank you."

CHAPTER 14

SIENNA WALKED TO THE market the following day with her mother and Jamie. She helped them unpack before heading to work.

Liam.

The man wouldn't leave her mind. They'd been together since leaving the gathering, and she missed him. Weird. Whatever they were, and whatever came next—her heart ached for him. Jamie's claim that he'd hit his head again worried her. Had he truly required rest, or was he injured and in need of medical attention? She should've grabbed his phone before fleeing the castle, but leaving it meant no one could add theft to the charges of abduction.

Still, she wished she could contact his home and let them know Liam was alive. Whether he was okay was another matter.

She fisted her hands until her fingernails dug into her palms, took a deep breath, and pushed through the double doors leading into the council offices. After yesterday, they were eerily quiet. Sienna glanced askance at Molly, who stared grimly at her computer screen.

"Is something wrong?" Sienna asked.

"Those bastards broke into the Pascoes' house last night." Molly's hands shook as she gripped her tea. "Sophie was...she'd shifted for the first time. They took her."

Sienna gasped, shock walloping her in the chest. She slid into her seat, stunned. "In her leopard form?"

"She's only thirteen. The first shift is terrifying enough without..." Molly shuddered. "God, I hope she stays in leopard form. Those men with a young girl."

It was easy to imagine what might happen, and the horror of it had Sienna's pulse racing.

Molly turned away, dashing away the moisture before anyone else noticed. "If her family acts recklessly, we'll have a bloodbath. Then more investigators will come, and possibly government agencies."

"What is the mayor up to?" Sienna demanded.

"Nothing," Molly said with harsh disapproval. "He says he warned everyone. If they didn't listen, it's their problem."

Sienna's skin crawled. "Really?"

"He says he's going to France for a prolonged holiday."

"A holiday? Now?"

"Probably guilt. Sophie is a child! She shifted in the privacy of her home," Molly said, glancing at the mayor's closed door, her expression one of distaste.

"We didn't receive a warning about the hunters. If it weren't for Jamie, we wouldn't have known."

Molly paled. "No one told you."

"No one," Sienna reiterated. "We were lucky the hunters didn't swoop down on the locals' homes earlier. They don't have authority, yet that isn't stopping their high-handed methods."

"The mayor is ignoring complaints," Molly said in disapproval. "Something else is going on with him. He hasn't been himself."

"He arranged for them to come to Stoneford," Sienna said.

"Heard that, did you? I don't know how Cormoran Richards can look you in the face. I saw Kitto and Jules together one night. They're friends. They were comfortable together, but I didn't see romantic intimacy."

"Kitto would never push himself on anyone. Our parents taught us better." She'd do everything in her power to put this situation right.

Molly offered Sienna a sad smile. "I was glad when the mayor agreed we should employ you. You have a work ethic young people should aspire to emulate. Your entire family works hard." She shook her head. "Villagers could learn a lot about life if they paid attention to your household."

"Thank you. Do you know Sophie's parents?"

"No one is helping them," Molly said before Sienna could say more. "Not a single person."

Shock surged through Sienna again, this time mixed with disgust. "Where are the hunters holding Sophie? Are they still in the village? Are any of the hunters still at the house?"

"No, Sienna," Molly said. "The mayor will sack you if you interfere."

"How much are they paying him?" Sienna asked.

Molly grimaced. "I don't know."

"But he's gaining more from this than separating my brother and his daughter?"

"That's my assumption."

Sienna snorted. The mayor had gone way down in her estimation. "Where would they keep Sophie, and who would help in a rescue attempt?"

"Sienna, it's too dangerous."

"Someone has to help her family. They can't do it on their own. Sophie is a child," Sienna snapped. "I can't live with knowing I didn't help try to save her."

"Your brothers would assist? After everything that has happened?"

"Yes," Sienna said. "Is the mayor in his office? A rude man called late yesterday and wanted to see him about the mall project. Said it was urgent and the mayor should stop avoiding him."

"No, he's working from home for the rest of the week before he leaves for France."

Of course, he was. He didn't want to be available to people right now, and if that didn't spell guilt, then Sienna had two heads. "If I left work now to put together a plan to save Sophie, would you tell him?"

"He'll find out. He has spies everywhere."

They were leaving, so what did it matter? She didn't say this aloud. It was best not to broadcast their plans—not yet. "I can't sit here and do nothing."

After a long pause, Molly nodded. "I'll cover for you. I'll also ring around and help assemble a team of shifters willing to help with Sophie's rescue."

"Thank you." Sienna stood and strode from the office. She

rushed to the market and was relieved to find Jamie still with her mother.

"Sienna, is something wrong?" her mother asked.

"Have you heard about Sophie Pascoe?" she asked in an undertone.

"What about Sophie?" Tony said, overhearing. "My wife is friends with her mother."

Sienna smelled human, but he also carried a distinct feline scent, so she took a calculated risk and included him in the conversation. "Hunters pushed into the Pascoe house last night and discovered Sophie in her feline form. They captured her and took her away."

"Fuck," Tony said in understatement.

"That's not legal, surely?" her mother said. "What is the mayor doing?"

Sienna's lips twisted. "The mayor is doing nothing. He warned everyone about the hunters, and now it is up to them to maintain their safety. He seems more worried about his business interests."

"I never liked the man," Tony muttered. "Too interested in money. I need to leave early. My wife will need me."

"Wait," Sienna said. "Before you go, I want to gather a team to rescue Sophie. It won't be easy, but we must try."

"Count me in," Tony said. "I'll put the word out. Where should I tell them to meet?"

"Would they be willing to gather at our place?" Sienna asked. "It would be best not to draw attention. Our cottage is out of town."

"I've heard rumors but never met your father or siblings. You've been nothing but kind and generous to me, especially since we've gone into business together. I'm willing to help. My friends will too. Sophie is a kid."

The man hurriedly served the few lingering customers and packed up his stall.

"Jamie, could you let Papa and the boys know what has happened? We'll need their help if we want to free Sophie."

"I'll leave now," Jamie said.

Tamsin gave him a quick hug. "Be careful. Don't attract attention."

He nodded and hurried away.

"I'd better pack up," her mother said.

"No, Ma. You should stay here and sell what you can before returning home. We need the income, especially if I end up losing my job."

A muscle in her mother's face twitched, and for an instant, Sienna saw the pain she couldn't hide. This weighed heavily on her, and she'd given up a lot to mate with Hedrek Teague. Her parents had disowned her, and life had been a constant struggle.

Sienna gave her mother a robust hug. "I'm sorry, Ma. None of us is making life easy for you."

"I'm scared, Sienna. Lately, every day, I wonder if someone will take your father or your brothers away from us. I wonder about our food situation." Her slender shoulders shook. "I wonder what fresh horror will arrive next."

Tears stung Sienna's eyes. "I kidnapped Liam."

Her mother gripped her shoulders. "And what a godsend that turned out to be. Liam is the one bright spot in our world."

"He'll want to go home to New Zealand," Sienna said.

"Listen, Ma. I need to discover where the hunters are keeping Sophie and what they plan. No matter the mayor's excuses, we can't turn our backs on her. I can't."

"Be careful, Sienna. I couldn't bear to lose you."

Sienna squeezed her mother's biceps. "I'll be careful. All I'm doing is gathering information. We'll make a plan once Liam, Pa, and the boys get home. I'll try to find others to help."

"Ask them to meet at our home," her mother said. "If they're willing to meet Hedrek, I might trust them." Her mother's tone held defiance.

"I love you, Ma. You're the strongest person I know." An understatement.

Her mother patted her cheek. "You take after me, Sienna."

They grinned at each other before a woman and her two teenage daughters stopped to ask about the hearts. Sienna left her mother telling the customers about the local artists who made the hearts and hand-painted the designs. She wandered down the street, pretending to window-shop but using the reflection in the shop windows to check if anyone was watching her. Two hunters entered a coffee shop, but Sienna saw no sign of the others in the village.

Gradually, she made her way to the Pascoe house, hoping there might be visitors or people who could offer help, perhaps even provide a rescue plan. The other villagers' absence was conspicuous, and Sienna's anger bloomed. She tapped on the door, feeling the weight of the neighbor's stares as she waited for someone to answer.

Sophie's father, Arthur, answered the door. His eyes were red as if he'd been weeping.

"Hello, Mr. Pascoe. Can I come inside? I want to help."

A quick glimpse of disbelief showed before he stood aside in a wordless invitation for her to enter. Sienna waited while he closed the door. His two older brothers and their wives were in the sitting room with Sophie's distraught mother.

"How can you help?" Arthur's brother demanded while his wife tried to comfort Sophie's sobbing mother. "We tried to fight them off last night and failed. Tonight we'll try again."

The instinct to snarl struck Sienna first, but she fought for calm. This wasn't about her or her family. This was about an innocent young shifter girl sucked into this mess through no fault of her own.

"I'm not sure yet. I want to spend the day gathering information and arranging a meeting at our house for anyone willing to help. Do you know where they're holding Sophie? Has anyone heard whether the hunters plan to leave soon?"

"The mayor let them stay in one of his rental properties." Arthur's voice cracked. "And now...now that monster wants to come see his prize."

"Do we know when he's expected?" Sienna asked. Timing would be critical.

Arthur scowled. "Butcher said this afternoon. Flying in from Scotland."

Scotland? That was where they had intended to seek safety. They'd have to reconsider this or at least investigate the reclusive man to determine if he'd pose a danger to them.

His wife burst into noisy tears, and Arthur sent Sienna an apologetic look.

"So they're keeping Sophie at the rental?" Sienna asked.

"We think so, although we don't know for certain," one brother said.

Okay. She needed to confirm this info. "Are the rest of the hunters staying there, or are they still at the hotel where they've been to date?"

"The hotel. I saw four men returning from the hunt this morning when I was going to work." One of Arthur's brothers spoke up. "Two men at the holiday home."

"How do you know?" Sienna asked.

"Asked around, then went to see myself." He shot a glance at Arthur. "I couldn't do nothing."

They'd need to strike before the boss arrived, in case he brought more men with him. He'd need someone to look after his prize and maintain Sophie's health. An involuntary shudder rippled through her. They had to move fast. The hunters weren't stupid. Soon, someone would connect the clues and realize the number of shifter sightings might bear closer scrutiny.

Everyone was in danger, and doing nothing was the greatest threat of all.

CHAPTER 15

THEIR PLAN WAS SIMPLE.

They'd distract the hunters standing watch at the rental home and pick them off one at a time. For once, fortune favored them—fog had delayed the boss's plane. Sienna had overheard that bit of intelligence while skulking around the house, trying to learn the hunters' positions.

Now, she and the others—an unlikely mix of family and allies—closed in on the holiday home. Sienna had hoped more village men would step up, but most wanted to avoid trouble and protect their families. She understood. She did. But didn't they see? If that billionaire collector left Stoneford with Sophie, the child might never see her kin again. And if the vets drew blood, it could spell trouble for them all.

"Stop stewing. It won't change the locals' opinion or their inaction. We're doing the right thing," Liam said.

"I know. Liam, I'm so sorry I kidnapped you. I can't make it right, but I am sorry."

"I'm not."

She stopped in her tracks and stared at him.

"Head in the game," he whispered. "We'll talk once we ensure Sophie's safety."

It sounded like forgiveness, but his casual tone left her stunned. Could it be that simple? Had he dismissed her crime with a single word...or was it a distraction for the mission?

She shook herself and gathered her thoughts. Liam was right. Each of them needed to focus and do their part of the plan. The window of opportunity was incredibly tight with Edwin Smith on the way to Stoneford.

When they neared the rear of the rental home, they split into pairs and waited. Jago undressed and placed his clothes under a handy bush. He shifted, and after a nod at her and Liam, he padded through the thick undergrowth, a silent and deadly predator.

Today, they didn't intend to kill anyone, but they would render them unconscious if necessary and leave them bound and gagged.

Jago released a soft growl.

The guard they were targeting heard because he whirled and peered into the undergrowth. His hand twitched toward his weapon, body rigid, before he called out, "Who's there? Come out where I can see you."

Sienna and Liam slipped behind the hunter and waited for Jago to appear. Long seconds passed before Jago growled again.

The hunter cursed and fumbled for his radio. Before he could make the call, Jago darted forward and bit his leg while Sienna and Liam pounced. The hunter's strangled cry barely carried beyond the trees, and Sienna didn't think anyone heard before they gagged, blindfolded, and restrained him.

One down.

Her father and one of Sophie's uncles slinked deeper into the rental grounds. They disappeared into the wisps of fog and the growing gloom of the late afternoon.

She, Liam, and Jago took out the next guard using the same plan. Two more team members slipped inside to help in case there were unseen hunters. They now had their best people inside, equipped with tools to cut through padlocks and steel bolts.

Creeping around the house toward their next target, Sienna and the others approached the trickiest part of the plan—the section facing the road. Several homes lined the street, and none of the residents knew shifters existed.

Even as Sienna considered this, a car crawled along the road, its headlights attempting to spear the mist. Sienna thought the vehicle would continue past, but at the last moment, it swung into the driveway.

"The boss man has arrived early," Liam said as they studied the flashy limousine.

"They need more time to free Sophie," Sienna said. "We should give him something to see. Offer a distraction."

"I'll do it." Calan was already tearing off his clothes. A moment later, he shifted.

"Wait," Liam said. "This man is wealthy. He'll have security with him. I bet they're armed."

"That's not legal in the UK," Sienna said. "If this man's team carries weapons, it will be unlawful."

"Try telling him that when they're shooting at you," Liam

fired back.

"He's right," Hedrek said, "but I don't see we have another option. How about this? Sienna, you help with Sophie. She'll do better with a woman present. The rest of us will shift and distract the big man."

Sienna slipped inside the house, and she found Sophie's father working on the locked door on the second floor.

"Sophie, are you there? It's Papa."

A weak mewling came from the other side—not the strong feline growl Sienna had expected.

"Something's wrong," she whispered, her stomach plunging.

When they forced the door open, Sophie lay curled in the corner in her leopard form. Her movements were sluggish and uncoordinated. Her ears flattened at the sight of them—even her father.

"They've drugged her," Sophie's father said, anguish cracking his voice. "Sophie, kitten, it's Papa. You're safe now."

Sienna kneeled beside the girl, her mind racing. The same sick feeling she'd had watching Liam's confusion filled her chest. "We can't carry her out like this. If the sedative is wrong for shifters, we might make the situation worse."

"Delta-2, status report." The radio crackle from downstairs made everyone freeze.

"Delta-3, acknowledged. Checking perimeter now," came another voice.

Jago appeared in the doorway. "First guard we took out missed his check-in. Backup's probably already en route."

"She needs to shift back," Sienna said. "But someone has to stay with her—watch her breathing, make sure the drugs and the shift don't send her into shock."

"Shift, kitten," Sophie's father whispered.

Gunshots cracked from outside—too many, too close together. A chill rippled down Sienna's spine, her hands trembling as adrenaline surged through her.

She bit her lip hard as Sophie shifted from leopard to human. The change dragged, as if her body resisted every step of the transformation. Copper filled Sienna's mouth before Sophie was fully herself again.

"Can you walk?" Sienna slid an arm under Sophie's to brace her.

Sophie nodded groggily but stumbled when she tried to take a few steps.

More shots rang out, followed by a man's shout of pain—terrifyingly familiar. Sienna's instincts screamed at her to run outside, to help, to find Liam. Her chest tightened, breath shallow, as she gripped Sophie's arm with shaking hands. But Sophie wouldn't make it without support, and with her experience handling Liam's drugged confusion, Sienna was the logical choice to stay.

"Come on," she murmured to Sophie, wrapping the girl's arm around her shoulders. "We're getting you out of here."

Sienna trembled under Sophie's weight, realizing she couldn't manage the distance alone. Sophie's father took over without hesitation, lifting his daughter effortlessly.

As they stumbled toward the servants' stairs, Sienna kicked over a table. The glass vase perched on it wobbled precariously. She reached out to catch it, but it crashed to the wooden floor, the sound echoing down the hallway. It was a clumsy move, but one that drew the remaining guards toward her, diverting them from reinforcing the outside.

Immediately, heavy footsteps pounded up the front stairs. "Contact! Second floor!" someone shouted.

Sienna turned back and wedged a chair under the doorknob. When guards came looking, they'd waste precious seconds getting through.

Another shot sounded outside, rapidly followed by a second. A high-pitched feline yowl of pain had Sienna jolting. A man screamed seconds later, and Sienna winced. It didn't sound as if their rescue mission was going well.

Jago growled, an order for her to get her head in the game, just as a radio blasted to life again.

"Where's Jameson?" a man demanded.

Sienna grabbed a coat at the bottom of the stairs, enough to cover Sophie until she could find her own clothes.

She handed it over as they burst outside. The servants' entrance opened onto a narrow alley leading away from the main garden and past a walled vegetable plot—precisely what they needed.

"Take Sophie and get out. If you come across any of our group, take them with you. Don't go home—head to our cottage. I think you'll be safer there than in your house."

"Thank you," Sophie's father said. "Really, thank you. If you need anything, please ask."

"No thanks necessary. I'll see you later." Sienna flinched as another burst of gunfire erupted.

Outside, a deep voice issued crisp orders, every syllable radiating authority.

"Quick, exit through the rear gate. Apart from Jago and me, everyone in the house should regroup at our meeting point."

She paused. "Or better yet, leave town entirely. Spend time with out-of-town relatives. This will have repercussions."

"Aye," Sophie's father said. "Thank you again." He squeezed Sienna's shoulder and hurried away, clasping his daughter's hand as if he'd never let go.

She watched them leave before turning to a silent Jago.

"Any plan?"

He shook his head, then grinned, revealing sharp teeth.

"Let's hit them from behind. Let out a victory roar to signal success. Then we fall back and split up—make it harder for them to chase everyone."

Jago nudged her knee and slipped past the garden.

"Guess my strategy meets with approval."

She zipped her jacket and followed. Mist had fallen, shrouding the surroundings in murk and limiting visibility.

They listened as the battle continued near the house. Jago released a roar. Moments later, a man cursed—no feline growls this time.

"Where have they gone? Damn it! Don't let them get away!" The boss shouted orders.

Sienna hesitated, but Jago nudged her firmly, big-brother bossiness demanding she follow their game plan. They had to get back to the cottage, take stock, and decide their next move. Using her feline senses, Sienna navigated the fog with Jago keeping pace.

"Search the grounds!" the boss shouted.

A man ran toward them. Sienna and Jago froze, pressing against the trunk of an old oak with low-hanging branches.

Voices drifted through the fog—organized, methodical.

"Thermal shows movement northwest section."

"Copy that. Switching to night vision."

The hunters weren't bumbling anymore; they were adapting.

Jago nudged Sienna again, and she slipped away stealthily. It took them over half an hour to navigate the village, dodging hunters and wary locals, before reaching home.

Those who had beaten the hunters back were there—Sophie, her father, Sophie's mother, and her siblings. They huddled in a tight group, seeking comfort in each other after their ordeal. Sophie clung to her mother, her slight frame trembling.

Mama and Papa were busy brewing tea, passing cups around with Jamie's help.

Where was Liam? Kitto and Calan?

Sophie's two uncles arrived, breathless and red-faced. They scanned the group, relief flooding them when they spotted Sophie.

Jago had shifted and changed, then joined Sienna when she stepped outside.

"I can't see Liam, Kitto, or Calan."

"They'll be here," Jago said.

His confidence didn't ease the fear flooding Sienna.

"But we heard shots fired. Those men had guns."

"Everyone else is here. We took longer because we had to dodge hunters in the village. The boss man has everyone on high alert, so they probably had to backtrack to avoid hunters. Don't worry. They'll be here."

Jago was right.

Sienna scanned the foggy path to the village. The mist hung low, typical for this time of year.

"We were lucky with the weather."

"True. At least Sophie seems none the worse for her ordeal," Jago said, frowning. "But it's not safe for them to return home. Those hunters act like they're above the law."

"We might've made things worse. Even here, it's dangerous. The boss man saw leopards and will wonder why his hunters have spotted so many around town."

"He will if he's got any sense," Jago agreed. "We should move up our plans. Pack up and leave Stoneford—even if Pa refuses."

Sienna shook her head even though she agreed with her brother. "Papa loves the land. He always says as long as we pay taxes, no one can take it."

"This will be hard, but Liam's right. With hunters here, we must adapt."

"But money..." Sienna's worry returned. "We barely have enough to rent a vehicle. The mayor started this mess—I should ask him for help."

"Shifter families have been leaving all day. At least, that's my guess. The village was unusually quiet, with only hunters out."

"They will if they're smart," Sienna said. "Do you think Liam, Calan, and Kitto are okay?"Jago nodded, one ear pricked from beneath his hair. "Liam's clever. He'll watch over our brothers."

"Should we search for them?"

"No, wait longer. Returning to the rental now would put us in danger. You heard the man in charge—his orders showed how seriously he takes this."

"His arrogance," Sienna muttered. "He won't give up. Money and power are his weapons, and no one who stands in his way will win."

"That, too," Jago said. "I'm going to talk to Sophie—see what she remembers about her time with the hunters."

"I'll help Ma." Sienna needed to gauge her parents' feelings. She hated the thought of forcing them from their home, but staying was dangerous.

Sienna moved among the group, mentally making a list of necessities. Clothes and food, of course, but also the goods her father and brother had crafted, the paints and ribbons for hearts, and any tools her father deemed essential.

Despite her focus on practicalities, her thoughts kept drifting to Liam. Where was he? Kitto? Calan? Her gaze darted to the window and the path beyond, still empty. Her hands twisted the hem of her shirt, pulse fluttering faster with each tick of the clock.

"Thank you for helping with Sophie," one of Sophie's uncles said.

Sienna blinked, dragging her focus from the world outside to the man speaking. "I couldn't stand by and do nothing, though we may have made things worse. The man in charge didn't earn his millions by being stupid."

"No," the uncle agreed, a tall man with a broad frame and graying hair. "We're collecting vans and will pick up the bags Sophie's mother packed. We're leaving town. You should go too."

Sienna sighed. "We don't have transportation."

"We can squeeze you in and give you a ride to the neighboring town. You could rent a vehicle there. Do you have a plan?"

She nodded but kept the details to herself. He didn't ask.

"I'll talk to my parents, but there's little time to prepare."

"Better to leave possessions behind than risk captivity," he said.

"Thanks. I'll let you know when we're ready."

Sienna knew her parents would worry, but leaving Stoneford was the only sensible course of action. Now all she could do was wait—and hope Liam and her brothers were still alive.

CHAPTER 16

THE BULLET HOLE IN Liam's shoulder pulsed in the beat of a war drum—slow, savage, and impossible to ignore. He'd made it three miles through back alleys and fog-thick streets, slipping past hunters swarming the village like furious wasps. Now, slumped on the local vet's metal examination table, the shock was peeling away, leaving a raw electric ache coursing through him and the oppressive weight of what came next.

"Hold still," Gregory muttered in his soft Irish brogue, forceps deep in the wound. Metal scraped bone, and Liam's vision flashed white as pain lit up his nerves.

Calan and Kitto flanked him, and their solid presence steadied him. The vet kept casting anxious glances at Calan's twitching ears and the patchy dark fur on Kitto's forearms. Liam sensed the tension beneath the vet's calm exterior, the way his hands trembled a fraction, though he kept his voice steady and measured.

Gregory's forceps clamped down, and a sharp tug sent fire

racing down Liam's arm. The bullet clinked against a metal tray. "Got it."

A groan escaped Liam, and it was closer to a yowl than he'd like to admit. Kitto's hand clamped over his mouth.

"Easy," Kitto murmured. "We need you conscious. We can't exactly carry you through the village."

"The hunters are everywhere," Calan added, worry threading his voice. "We're not going anywhere until they calm down or take a break."

"You can't stay here." Panic edged Gregory's brogue as he began cleaning the wound. "I have my wife and children to consider."

Sienna. The not-knowing clawed at him worse than the bullet wound. Had she made it home? Was she safe, or was she lying somewhere, hurt and alone while he was stuck here, useless?

"Sienna," he whispered.

"She was heading home with the others," Kitto said. "Don't worry. Papa trained us well."

Liam kept his eyes squeezed shut while the vet worked, focusing on that certainty. Hedrek *had* trained them well. Sienna was smart, capable, and fierce when protecting those she loved. She'd made it home. *She was safe.*

"I like your parents," he muttered as the vet began stitching. "Much better than mine ever were."

"You can tell us later." Kitto squeezed his good shoulder. "Gregory's nearly done."

The sharp hiss of an aerosol can was his only warning before the antiseptic hit the wound. Raw agony lanced down his arm, and this time he couldn't muffle the scream. His vision grayed at the edges.

"There's no need to hurt him," Kitto snapped. "Liam got injured rescuing Sophie."

"And he's placed us all in danger," Gregory shot back, his tone ice-cold. "Because of your family, I have to leave the village to keep my wife and kids safe. Do you know how much I hate staying with my in-laws?"

"Selfish, aren't you? Only thinking of yourself." Calan's voice carried an edge Liam had never heard before.

"If you freaks didn't live in our village, none of this would've happened. The mayor wouldn't have called in the hunters and the animal collector."

"Animal collector?" Kitto seized on the words.

"So this isn't about the Bodmin Beast?" Calan pressed.

"Your kind *are* beasts," Gregory spat.

A thunderous pounding echoed from the front of the house, followed by raised voices. Everyone froze.

"My wife. My kids." Gregory stripped off his bloody gloves and bolted from the surgery, terror rolling off him in waves.

Liam forced his eyes open and struggled to sit up. Gentle hands held him in place.

"Stay," Calan murmured. "Gregory isn't stupid. If he tells the hunters about us, he endangers every villager, himself included. Those men saw several of us in leopard form tonight. They know something's not normal in this town."

It was the longest speech Liam had heard from the quietest Teague brother.

"We need transport," Liam said through gritted teeth. "Does anyone know where we can get a vehicle?"

"Not unless we steal one," Kitto said. "The problem is,

you're in no shape to drive, and Calan and I have never learned."

"I'll teach you." Liam tried to rise again, swayed, and nearly pitched forward, but Kitto grabbed him. "After I can see straight again."

"You barely made it this far. I doubt you'll get much farther without face-planting," Calan pointed out.

"But Liam's right about moving," Kitto said. "We can't stay—Gregory might trade us for his family's safety. I have an idea, though. There's somewhere we can hide until things settle."

Voices in the front room grew louder, Gregory's placating tone mixing with deeper voices demanding answers.

"Where?" Calan asked.

Kitto's ears flattened against his skull. "Jules has a painting studio. Her father doesn't know I still visit."

Calan gaped. "The mayor's daughter? The same one who called in those hunters? The one who got you beaten to a pulp?"

"We're friends. She helps me with art techniques. I help her with other things."

"Other things?" Calan's eyebrows lifted. "Kitto, you've been holding out on us."

"It's not like that." Pink crept up Kitto's neck. "We paint together. She's got a studio in her garden that her parents never visit because they hate the smell."

Gregory returned, opening the door so abruptly that all three of them jumped.

"They've gone, but you need to leave. Now."

"We will," Kitto said. "Thank you for treating Liam's

wound. What do we owe you?"

Gregory's expression softened fractionally. "Nothing. You saved Sophie when everyone else turned their backs." He paused. "But don't get caught. I doubt anyone else will bother helping you."

Liam groaned as he hauled himself off the examination table. His legs went rubbery, and only Kitto's quick reflexes kept him upright.

"Rear exit?" Calan asked.

Gregory led them through his cottage and cracked open the back door, peering both ways. "Clear for now. Move fast."

The fog had rolled in heavier while they were inside, a veil that offered cover but made every step treacherous. Each slow shuffle sent jolts through Liam's shoulder, and he had to grit his teeth to keep silent.

"This way." Kitto guided them away from the village center, taking a route Liam wouldn't have expected.

They glided like ghosts through the narrow lanes between cottages, pausing whenever voices echoed through the fog. Twice, they had to duck into doorways as hunters passed, their heavy boots and easy chatter marking them as confident predators. Occasionally, their radios squawked.

By the time they arrived at the edge of the mayor's property, Liam's vision was swimming. Sweat beaded his forehead despite the cool, damp air.

"How much farther?" he mumbled.

"Just to that building." Kitto pointed through the gloom toward a small structure barely visible beyond an ornate fountain. "Wait here while I check if Jules is around."

He melted into the shadows, leaving Liam swaying against

Calan's steady bulk.

"My brother is full of secrets," Calan muttered, but there was affection in his tone.

Kitto returned within minutes. "Jules is here. She says it's safe to come in."

"Will she tell her father we're here?"

"No." Kitto's voice held absolute certainty. "She's furious with him for bringing danger to the village. Her mother isn't speaking to him either."

They skirted the fountain—a Greek goddess pouring water from an urn—and Liam tried not to look at the dark windows of the mayor's mansion. His legs were barely holding him up, and paranoia whispered that someone was watching from behind those curtains.

Kitto tapped on a door. It opened right away, and a pretty blonde stepped aside, her movements smooth, her gaze already scanning the street behind them.

Jules wasn't who Liam had expected. Beautiful, yes, but her bright blue eyes held intelligence and determination rather than the vapid entitlement he'd expected from the mayor's daughter. She took in his condition with one sweeping glance before springing into action.

"Put him on the couch," she said, closing and locking the door behind them. "He needs to lie down before he falls."

The studio was larger than it had appeared from outside, with easels and canvases arranged around the space. The sharp, pungent scent of turpentine and oil paints filled the air. Under any other circumstances, Liam would have been curious about her work.

They guided Liam to a paint-spattered couch, and his knees

gave out the moment they let go. He collapsed onto the cushions with a pained grunt.

"Easy," Kitto murmured, guiding him back. "Rest while we figure out the next step."

"I should help plan," Liam said, his voice thin.

"You've had two head injuries and got shot tonight," Calan replied. "Rest. We'll need you tomorrow. You're no use to us if you're unconscious."

Liam blinked up at him, some of the tension easing from his shoulders. The quietest Teague brother was speaking up, and his words carried the same steady weight as his father's.

Around them, low conversation stirred as the others mapped their next move. Outside, hunters prowled with renewed purpose. And somewhere in the fog, Edwin Smith was likely plotting how to grow his collection.

But here, surrounded by the fierce loyalty of the Teague family and an unexpected ally, Liam let himself relax. They'd rescued Sophie. They'd bloodied the billionaire's nose.

Tomorrow would bring new challenges, but tonight, they were alive and together.

That had to be enough.

CHAPTER 17

THE NOT KNOWING WAS killing her.

The Pascoe family left, and Sienna watched as they drove away. With their departure, the window of escape they'd offered disappeared. Her family would have to find another way to leave Stoneford.

Without even considering the consequences, she jumped to her feet. "Mama, Papa. I'm going to work. We need information if we're going to make smart decisions."

Both of them snapped their gazes to her.

Mama opened her mouth—likely to object—but Papa murmured something low, and Mama gave a reluctant nod.

"Be careful," she whispered.

Sienna grabbed her coat and handbag and left, her steps brisk. She didn't see another soul until she reached the main road to the marketplace. An elderly woman pushed a shopping trolley along the footpath—Mrs. Watson, the retired librarian. Human.

A few people were setting up market stalls as Sienna passed, heading for the council offices. They were also human. Had all the shifters left town? It certainly looked that way. The scent of baking bread curled from the nearby coffee shop and bakery—heady, warm, deceptively normal.

A squawk of radio static made her slow. Male voices followed. Sienna pressed against the bakery's stone wall, heart pounding, just as boots clomped past on the cobblestones. Three hunters talking in low, clipped tones. She caught fragments: "...blood trail...vet's place...lock down the whole bloody village."

Her breath caught.

The jump toward a gunshot injury wasn't a massive leap.

Her feet were moving before the thought fully formed.

If she cut across the road and down the lane behind the council offices, she could beat them to the vet, but she'd have to move fast. As she passed her workplace, a pang of regret twisted in her gut. No time to mourn a job.

She sprinted down the lane, startling a blackbird from the gutter. By the time she skidded to a stop opposite the vet's surgery, her chest was heaving. His vehicle was gone. No patients waited outside.

A notice in the window caught her eye. She glanced over her shoulder, then darted closer for a better look.

The vet was away indefinitely due to a family emergency. His receptionist, another human, had signed the note. Every shifter who could leave Stoneford had already left.

"Hey, you!" a man shouted, skidding around the corner.

Sienna jerked left, evading his grasping hands, and bolted, her footsteps echoing off the narrow stone walls.

"Grab her!" he yelled.

Hunters in heavy boots bore down on her, their steps uneven on the unforgiving cobblestones. Sienna's lungs burned as she pushed harder, darting through an open gate into Mrs. Henderson's prized garden. The elderly woman would have a fit, but desperate times.

A curse rang out behind her as the hunter crashed through the rose bushes she'd nimbly avoided. Her muscles coiled, and she vaulted the six-foot fence in one smooth motion, landing on the balls of her feet.

"Did you see that?" one man panted. "No human jumps like that."

Shit. Her blood chilled even as sweat stung her eyes. She'd blown her cover.

She couldn't keep up this pace. Her chest burned with every gasp, and her legs shook like a newborn foal's.

Think, Sienna.

Where could a local go that strangers wouldn't?

The old mine shaft.

Dangerous, yes. Every parent had warned them to keep away as kids, but she knew the safe path. Jago and Calan had shown her years ago, swearing her to secrecy.

She veered left down a narrow alley most people didn't even notice, squeezing between two cottages so close together she had to turn sideways. Rough stone scraped her shoulders through her coat. Behind her, she heard a man try to follow and get stuck.

"Where the hell did she go?"

"There's a gap here, but I can't fit through."

"Go around. Cut her off at the other end!"

Sienna burst onto the moor, her feet sinking into boggy ground. Out here, local knowledge meant everything. One wrong step could leave her waist-deep in marsh water. She stuck to the hidden path only locals knew, stepping where generations of Teagues had walked.

A gunshot cracked.

She dropped instinctively, heart hammering like it might tear free. Were they shooting at her?

Another shot. Then shouting from a different direction.

"We've got movement by the old mine workings!"

Relief and fear tangled in her chest. They weren't after her, but they'd found someone. Who?

Staying low, she crawled to a crumbling stone wall, part of the old mining site, and peered over. Three hunters stood at the shaft entrance, gesturing wildly. One spoke into his radio.

"...definitely heard something...big cat...went into the old mine..."

"Should we follow it in?"

"Are you mental? That place is a death trap. We'll smoke it out."

A low rumble echoed from deep in the mine shaft—definitely feline. But something about the call seemed off. The call was too regular. Too perfectly timed.

"What if it dies down there?"

"Then we drag out the body and claim the bounty. Smith doesn't care whether it's alive or dead. If it's dead, he'll stuff it and mount it for display. All he wants is his prize."

The casual way they discussed murder made her sick. But that sound bothered her. She'd heard her brothers and father make distress calls, and this wasn't right.

As she watched, one hunter held up a hand for silence. The rumbling ceased, then started again with the same pitch.

"That's not a bloody cat," the hunter muttered. "That's a recording."

"What?"

"Listen to it. Same sound, same timing. Someone's playing games with us."

Sienna blinked, the pieces finally falling into place. The smugglers. Jamie had mentioned they used the old mine workings. They must have set up the recording to scare off anyone who got too close to their hiding spots.

"Check for footprints. Recent ones."

"The boss won't like this. We've been chasing shadows while the actual targets slip away."

One hunter kicked a loose stone. "The locals are playing us for fools."

Sienna had heard enough. The hunters were desperate now. Angry and unpredictable. She eased back, her mind racing. If the smugglers were using recordings to throw them off, how long before the hunters realized real shifters were still in town?

She had to get home. They needed to leave. Soon.

Each step was slow and deliberate until she was far enough to risk running. Then she bolted, tears streaking her face.

Whoever was down there in the mine would have to survive on their own.

Her family couldn't save everyone—they could barely save themselves.

She puffed out a sigh of relief when she entered the front door of the cottage almost two hours later.

"Sienna?" Jago appeared, his brow creased. "Your face is red.

You okay?"

Jamie loitered behind him, concern on his youthful face.

Sienna inhaled, trying to steady her breath. She'd never run so fast, but fleeing a hunter made it easy. "Most of the shifters are gone. We need to leave too. A van."

"What happened?" Jago asked.

"The hunters chased me. I didn't see any sign of Liam, Kitto, or Calan, but the hunters were following a blood trail." She brought him and Jamie up to speed.

Jago frowned. "Who in the village has a suitable vehicle?"

She knitted her brows. "What are you thinking?"

"We borrow it," Jago said. "Just long enough to get to the neighboring town. We can leave it there. It mightn't be legal, but these people owe us."

Sienna didn't disagree. "Pa won't like it."

Jago snorted, his cat ears pricking. "You kidnapped Liam."

"Yeah, okay." Sienna pulled a face. "Fair point. The mayor has a campervan."

"Huh! If the mayor is smart, he will have taken his wife and kids and gone already. I'll talk to Papa and Mama." Jago squared his shoulders. "Wish me luck."

Jago waved a hand and knocked on their parents' bedroom door. "Mama? Papa? We need to talk."

Jamie returned to the kitchen table, where Sienna's arrival had interrupted his work, threading ribbons through clay hearts. She sat beside him, her hands automatically taking up the task as she listened to the muffled voices from the bedroom.

"Leaving?" Papa's voice rang out, thick with disbelief. "Jago, this is our home."

"It's not safe anymore, Papa. They're hunting us."

"This land's been in my family for four generations," Papa said, his tone sharpening. "My great-grandfather built this cottage by hand. Every stone, every beam."

"The clay here is unique," Mama added, voice tight with worry. "Without it, we're ordinary potters competing with mass production. How will we survive?"

Jamie's fingers stilled on the ribbon he was threading. Sienna caught his eye and saw her own anxiety reflected there.

"At least here we know which people to avoid," Papa continued. "Out there, we'll be strangers everywhere. What if we can't find work? What if the boys get sick on the road?"

"Kitto and Calan are missing, possibly hurt, and you're worried about *clay*?" Jago's voice cracked with frustration. "I'm tired of being ashamed of what we look like. Maybe somewhere else, we could live instead of just survive—thrive."

A long silence followed. When Mama spoke again, her voice was smaller. "We have no references, no connections. Who will hire a family like us?"

"The Pascoes didn't hesitate," Jamie said, his voice carrying loud enough for Sienna to hear. "They left."

Sienna suddenly felt too hot. She pushed back from the table. "I need some air."

The evening had grown cool, mist beginning to creep in from the moor. She wrapped her arms around herself and walked to the edge of their small garden, where the land dropped away toward the valley. In daylight, she could see for miles: rolling hills dotted with sheep, the glint of the stream where she and her brothers had played as children, and the tor where Papa had taught them to shift safely away from prying eyes.

How many times had she stood in this spot? As a child, dreaming of adventures beyond the horizon. As a teenager, yearning to escape whispers and stares. Now, facing the reality of leaving, all she could see were the memories soaked into the rocky soil: the old oak where Kitto had fallen and broken his arm, Mama's herb garden, its scent carried on every breeze, and Papa's workshop, where clay became magic in her family's hands.

Behind her, voices rose and fell in the cottage, Papa's resistance crumbling under the weight of reality, Mama's fears giving way to fierce protectiveness. They would leave. She knew it with the same certainty that she knew this view by heart.

A night bird called from the copse of trees near the stream, its cry lonely in the gathering darkness. Soon, even that sound would be a memory.

Sienna pressed her hand to her chest, trying to hold on to this moment—the familiar ache of home, the bittersweet knowledge that sometimes love meant leaving everything you'd ever known behind.

When she turned back toward the cottage, golden light spilled from the windows, warm and welcoming. But for how much longer?

"Sienna?" Jamie's voice drifted from the doorway. "They've decided. We're leaving tomorrow."

She inclined her head, silent, before taking one last look at the valley that had formed her life.

"Where are you, Liam?" she muttered, peering toward the town. She prayed that he and her brothers were safe because she couldn't live with herself if something happened to them.

Then she walked toward the light, toward her family, toward whatever the future held.

"Jago and I will do a quick run to camp and return tomorrow with the equipment we should take with us," her father said. "Jamie, would you like to come?"

Jamie nodded.

"Please be careful," her mother said. "It will be dangerous out tonight."

Her father nodded. "Always, sweetheart. Always."

He, Jago, and Jamie collected packs and shrugged them onto their backs.

"See you in the morning," her father said.

Her mother's brow furrowed when she closed the door after them. "Are we doing the right thing?"

"Staying isn't an option, Mama."

As darkness fell, they finished the chores and sat in the kitchen, each cradling a mug of tea.

A heavy thump at the door made them tense. A second, then a third bang—definitely not her brothers.

Sienna stood, her inner cat bristling. "Hunters?"

"Be careful," her mother warned.

Sienna approached the door and inhaled. Two strangers—neither scent familiar. She smoothed her palms over her jeans and drew a steadying breath before cracking the door open.

The frown came naturally.

"Why are you banging on our door in the middle of the night?" she snapped, not opening it fully.

Two hunters loomed on the doorstep, broad-shouldered and stone-faced, their gaze sweeping her like predators sizing up prey.

"Who lives here?" one demanded.

"Who wants to know? And why?" Sienna shot back.

"We're doing house-to-house searches," the second said.

"Why?"

"For leopards."

"In our house?" Sienna scoffed. "No animals here. Not one."

"We're also looking for a man with a gunshot wound," the first said.

Her stomach hollowed. Liam? One of her brothers? She fought to keep her face blank. "Just my mother and me," Sienna said, planting her feet firmly in the threshold.

"Can we come in?"

"No," Sienna said.

"If you don't let us in, we'll assume you're hiding something," the man warned, edging forward.

Sienna snorted. "You wouldn't let me into your homes, so don't expect entry here." She shut the door, sliding the lock across, catching them off guard.

Who did they think they were? If they pushed it, she'd call the cops in the next village.

Tense, she pressed her ear to the door.

A muffled voice said, "We'll return when they least expect it. Tomorrow night. More men. We'll distract from the front, while others sneak in the back."

Sienna huffed, exasperated. They didn't have a rear entrance.

"We're lucky Hedrek and the boys left earlier," her mother said.

"Yeah. Ma, we can't keep living like this, wondering when

169

we'll fall a step behind instead of ahead. We need to change the narrative."

"I understand. Hedrek feels it too. But leaving everything familiar behind and stepping into uncertainty—it's terrifying. We're putting Hedrek and the boys at risk."

Sienna let out a shaky breath, a restless energy coiling beneath her skin. "Do you think the boys are okay? I'm so worried about Liam."

"If the hunters had caught Kitto or Calan, they'd be tearing through houses by now. Liam's still with them. He wouldn't abandon them."

"You like him," Sienna said.

"He'd make a fine son-in-law."

"I wouldn't count chickens." Sienna's gut twisted with worry and longing. "He might want to go home, and I wouldn't blame him."

"Don't borrow trouble," her mother said briskly. "I'll start packing. With eight of us, space will be tight. I'll pack a set of clothes for each boy and Hedrek, and one for each of us."

Sienna gathered food supplies, organizing them into the bigger, sturdier pack her mother recommended. Quietly, they worked side by side, the tension hanging between them.

"Should we find a phone and call the castle?" her mother asked, folding a shirt.

"And say what? I didn't make friends there. It's better to arrive and assess the situation first."

Her mother nodded and stowed the last items. A yawn escaped her.

"We should try to sleep," Sienna said, setting down the pack. "We'll need all the rest we can get if we're driving up to

Scotland."

"Agreed. Good night, Sienna. Don't worry. Hedrek and Jago will be back by morning. Liam and the others, too."

Sienna had always appreciated her mother's sunny disposition, but right now, she couldn't dredge up the same optimism.

"Good night, Mama. I've checked the windows, and they're locked. Hopefully, the hunters will stay away, at least until tomorrow."

Sienna closed her bedroom door and prepared for bed. When she slid between the sheets, Liam's scent washed over her. She tugged the covers up to her chin and inhaled deeply. Lord, she missed him and hoped he was okay. Her brothers, too. Her family would fall apart if anything were to happen to one of them.

She must have dozed, because the rumble of an engine jerked her awake. Sienna sat up, disoriented. What time was it? The cottage was dark, silent except for her mother's soft breathing in the next room.

Papa and Jago weren't supposed to return until morning.

Heart hammering, she slipped from bed and crept to the window. Through a gap in the curtains, headlights swept across their garden.

A vehicle rumbled up the path toward their cottage. Sienna peered through the curtain and gasped. Oh, no. It wasn't Papa and Jago returning. It was a black SUV with hunters inside.

CHAPTER 18

SIENNA SLIPPED THROUGH THE door into pre-dawn darkness, water bucket in hand. Exhaustion weighed on her after the night's chaos.

"Sienna."

She spun, bucket raised like a weapon. "Calan?"

"Yeah."

Relief washed over her, but worry for Liam and Kitto settled deep.

From the deep shadows near a towering schist pile, her brother stepped forward. "The hunters are still out. I had to take the long way around to avoid them."

"Where are Kitto and Liam?" Her heart banged against her ribs on spotting her brother's expression.

"Liam got shot. The vet removed the bullet and gave us antibiotics, but he spiked a fever overnight. Jules is watching him while Kitto gets some rest."

A low growl hummed in Sienna's throat at the unfamiliar

name. Jules? Who was that? She'd feel better once she saw Liam herself.

"Pa, Jago, and Jamie went to the camp to grab equipment. Ma and I packed. Now we have to figure out how to get out of the village."

"We have a vehicle," Calan said, grinning as he took the water bucket from Sienna.

"A vehicle? Big enough for everyone?"

His grin widened. "You know the mayor's campervan? We have it."

Sienna gasped. "He'll have you arrested for stealing."

"Nope. Jules said her father left for France yesterday morning—took the family car with her mother and sisters and told Jules to follow in the campervan. She's supposed to meet them there but decided to help us first."

"You told her where we're headed?"

"No, but Kitto trusts her—they've been friends for ages. I think we can too."

"I don't know—"

"Judge for yourself," Calan said.

"Where are they waiting?"

"Near the old campgrounds. We didn't see any hunters down there. From the gossip we picked up, they searched near the mayor's rental home."

"They came to the house, but I refused to let them inside."

Calan wrinkled his nose. "They've been out all night. I kid you not. I didn't get much sleep either."

"Since you're here, is there anything you need to take, bearing in mind we won't have much room, even in a campervan?"

"This one is large," Calan said.

"We'll need to drive via the back roads. Navigating some country roads will be difficult if the vehicle is too big." Sienna led the way into the cottage.

When her mother spotted Calan, she gave a glad cry, engulfing him in a crushing hug even though he towered over her. Sienna busied herself making coffee because she expected her father to arrive soon.

"Calan, can you help me stow the camping equipment inside the cottage? We mightn't be able to take it with us, but there is no sense in leaving it to get damaged outside," their mother said.

Calan busied himself following their mother's instructions, and by the time her father, older brother, and Jamie arrived, they had packed everything away.

They had a quick coffee, did a final clean, and prepared to leave.

Papa moved through the cottage slowly, his fingers trailing along the wooden mantelpiece he'd carved when Jago was born. In the kitchen, Mama paused at the window overlooking her herb garden, her hand pressed against the glass.

"Ready?" Sienna asked, compassion welling inside her. Leaving was difficult, but it had to be so much harder for her parents, who'd built their lives here and raised a family.

Her father nodded but didn't move, years of memories anchoring him here. Slowly, he shuffled to the door, the last to step outside. His weathered hand lingered on the frame, tracing the worn marks that measured his children's growth.

"We'll be back," Tamsin whispered, her voice faltering.

Hedrek closed the door with a soft click, final and heavy.

Jamie appeared at Hedrek's elbow without being asked, shouldering the heaviest pack before any of her brothers could protest. "I've got this," he said, and Hedrek's grateful nod said everything.

Without speaking, they hastened away from the village, taking the less-traveled path down to a gravel road. Each of them carried a pack and had to ensure the contents didn't rattle and reveal their location.

Sienna took one last glance at the cottage that had been her home for her entire life. Sadness filled her as she reflected on how they'd mostly had a good life here until the mayor had brought change. The indistinct murmur of voices drifted to her seconds before two hunters appeared. Sienna didn't dart, but glided to the right until she was out of sight. They'd been lucky this morning. Very lucky.

They kept moving in single file, with Sienna taking up the rear. They didn't speak, each aware of the danger of voices carrying. She promised herself they'd keep the land taxes current because if they ever returned, she wanted the land and cottage to be there for her parents.

It took an hour to walk to the campgrounds. Sienna didn't initially see the campervan because Jules had parked it behind a tall hedge, which did an excellent job of camouflage.

Sienna burst into a sprint when she saw her younger brother. "Kitto, how is Liam?"

Kitto frowned as she pushed past him. "His forehead is hot, but he's sleeping comfortably. Jules thinks it's best to let him wake naturally. He's not due to have more antibiotics until tonight. Come and see for yourself. I'll introduce Jules before we pack and take off. Jules, have you met my sister, Sienna?"

Jules was a pretty blonde with bright blue eyes and loads of confidence. She didn't hesitate to shake hands with Sienna.

"My parents, Hedrek and Tamsin Teague," Kitto said, and Sienna realized Kitto had confidence too. His friendship with Jules helped him blossom. "You've met Calan already, and this is my older brother, Jago, and our friend, Jamie."

"It's a pleasure to meet you. Kitto talks about you often, so I feel as if I know you already."

"Where is Liam? I want to see him," Sienna said.

"He's in the back. Kitto will show you. I'll help everyone stow your gear," Jules said.

"She's bossy," Calan muttered.

Jago grinned and brushed past, lugging a heavy pack. Calan and Jamie followed while Sienna darted after Kitto.

"How is he? Truly?" she asked.

"He didn't sleep much during the night. I think he had bad dreams. He shouted a few times. Honestly, Sienna. I worried someone would hear him and come to investigate."

Kitto opened a side door and stood aside to let her enter before him.

She gasped because the entire vehicle interior was luxurious, with the rich scent of leather. Everything appeared top-of-the-line. No expense spared. Where *did* the mayor get his money?

Liam lay buried beneath a pile of blankets, only his ruffled dark hair visible. Sienna crossed the room in two strides and sank beside him, her nose wrinkling at the mix of antiseptic and sweat. She pressed a hand to his forehead and winced. Heat poured off him, and her feline instincts stirred, sharp with alarm. Dark shadows ringed his eyes, and his breathing was too shallow.

"You said he's on antibiotics?"

"Yeah, the vet told us to keep him comfortable and get him to drink plenty of fluids. He seemed fine last night. Tired, but he spoke to us."

"Okay, Ma and I will keep watch over him."

"No, you and Ma will need to sit up front with Jules. None of us can sit up there because we're taking the fastest way to get away from Stoneford. Jules can drop us somewhere quiet, and we can hire a vehicle to take us north. I'll watch Liam."

"But—"

"No, we have to appear normal. Anyone searching for us will look for men and women." The distant sound of engines made Kitto's jaw tighten. "No arguments. We need to move."

Sienna smoothed a lock of Liam's hair off his forehead and nodded before backing up and exiting the campervan. She made way for her father, brothers, and the few bags that hadn't fit in the side lockers.

Her mother hovered, her discomfort clear in her shuffling feet and lip biting.

"Ma, it's going to be all right. Kitto wants us to travel upfront with Jules."

"Can we trust her?" Ma whispered. "She's the mayor's daughter."

"Just because I'm his daughter, it doesn't mean I'll turn you in to the hunters. Kitto and I have been friends for months." She paused, and the attitude seeped right out of her. "I've never told my parents about Kitto and me because they would disapprove, but I think my younger sister saw and told my father. My father gave me a lecture about choosing friends wisely, and my parents sent me to boarding school. We kept seeing each other, but only when I was at home for the school holidays."

"Your father called in the hunters." Sienna tried not to sound accusing, but it leaked into her words.

"I know. Look, we can talk on the way. Kitto and I studied the map last night and have picked out three different campgrounds. We can discuss and choose the one you think will work best." She rounded the front of the vehicle and climbed into the driver's seat.

Sienna nudged her mother, and they entered via the passenger side. A door slammed shut, and Jules started the engine.

"Everyone ready?" she asked.

There was a chorus of assent from the rear, and Jules pulled away from their sheltered spot and onto the gravel road. Jules wasn't a tall girl, but she drove with confidence and skill.

"Won't your father notice you're gone?" her mother asked.

"He and Mama and my younger sister have already left for France, but Papa wants the campervan there too. I'll take it as I promised, but I intend to help you get out of Stoneford first. I detest what he has done to your family. Even before the hunters came, he pressured the other villagers into causing trouble. And it was all because of my friendship with Kitto. We've done nothing wrong. I trust Kitto and know he won't try to kiss me or attack me, or worse, because he's honorable. My father sees only his differences. I want to help, and I won't tell my father or the hunters a thing."

"Thank you," Mama said. "I believe you."

Silence fell while Jules navigated the country roads. They

passed several vehicles full of men heading into the village.

"That doesn't bode well," Jules said with a frown.

"Those poor people. Many have left the village, but what will happen to those who have to remain?" Ma asked.

"They'll be all right as long as they stay in their human form and don't panic," Jules said. "But if I were them and couldn't leave, I'd make a complaint to the cops in the neighboring town. The hunters are breaking the law and bullying everyone."

"None of them will consider the police," Ma said. "The Stoneford shifters are independent and won't think to complain to human authorities."

"So do it for them," Jules said. "I have a prepaid phone. Use the internet to find the number, then call and make a complaint."

"Sienna," her mother said. "What do you think?"

"I'll do it," Sienna said.

"The prepaid is in there," Jules said, pointing to a small compartment. "Use mine to look up the number."

Sienna found the number and plugged it into the prepaid phone. Within seconds, she was speaking to an officer at the police station.

"Have you heard about the hunters searching for the Beast of Bodmin?" she asked.

"In Stoneford," the man said.

"Yes," Sienna said and then recounted the threats and bullying and the way the hunters were barging into people's homes and terrorizing the locals. "Please, can you do something? My husband is afraid. I have small children, and I'm worried the hunters will shoot someone. They have weapons. Please, you must help." Sienna hung up.

"Good job," Jules said. "That will get them moving or at least investigating. Sienna, can you get out the map and help me navigate? I don't want to use the GPS because Pa might check, and he'll freak if he sees where I've been."

When they reached an isolated campsite late afternoon, Sienna was pleased to see Liam awake.

"How do you feel?" she asked.

"Like someone shot me," Liam muttered.

"Happens a lot, does it?" Jago asked.

"Smart arse."

"No, really," Sienna said. "Can I check your wound? Sit over here." She gestured at one of the deck chairs Calan had set out. Jago and Kitto were helping Papa set up a tent while her mother and Jules were sorting out dinner.

Liam shrugged out of his shirt with a pained grunt. "I feel like an invalid."

She refrained from telling him he was one. The truth—he'd had a rough spell with two knocks on the head and a gunshot wound. He was lucky he was still functioning.

Sienna peeled off the tape and pad covering the wound. What she saw didn't reassure her much. The edges of the wound were red and swollen, with a thin line of pus seeping from one corner. This wasn't normal healing. "Let me clean it for you before you take more antibiotics. How many do you have left?"

"Don't know. Kitto has them."

"Okay." She found the first aid box and cleaned the wound with an antiseptic wipe. The doctor had stitched it closed, and she hoped he'd cleaned it well because she didn't want to reopen the wound. It wasn't as if they could go to a vet now.

"Where are we?" Liam asked.

"Wales. Jules and Kitto figured it would be best to drive through more isolated places. We used main roads to get here, but from tomorrow we'll stay on the B roads. We're with Jules tomorrow, but she'll drop Ma and me in town to sort out a hire vehicle. After that, she's heading for France."

Liam gripped her arm. "Can we trust her?"

"Yes, I think so. We haven't told her our destination, and she hasn't asked."

Once they had the camp organized and the tent pitched, Kitto and Jules worked on decorating the unpainted hearts. Liam drifted off to sleep.

She brought out the ribbons, and the rest of them settled down to thread them through the painted hearts, readying them for sale, while her parents went for a walk.

"We found clay," her father said, excitement lighting up his gaze. "It's a little different from ours, but it will work with our equipment. What do you say about staying here for longer? It's quiet, and I haven't seen anyone else since we arrived. What do you think?"

"You won't have access to cooking stuff once I leave," Jules pointed out.

"We could use the barbecue over there," Ma said.

Sienna shared a glance with her brothers before turning back to her parents. "We could stay, but we'll need to hire a vehicle."

"We have enough cash," her father said.

"Pa, they'll need a credit card or it will seem suspicious," Sienna said.

"I have a better idea. Staying here is fine, but use my credit card. I'll hire the vehicle and hand it over to you later." Jules bit her lip, momentarily losing some of her confidence. "Though I'll have some explaining to do when the charges show up."

"We don't want to get you in trouble."

Jules straightened. "My father owes you."

Sienna shared another glance with her brothers and nodded. "We're not sure of our destination. It will depend on local shifters and if they're welcoming. And we have to find an isolated place."

"A location with clay so we can make pottery to sell," Hedrek said.

"A north destination," Jules said. "Why don't I tell them I'll drop the vehicle at Edinburgh Airport? You can get someone else to deliver it if necessary."

Sienna nodded. "All right. Can we hire a van tomorrow, and I'll give you the equivalent in cash?"

"Check to see if they have any markets where we can hire a stall or sell from our van," Hedrek said.

The vehicle rental went through without a hitch, and she and Jules parted. Sienna scoped out the town and learned they had a market in two days. She booked a spot and purchased fresh bread, fruit, and vegetables from the market before heading back to their camping spot.

"Liam's not good," her mother said. "The wound looks infected. A scrap of foreign material may still be present."

"What do we do?" Sienna asked.

"We reopen the wound and clean it properly," Mama said, her tone grim. "I have my herbal supplies, and there are still the antibiotics."

"Ma," Sienna said, unease coiling inside her, rousing her

feline.

Her mother squeezed her hand. "The sooner we do this, the better."

"But what if he dies?" Sienna fervently wished she could turn back time because she'd made one mistake after another.

"We won't let him," her mother said.

CHAPTER 19

WATCHING LIAM RECOVER TESTED Sienna's patience. It took weeks before he could walk unaided, and he lost weight—heck, they all did—but at least they'd survived. She was grateful the campground stayed quiet, and the weekend market gave them a way to sell their hearts and tumblers and pad their savings despite the extended car rental.

They had Jule's card on file but no way to send her the cash. Sienna hoped they could pay part of the bill in person when they returned the vehicle. Just one more thing to worry about.

Once Liam was fit to travel, they packed up their gear and headed north to Scotland. Sienna had a plan, but she kept it to herself. She searched for a campground near Glenkirk and found one backing onto a forest.

"I'll head into town, see if there's a market where we can sell our hearts," she said. "Ma, you coming along?"

"No, I'll stay put. That was a long drive yesterday, and I tossed and turned last night."

None of them were sleeping well, stress taking its toll. Sienna knew it. Something had to change. They couldn't keep wild camping and scraping by, with no end in sight. Liam needed to go home, and she had to confess to the shifters who'd organized the gathering.

She didn't think they'd report her. At least, she hoped not. Whatever punishment they handed down, she'd accept. It was only fair.

Sienna forced a smile. "All right. I won't be long. I'll top up the diesel and see if I can find some cheap fruit and veg."

"Sausages? Or some soup bones?" her mother asked. "We need meat. Oh, look. Rabbits." She brightened. "I'll get the boys to go hunting."

Sienna nodded and grabbed cash before heading to the van. She glanced at Liam, sitting with Kitto and helping with painting.

Tears stung her eyes as she yanked her gaze from him. He was still pale, still paying the price for her selfish desperation. She had to fix this for him and for her own conscience.

It didn't matter that letting him go would break her heart. She'd gone and done the stupid thing—fallen for him. And despite everything, he'd never blamed her or her family.

But his dreams haunted her as much as they did him. He shut her out when the nightmares came, and she couldn't shake the dread that they were her fault. Another scar left by what she'd done.

Once she arrived in the town of Glenkirk, Sienna asked around and learned the village held a twice-weekly market. She booked a stall for both days, paid in cash, and pocketed the receipt.

Then came the part she could no longer avoid. She parked in the visitor car park and trudged to the castle gates, her heart beating way too fast.

At the gatehouse, her steps faltered, her feet like lead. The young man inside looked up, and for one wild second, she almost blurted she was in the wrong place and begged for directions to anywhere but here.

Instead, she stepped forward and cleared her throat. "I'd like to speak with Mr. Falconer, please." The words tumbled out, and it was like stepping off the edge of a cliff.

"An' who should I say's askin' for him?" the young man asked, his Scottish lilt carrying easily to her ears.

"My name is Sienna Teague. I attended the most recent gathering." She bit back the rest. Best not to say more.

"I'll put a call through now." He stalked over to a desktop phone, kilt swishing, and picked up the receiver.

Anxiously, Sienna waited. He was speaking, but all she heard was a low murmur. And she couldn't decipher his expression. The urge to fidget sent her away from the gatehouse and back again before she forced herself to still. Pacing wouldn't help her stay calm or explain things clearly.

Maybe she should've brought Liam. He hadn't offered to come—another worry. His memory had returned, but he wasn't the same. Whatever the bullet had done, it had taken pieces of him she couldn't fix. He was quieter now. And it scared her.

The truth—her father and the boys weren't doing well either. They were used to shifting at will and running. Here, they had to be extremely careful, even at the isolated campgrounds they favored. Sienna worried she'd steered them in the wrong direction, even though they'd all agreed to leave Stoneford.

"Ms. Teague, Mr. Falconer said to send ye through. Just follow the path and give a knock at the front door. He's dealin' wi' a supplier just now, but he'll see ye as soon as he's done."

Sienna nodded and wiped her damp palms on her jeans. The young man smiled, but her pulse kept racing.

"Dinna worry. Mr. Falconer barks more than he bites," he said with a wink.

Sienna forced a laugh, although it emerged rusty and fake. There was nothing funny—nothing at all. Every step brought her closer to her own undoing. "I know," she managed. "I have met him before."

The gatehouse phone rang, and the young man returned to his booth, leaving Sienna alone. She sucked in a breath and started walking. The scent of roses and lavender drifted in the air. Not that she took pleasure in the divine perfume. Instead, with each step, her limbs trembled, her knees threatening to buckle. She reached the immense wooden door—the entrance to the castle's foyer—and knocked. It opened way before Sienna was ready.

"Hello," a cheerful voice said.

Sienna froze on seeing the trim woman with her black hair in a braid and her welcoming grin. And her accent. It was like listening to Liam, but the feminine version. And she was familiar, but Sienna couldn't place where she'd seen her. No, it had to be at the gathering. Was this woman one of Liam's friends?

"Angus is still busy and asked me to escort you to the receiving room. He'll be at least half an hour, so I've ordered us tea." Her green eyes twinkled. "You look familiar. Have we met before?"

"I thought that," Sienna said while she willed herself to calm. "Were you at the last gathering?"

Sienna barely registered the surrounding grandeur. Ancient swords gleamed under modern lights, and tapestries whispered of centuries past as the woman led her deeper into the castle. The receiving room's mix of medieval stone and contemporary comfort should have been reassuring. But all she could focus on was the enormous fireplace, looming over her like a judge's bench.

The woman laughed. "I was."

"Me too." Sienna swallowed hard. "Your accent. Where are you from?"

"Ah, I come from New Zealand but live in Scotland now. I married the castle owner. My name is Suzie, by the way."

"Sienna."

"Ah, here's the tea," Suzie said. "Thanks, Moira. Please tell Steve I'll be late for my cooking lesson and to go over the menus for the upcoming function."

Moira, dressed in jeans and a T-shirt depicting a coat of arms, shook her head. "He'll shout."

Suzie rolled her eyes, her gaze full of mischief. "No doubt, but tell him I'm determined to perfect my shortbread, and I'll be there soon."

"I will, Miss Suzie." Moira unloaded the tea things off her tray and bustled away, humming.

Suzie picked up the teapot. "Do you take milk?"

"No, thank you." Sienna wasn't sure she could swallow tea. Her stomach was in knots, but holding a cup might give her hands something to do.

Her mind sharpened. She recognized the woman now—she'd seen her with Liam and his friend at the start of the gathering. There had been a larger group then, their number slowly dwindling.

Sienna swallowed hard. "I know Liam."

Suzie almost dropped the teapot before setting it down. "Liam? From the gathering?"

Sienna nodded, unable to meet her gaze. She'd expected this to be hard, but Suzie's stare pinned her like a leopard ready to pounce.

"I... ah." Her voice cracked. *Tell her.*

"I took him," she said. "From the castle. I drugged him and—"

Suzie's sharp intake of breath cut through the air, and the physical noise stabbed at Sienna.

"I kidnapped him." Her throat tightened, and she didn't dare touch the bone china cup, given the tremor of her hands. It looked valuable. A cold draft sent a shiver through her, but it might have been her conscience rather than the castle.

"Tell me," Suzie said, her gaze narrowing, all good cheer fading away. "Have you seen Liam?"

Sienna nodded, and Suzie jumped to her feet. "Niall!" she hollered.

A loud growl rumbled down the nearby stairwell, and an instant later, a massive man filled the doorway. He moved with surprising stealth for someone of his size, and his presence made the spacious room seem smaller.

"What's wrong?" His deep voice carried a calm authority as he strode to Suzie, one large hand settling protectively on her back. "Tell me."

"She knows Liam and his location," Suzie said.

A tall, thin man burst through the doorway—probably from the kitchen. Gray hair, lined face, and yet he moved with surprising speed. Sienna balled her hands into fists. Mr. Falconer, the castle steward.

"What's all the kerfuffle about? I can't see blood."

Suzie pointed at Sienna. "Angus, she knows Liam."

All three stared at her, and Sienna trembled. She had to do this. Tell them the truth. They were studying her as if she'd committed a terrible crime, and it was true. She had. She'd upended Liam's life.

"If you know where Liam is, you must tell us," Mr. Falconer said in a calm voice.

Beside him, Suzie trembled, every muscle coiled to pounce.

"He's here. I'll take you to him," Sienna said, her shoulders hunching as guilt washed over her. She couldn't look them in the eye.

"As long as he's safe," Mr. Falconer said.

"He hasn't been well—"

"Did you hurt him?" Suzie demanded, her teeth bared in a feline snarl.

Suzie's words landed hard, leaving Sienna reeling. She wanted to defend herself, to explain she'd never meant for any of this to happen, but the raw pain in Suzie's voice froze her. This was the cost of her selfishness—not just Liam's time, but the peace of mind of everyone who cared for him.

"Answer me," Suzie snapped.

"He knocked his head and suffered a severe concussion. He also picked up a flu bug after the bullet wound. We all did, but it hit Liam harder than the rest of us."

Sienna stood, more to put space between herself and a furious Suzie than for any other reason.

"Bullet wound?" Suzie growled, springing to her feet with a feline speed that made Sienna blink. Niall stepped between them before Suzie could reach her.

"Easy." Niall's enormous frame blocked Suzie's path without apparent effort, one hand gently but firmly on her shoulder. "Violence won't help anyone."

"Liam has been missing for months. Months! We had no idea where he was or what had happened. We've searched and searched for him, liaising with Saber and contacting shifter groups and every gathering attendee we could locate. His phone went to voicemail, and he didn't have his passport or wallet. He didn't touch his bank account. Now she waltzes into our home and tells us she knows his location. Why didn't Liam come with you? Are you holding him captive?"

"No! Of course not. I didn't push him when he said he wanted to stay with my brothers." Sienna swallowed hard, but the lump in her throat was stubborn about shifting.

"Explain the bullet wound," Suzie demanded.

"It was the hunters. The police shut them down," Sienna said, darting an uncertain glance at Suzie. The woman looked ready to do murder. "Edwin Smith moved his operations to South America, last I heard. But the village... We couldn't go back. Too much bad blood." Aware that she was babbling, she stopped talking.

"Please, Ms. Teague. Take a seat and tell us about Liam," Mr. Falconer said, a calm port in the storm that was Suzie's fury.

Yet Sienna didn't blame Suzie. She was Liam's friend. She'd

worried about him, searched for him, wanting answers. Envy crept in. She loved her family and cared for Liam. She'd grown to like him immensely. Before he became sick and slowed their journey to Scotland, he'd talked about his life in Middlemarch—the farm, his friends, his social life. They'd discussed so many things, and she'd miss the companionship when he left.

But this wasn't about her.

It was about Liam.

Sienna braced herself, spine stiff with resolve. The truth hovered on her tongue, and she let it out. She told them about her family and how much they were struggling. They'd scraped together money they didn't have so that she could attend the gathering.

She gave them facts, wincing at Suzie's growl when she got to the part about abducting Liam. She shared about his head injury and losing his memory. The hunter's arrival and Liam regaining his memory. She mentioned Sophie's rescue and how they'd concluded they'd have to leave their home because none of them were safe. About the slow journey to Scotland when they'd become ill, but they'd arrived in Glenkirk this morning, and she'd come straight here.

"Without Liam," Suzie gritted out.

"I asked him to come with me. He said he was tired. Would you have me drag him here?"

"You had no trouble dragging him away," Suzie pointed out, her tone sweet.

"Enough," Mr. Falconer said. "Niall, a word?"

The two men retreated, their heads together as they whispered in undertones. Despite her feline advantages,

Sienna couldn't make out a single word.

"How did you get Liam out of the castle unseen?" Banked fury glittered in Suzie's green eyes, and she aimed that anger solely at her.

Sienna managed not to wince this time, but it was a close-run thing. She deserved every bit of Suzie's anger. What she'd done to Liam was unforgivable, despite the reasons behind her decision. Involving another person in her crap wasn't the correct way to solve a problem.

"Well?" Suzie demanded.

"I took Liam out through a rear entrance, and it was pure luck no one spotted me."

Suzie sneered and was about to fire more cutting words when the two men returned.

"This is what we'll do." Niall's tone brooked no argument—the voice of a man used to making decisions worth millions. "We're coming with you. Your family comes back with us. The staff will see you, but they're all shifters," he added as Sienna started to protest. "No one here will harm your family or make them feel uncomfortable. We have no functions or human guests at present, so it will be safe for them to wander the gardens, run in the forest, or around the lake in either form."

"What?" Sienna said in unison with Suzie's pithy comment.

"Didn't you hear her?" Suzie said. "She abducted Liam and stole six months of his life. They've even replaced him at the farm, and he loved his job."

Sienna winced at the verbal jab, even though it was a statement of fact. Liam loved his job. Once his memories had returned, he'd talked about it often. It hurt her to know she'd caused this. "I'm sorry. I never meant to cause him harm. Believe me."

Suzie snorted.

"Your family will be safe with us. You have my word," Niall reiterated. "You said Liam and your family have been unwell. We have a shifter doctor who—"

"We're fine," Sienna said.

Her father would be wary of trusting strangers. Her brothers, too, but she'd be happier if someone more knowledgeable than her and her mother checked out Liam. His lethargy worried her, and she didn't mind admitting it.

"But you could be better," Mr. Falconer said. "You're struggling after leaving the only haven you knew. It can't be easy for any of you. We have dozens of empty rooms, hot showers, and healthy food. Stay for a few days at least, and if you want to leave after that, you can."

"You won't hurt my family? Or make fun of them?" Sienna asked, her mind turning over the pitfalls. The benefits. They could all get a good night's sleep and a hot shower. A nutritious meal, but they'd have to trust these strangers. Liam was friends with Suzie. She'd seen them interact. She didn't know Niall, but Mr. Falconer, the steward—he'd been decent to her. But still...

"Okay, let's be real. You don't have a choice," Suzie said. "We want Liam back. Take us to him and decide if you're coming to the castle or moving on without him."

"Suzie!" Mr. Falconer said, his expression full of disapproval. "Put your anger aside and place yourself in Sienna's shoes for one minute. How would you have reacted? If you were desperate, what would you do?"

Suzie's mouth opened and closed like a fish. "I wouldn't have kidnapped Liam."

A bell chimed in the distance, and Angus excused himself to answer the summons.

"What would you have done?" Sienna demanded, tired of this woman sniping at her. Yes, she deserved it, but she wasn't a doormat either. She was trying to make things right.

"I would never resort to kidnapping Liam," Suzie repeated, fire in her gaze.

All the *oomph* seeped out of Sienna. Her shoulders slumped, and tears pricked her eyes. There it was. The truth. She shouldn't have done it either. She should've found another way. "Don't you think I know that?" she whispered. "I'm doing my best to fix this."

"Ms. Teague." Angus returned, out of breath. "It seems your companions grew concerned when you didn't return as expected. He's been asking questions in the village about your movements." Before anyone could respond, the door knocker sounded again. "That'll be him now," Angus said with a slight smile. "A young man with a scar, asking after a Sienna Teague?"

Niall was already moving toward the door. "Liam," he said, as if he'd sensed his approach.

Liam strode inside. Sienna blinked because he appeared much better than this morning. He was still pale. Still thin, but he had an air of purpose about him.

"Liam!" Suzie sobbed as she launched herself at him, and he caught her automatically, feeling her tremble against his chest. "God, when you just vanished—" Her words tumbled out in a rush. "Your phone, your wallet, everything was still in your room. We searched everywhere."

"I know. I'm sorry." He held her tight, breathing in the familiar scent of her shampoo. How many nights had he lain awake thinking about home?

When Suzie stepped back, Niall was there. The big man's gaze was suspiciously bright as he pulled Liam into a careful embrace. "Six months," Niall said. "Six bloody months of not knowing if you were alive or dead."

"I'm harder to kill than that," Liam managed, his voice rough around the edges.

"You'd better be." Niall's hand lingered on his shoulder. "Suzie nearly organized her own search party to scour every inch of Scotland."

As he hugged his friends, Liam's gaze found Sienna over Suzie's shoulder. She sat frozen, watching their reunion with a mix of longing and guilt. She thought this was the end. That she'd delivered him back to his real life and could disappear with her family into the Scottish wilderness. She was wrong.

"Let's have a conversation," he said, his voice carrying across the room. "All of us. About what happens next."

CHAPTER 20

"YOU COMMITTED A CRIME, and you shouldn't get away with it."

Suzie's accusation hung in the air, sharp and relentless. Sienna's face drained of color, her hands trembling as she gripped the edge of her chair. She looked just as she had those first nights in Cornwall—terrified, guilty, braced for the next blow.

Liam watched as Suzie's words stripped Sienna of her composure. With her shoulders hunched and her chin lowered, she looked like a cat trying to disappear.

Fierce protectiveness surged in Liam's chest.

"Enough." His voice cut through the tension, sharper than he intended. All eyes turned to him, but he kept his focus on Suzie.

"She's not getting away with anything. Look at her—she's drowning in guilt."

Suzie opened her mouth, but Liam pushed on.

"You want to punish her? She's been punishing herself for months. Barely sleeps, and she watches me like I'll collapse or vanish, convinced every setback is her fault."

He stepped closer to Sienna—not quite touching, but near enough that she could feel his presence.

"She came here alone, knowing you'd be furious, knowing she might face consequences because she wanted to make things right."

The silence thickened. Outside the tall windows, gray Scottish clouds pressed against the glass, mirroring the weight in the room.

"That doesn't excuse—" Suzie started.

"No, it doesn't," Liam said, his tone softening. "But it explains a lot. And if you'd met her family, you'd understand why she was desperate enough to take such a risk." Sienna finally lifted her gaze, her brown eyes glistening with unshed tears. "Liam, it's not necessary for you—"

"It is," he said, his fingers brushing her shoulder. "Because I know who you are, Sienna Teague. And I know what your family means to you."

The room fell quiet except for the distant sound of wind rattling the castle's ancient stones. Angus cleared his throat, breaking the spell.

"Perhaps," he said diplomatically, "we should focus on the present situation rather than assigning blame."

Niall stepped forward, smiling. "We'd like to meet your family. Not to judge them, but to know them better."

"They don't need your understanding," Sienna said, though the heat had left her voice. She looked spent, as if the confession and Suzie's anger had wrung out what little fight she had left.

"Maybe not," Niall said. "But we'd like to help all the same."

Suzie was studying Sienna with a different expression now—still wary, but no longer openly hostile. "How long have you been camping?"

"Weeks." Sienna's answer was barely audible. "We had to leave everything. Our home, our pottery business, the land that's been in Papa's family for generations."

"Because of the hunters," Liam added. "The ones I mentioned. They took a young teen from her home. Dragged her away in her leopard form."

Suzie's breath caught. "A child?"

"We got her back," Sienna said, lifting her chin in a flash of old defiance. "But it only made things worse. Edwin Smith—the one funding the hunt—sent more men. It wasn't safe for anyone with feline blood."

"So you ran," Angus said, not unkindly.

"We survived." The words came out harsher than she likely meant. "My father and brothers can't hide what they are when they shift back. Ears, tails, patches of fur. They're different. Always have been. The villagers of Stoneford barely tolerated us before the hunters showed up."

Clouds gathered outside, dimming the room as Angus moved to switch on a lamp. The warm light caught the exhaustion etched on Sienna's face, the way her clothes hung loose from weight loss, and the careful way she held herself, as if she were bracing for another blow.

Liam saw the instant Suzie's anger gave way to surprise, her shoulders easing as the fight drained out of her. She was seeing what he'd seen for months—a woman pushed to her breaking point, fighting for those she loved.

"Where are they now?" Suzie asked.

"About twenty minutes away. At a campsite." Sienna glanced toward the window, where rain splattered against the glass. "They'll be wondering where I've gone."

"Camping in this weather?" Niall frowned, following her gaze. "That can't be comfortable."

"We've managed worse." But there was no pride in Sienna's voice now, only weariness.

Liam stepped closer to her chair. "What if we all went back together? You could introduce everyone properly. No pressure, no expectations—a conversation."

Sienna shook her head, her voice sharp. "It's not that they won't believe you... It's that they won't *trust* outsiders. The last time strangers came, hunters followed."

Liam's gaze didn't waver, but his tone softened. "I'm not expecting them to open up right away. But your family knows me. That's a start."

"All right," she said, after a long pause.

Sienna was quiet during the drive back, her knuckles white where she gripped the steering wheel. In the rearview mirror, Liam could see Niall's Range Rover following them through the increasingly heavy rain. The windshield wipers struggled against the downpour, and he leaned forward to peer through the gray curtain of water.

"They're going to think I've lost my mind. Bringing strangers to our camp."

"Your father will understand once he meets them."

"Will he?" She took a sharp turn onto the narrower road leading to the campsite. "Papa's spent his whole life being stared at, judged, rejected. And now I'm asking him to trust the friends of the man I kidnapped."

The campsite entrance appeared through the rain, marked by a weathered wooden sign. Sienna slowed as they passed the main facilities block, deserted except for one hardy camper's car, and continued toward the back, where the trees provided more shelter.

"There," she said, pointing to a cluster of tents barely visible through the pines.

Even from this distance, Liam noted how carefully they'd positioned everything. The Teagues had tucked their tents deep into the tree line, hidden from casual view. A tarp stretched between several oaks created a makeshift shelter where thin wisps of smoke rose from the concealed camp stove.

As they pulled up, figures emerged from the shelter. Hedrek appeared first, his distinctive silhouette unmistakable even in the rain. The boys flanked him protectively, while Tamsin hung back in the deeper shadows. Their positioning spoke of months of practiced caution.

"They look like they're ready to run," Niall observed quietly as he and Suzie joined them beside the vans.

"They probably are," Liam said. "It's become second nature."

Hedrek stepped forward as they approached, his leonine features set in polite wariness. His dark eyes took in Niall and Suzie with the quick assessment of someone who'd learned to read potential threats instantly.

"Papa," Sienna said, her voice carrying despite the rain drumming on the tarp above them. "These are Liam's friends from the castle. Niall Sinclair and his mate, Suzie."

"Mr. Teague." Niall extended his hand without hesitation, seemingly unbothered by the water dripping from his hair. "I'm pleased to meet you."

Hedrek scrutinized him before accepting the handshake. Behind him, Liam noticed Jago and Calan moving closer to their parents, protective and ready. Even Jamie edged nearer, his young gaze watchful.

"You're the castle owner Sienna mentioned," Hedrek said. It wasn't quite a question.

"I am. Though Angus, our steward, does most of the actual work." Niall's smile was easy and genuine. "I understand you've had an arduous journey."

Tamsin emerged from the shadows then, and Liam saw Suzie's intake of breath. Sienna's mother had always been elegant, but weeks of rough living had taken their toll. Her clothes hung loosely, her face looked gaunt, and the dark circles under her eyes spoke of many sleepless nights.

"Mrs. Teague," Suzie said, stepping forward with sudden purpose. "You must be exhausted. Camping in this weather can't be easy."

"We manage," Tamsin replied with quiet dignity.

The rain chose that moment to intensify, driving harder against their makeshift shelter. Water dripped through gaps in the tarp, and Jago darted over to adjust the sagging corner.

"This is madness," Suzie said, loud enough for everyone to hear. "You can't stay out here in this. Mr. Teague, we have warm, dry rooms at the castle. Hot water, proper beds, and decent food. Please, at least come in out of this storm."

Hedrek glanced at his wife, and Liam caught the silent

communication that passed between them. Tamsin's slight nod was almost imperceptible, but he saw Hedrek's shoulders relax fractionally.

"We appreciate the offer, but we don't want to impose."

"Papa." The word came from Jago, barely audible above the rain. He was still holding the corner of the tarp, water streaming down his face. "Mama's cough is getting worse."

Tamsin shot her oldest son a reproving look, but she couldn't quite suppress the harsh sound that escaped her throat as if summoned by his words.

"It's a cold," she insisted, but her voice was hoarse.

Suzie moved closer, her earlier anger completely forgotten. "How long have you had that cough?"

"A few days. It's nothing."

"In this damp?" Suzie shook her head. "Mrs. Teague, I'm not a doctor, but I know enough to recognize when someone needs to get warm and dry." She looked around the campsite, taking in the water pooling despite their best efforts, the steam rising from wet clothes, the way everyone unconsciously hunched against the cold. "This isn't safe for any of you."

A fierce gust of wind sent water cascading through a new gap in the tarp, and Jamie, who'd been silently helping Calan secure their gear, looked up, strands of hair plastered to his wet face.

"At least the hearts are safe," he said, patting a waterproof container. "We finished the new batch yesterday."

"Hearts?" Niall asked.

"Pottery," Jago explained, unconsciously moving to shield the container from the worst of the rain. "Papa, Calan, and I design them. Jamie and Kitto paint them. We sell them at markets."

"They're beautiful and popular with the tourists. The family has done well with them," Liam said.

Niall's eyebrows rose with interest. "Really? We get coachloads of tourists every year. I'm always looking for authentic Scottish crafts."

"These aren't Scottish," Calan said quickly, as if he was worried about being accused of false advertising.

"No, but they're handmade by skilled artisans," Niall replied. "That's what people want. Something genuine, made with care."

Another violent gust shook their shelter, and this time, part of the tarp tore free entirely. Rain immediately soaked the area where they'd been standing.

"Right," Hedrek said, his decision made. "Boys, start packing the essentials. Quickly now."

"What about the rest?" Tamsin asked, looking around at their carefully organized camp.

"We'll come back for it tomorrow if the weather clears," Niall said. "Bring what you need for tonight."

The efficiency with which the family moved spoke of long practice. Within minutes, they'd gathered personal items, secured their pottery, and dismantled what they could of their camp. Liam helped Jago wrestle a tent into submission while Suzie assisted Tamsin in gathering cooking supplies.

"Travel light," Hedrek instructed his sons. "We can always return."

But Liam caught the way he said it, as if he didn't quite believe they would. As if this was another temporary stop in a series of escapes.

As they loaded the last of the immediate necessities into the vans, Tamsin paused beside the driver's door, looking back at what remained of their campsite. Her expression was unreadable, but Liam detected a flash of something like grief.

"Mrs. Teague?" Suzie appeared at her elbow. "Are you all right?"

"It's just..." Tamsin's voice was barely audible over the rain. "We've been running so long. Sometimes I wonder if we'll ever have a proper home again."

The raw honesty caught Suzie off guard. For a moment, she stood in the downpour, staring at a woman who'd lost everything yet held her dignity.

"You will," Suzie said, her voice fierce. "I promise."

The castle emerged from the rain like something from a fairy tale, its ancient stones darkened by water but somehow more imposing for it. Warm light spilled from dozens of windows, casting golden rectangles against the lead-colored afternoon.

Liam heard Kitto's sharp intake of breath from the back of the van. "Is that where we're going?"

"Aye," Jamie whispered in awe.

Even Sienna was stunned into silence as they neared the main entrance. She'd been here before, but arriving now seemed different.

Niall had radioed ahead because the massive front doors opened before they'd even stopped. A small, energetic woman with silver hair hurried out, accompanied by two younger staff members carrying umbrellas.

"Mrs. Fraser," Niall called as he climbed out of his Range Rover. "I should have known you'd be watching for us."

"Course I was. Can't have folk turning up to a cold

welcome. Come on then, all of ye. Let's get ye inside before ye catch your deaths," she said, her Scots accent warm and inviting.

The organized efficiency reminded Liam of military operations he'd seen in films. Within minutes, the Teague family found themselves ushered through an entrance hall that could have housed their entire cottage, past suits of armor and oil paintings that seemed to watch their passage.

"Mrs. Fraser is our head housekeeper," Angus explained as he appeared to help with bags. "She runs this place with an iron fist, and we're all terrified of her."

"Speak for yourself, Angus Falconer," Mrs. Fraser replied tartly, but her eyes twinkled. "Now then, who needs dry clothes? I can see you're all soaked through."

Tamsin's cough chose that moment to return, echoing off the stone walls with an alarming rasp. Mrs. Fraser was at her side an instant later.

"Right, ye're headin' straight to a warm room to get into dry clothes. I'll have Dr. Mackenzie take a look at that chest." She cast a quick, practiced eye over the group. "How many rooms will we be needin'?"

"I don't know—" Hedrek began.

"Six," Liam said. "Hedrek and Tamsin share one, and each of the boys—and Sienna—has a room." He caught Sienna's questioning look and added, "For now."

Mrs. Fraser nodded with approval. "Good. I've got the Blue Suite ready for Mr. and Mrs. Teague. It's got a bonnie view o' the loch, and there's a sittin' room if they want a bit o' privacy. The tower rooms are for the young men—they'll like them, good views and plenty o' space. Miss Teague can have the Rose

Room."

As they climbed a grand staircase that could have accommodated a small parade, Calan whispered to his brothers, "Are we sure this isn't a dream? Because if it is, don't wake me up."

"The portraits are watching us," Kitto murmured back, staring at the succession of stern-faced ancestors lining the walls.

"They've been watching everyone for centuries," Suzie said with a laugh. "You get used to it. That one there—" she pointed to a fierce-looking Highland warrior, "—we pretend that's Niall's great-great-grandfather, but Niall and Angus inherited the castle from Cameron Glenkirk. Family legend says Cameron's ancestor once held off an entire English army single-handedly."

"Did he really?" Jamie asked, momentarily forgetting his usual shyness.

"Probably not," Niall admitted. "But it makes a good story."

They reached a long corridor lined with doors, each bearing a small brass nameplate. Mrs. Fraser began directing traffic with the efficiency of a general deploying troops.

"Mr. and Mrs. Teague, ye're here. There are robes in the wardrobe and tea things on the sideboard. Ring if ye need aught at all." She moved on before they could protest. "Young men, your rooms are down this way. Hot baths drawn, fresh clothes laid oot. Don't fash yersels about sizes—we keep a selection."

Liam watched Hedrek's face as he took in the opulent surroundings. The older man's expression remained blank, but his gaze betrayed his wonder. Tamsin was less successful at hiding her amazement, her gaze traveling from the rich tapestries to the carved wooden ceilings.

"This is too much," she said quietly to Mrs. Fraser. "We can't impose."

"Nonsense," the housekeeper replied. "Mr. Niall's instructions were clear. We're to treat ye as honored guests. Now, I'll have dinner ready in two hours—nae fancy, just good Scottish cookin'. Will that suit ye?"

She addressed the group, but it felt like Mrs. Fraser was really asking Hedrek, recognizing that despite Niall's authority, he was the one who'd decide for his family.

"That's very kind," Hedrek said. "We're grateful."

"No thanks needed. Just get yerselves warm and dry." She bustled away, already calling orders to staff members who seemed to materialize from nowhere.

In the sudden quiet that followed, the Teague family stood clustered together in the hallway, looking somewhat overwhelmed by the grandeur surrounding them.

"Well," Jago said. "This is different."

Two hours later, Liam barely recognized the family he'd camped with for weeks. The hot baths and fresh clothes had transformed them beyond the physical. Color had returned to their cheeks, and their movements no longer carried an edge of wariness.

Sienna appeared at the top of the stairs, wearing a simple green dress that brought out the color of her eyes, her dark hair loose around her shoulders instead of pulled back in its usual practical braid. When she caught him looking, she smoothed the skirt self-consciously.

"Mrs. Fraser insisted," she said. "She took my clothes away

to be laundered."

"You look beautiful."

The compliment flushed her cheeks, but before she could respond, Kitto bounded down the stairs behind her, practically vibrating with excitement.

"Liam, you should see my room! There's a window seat that looks out over the loch, and there are books everywhere. Art books with pictures of paintings from all over the world!"

"And the bath," Calan added, appearing with Jamie close behind. "It's the size of a small swimming pool."

"Bit different from washing in icy streams," Jago observed dryly, but he was grinning.

Hedrek and Tamsin descended more sedately, but Liam could see the change in them too. Hedrek wore a simple shirt and trousers that fit him well, and his usual guarded expression had softened. Tamsin looked almost fragile in a soft blue dress, but her cough had already improved in the warm, dry air.

"The doctor says it's a chest cold," she said when Suzie inquired. "Nothing that rest and warmth won't cure."

Mrs. Fraser appeared as if summoned. "We'll serve dinner in the wee dining room. Less formal than the great hall. Thought ye'd be more comfortable there."

The small dining room could still seat twenty, but someone had arranged chairs around one end of the long table, creating an intimate atmosphere despite the room's grand proportions. Candles flickered in silver holders, and the smell of roasted meat and fresh bread filled the air.

"This is incredible," Tamsin said, taking in the scene.

"Mrs. Fraser's outdone herself," Niall agreed, pulling out chairs for the ladies. "Though I suspect she's been planning this feast since the moment I called ahead."

"Guilty as charged," Mrs. Fraser said, appearing with a procession of serving dishes. "Haven't had a proper family dinner in ages. Mr. Niall grabs something from the kitchen and eats while readin' reports, and Miss Suzie loses track o' time when she's writin' her music."

"She exaggerates," Niall protested, but his grin suggested otherwise.

As the food was served—roast lamb with rosemary, vegetables from the castle's gardens, and thick slices of fresh bread—Liam watched the Teague family relax in earnest. Jago and Kitto were engaged in an animated conversation with Suzie about New Zealand, while Calan peppered Niall with questions about the castle's history.

"How old is this place?" Calan asked, gesturing around them with his fork.

Niall smiled. "Parts of it date back to the thirteenth century. Though different lairds have added and modified it countless times. They built the dining room we're in now in the eighteenth century."

"It must be a lot of responsibility," Hedrek said.

"It is. But it's also a privilege. This place has sheltered people for centuries, and it seems right to continue that tradition."

The comment hung in the air for a moment, and Liam saw understanding pass between the two men. Hedrek nodded, as if recognizing something in Niall's words.

"Tell me about your pottery," Suzie said, turning to Tamsin. "Liam mentioned you have quite a business."

"Had," Tamsin corrected. "We're not sure what comes next."

"Why not?" Kitto asked, looking up from his plate. "We could set up anywhere, couldn't we? Find new clay sources, new markets?"

"It's not that easy," Sienna said. "People don't always welcome our kind of family."

An uncomfortable silence fell over the table. It was Jamie who broke it, his youthful voice cutting through the quiet room.

"They welcomed us here."

The simple truth landed hard, rippling through the room. Liam saw Suzie's eyes grow bright, saw Niall's expression soften further.

"Yes," Hedrek said, his voice rough with emotion. "They did."

Mrs. Fraser chose that moment to appear with dessert. It was a magnificent trifle that drew appreciative murmurs from around the table.

"If ye don't mind me sayin', sir, it's been far too quiet around here lately. Nice to have a proper family at the table again." She set down a large glass bowl layered with sponge, custard, and cream. "And before anyone asks—nae, it's no' a trifle. It's a Tipsy Laird, and there's a good splash o' whisky in it, so go easy unless ye fancy a nap afterward."

As she bustled away, Liam caught the look that passed between Hedrek and Tamsin. It was the same one he'd seen countless times during their journey—the silent communication of two people who'd faced the world together for decades.

But this time, instead of wariness, he saw something else.

Hope.

211

CHAPTER 21

AFTER DINNER, AS THE family drifted off to explore the castle or retire to their rooms, Sienna walked the corridor toward the Rose Room with Liam beside her. The castle was peaceful, the warm glow of electric sconces casting soft, dancing shadows on the ancient stone walls.

"Thank you for tonight," she said when they reached her door. "My parents look happier than they have in months."

"They deserve it," Liam said, though his attention lingered on her mouth, not her words.

She fumbled with the door handle, nerves flaring at the thought of sharing a room. "Are you sure you want to stay here? Mrs. Fraser said there are other rooms."

"I'm sure." His voice was firm, leaving no room for argument. "We need to talk."

The door swung open to reveal the elegant Rose Room, its four-poster bed framed by a view of the moonlit loch. Sienna stepped inside, hyperaware of Liam following and the door closing in his wake.

They were truly alone. No campers nearby, no family within earshot, no urgent travel plans. Just the two of them, one bed, and far too many unspoken words.

"Talk about what?" she asked, her pulse skittering as her thoughts scrambled ahead of her.

"Us. About what I want." He stepped closer, and she caught the familiar scent of pine and feline.

Her legs wobbled, and she lurched toward the bed, craving space between them.

"What do you want?" The question barely made it past her lips.

His blue-green eyes gleamed, and something in his gaze made her breath catch.

"Right now? I want a kiss."

She blinked once. Then again. "Why?"

"Because I've been thinking about kissing you for days," he said, taking another step forward. "But with no privacy, all the traveling, the camping, me being sick... There wasn't time. Wasn't space. I want more than that."

Panic fluttered in her chest. "I—I thought we were talking first."

"We are, but right now, I have other things on my mind." His gaze dipped to her mouth, and she didn't need to ask what those things were.

"Liam." She backed toward the window, putting the width of the room between them. "You wanted to go home. I didn't think we had a future. So much has happened...and we didn't start normally."

"We didn't." He padded after her, careful and quiet, every

step measured, ears alert to her slightest movement. "But that doesn't change how I feel."

"How...you feel?" Her voice wavered, soft and uncertain, like a whisker twitch before a pounce.

"Despite the rocky start, Sienna Teague, I like you. A lot." He paused, focus locked on her. "We've kissed before, and I enjoyed every moment. I want to see where this could go."

The room seemed to spin around her. This couldn't be real. Men didn't say things like this to her. Not when they knew about her family.

"You're playing games," she said, her shoulders hunching defensively. "I realize I deserve this, but no one wants a do-over more than me. I wish I could turn back time and put this entire sorry mess behind me."

Liam's expression shifted, hurt flickering across his features. "I don't play games, Sienna. I'm telling you how I feel."

"B-but you're going home." The stutter was back, embarrassing her further. "I don't even have a passport, and besides, I can't leave them." She gestured vaguely toward the door, meaning her family.

"Which is why I want you to consider moving to New Zealand. All of you."

"We're not mates." The words burst out of her, final and desperate.

Liam tilted his head, studying her with those too-perceptive gaze. "Are you sure?"

That question hung between them, loaded with possibility she didn't dare examine. When he lifted his hand and brushed a lock of hair from her cheek, the gentleness of the action made her tremble.

"What are you doing?" she whispered.

"What do you think I'm doing?"

She pulled away, putting a safe space between them again. Her back hit the stone wall beside the window. "P-playing games. I know I deserve this—"

"Stop." His voice cut clean through her spiral. "You keep saying you deserve punishment, but I'm not here to hurt you. I'm trying to tell you I care."

"Why?" The word came out raw, torn from somewhere deep inside her. "Why would you want me? You know what my family is. The genetics, the rumors, the whispers—no one wants the bad seed of the Teague bloodline."

Something fierce flickered in Liam. "Is that what you think? That I'd judge you based on gossip and fear?"

"Everyone else does." Tears burned, but she blinked them back hard. "The boys at home made it clear—I'm good for a fling, maybe, but nothing serious. Who wants children that might not shift properly? Who wants to be tied to a family that everyone shuns?"

"I would." His voice held such quiet certainty that her breath caught. "I want to have children with you. And if they inherited your father's traits, I'd love them just as fiercely as I've come to love your brothers."

"You don't mean that." Her voice was barely audible.

"I would've thought you'd trust me by now," he said, and she heard the frustration building in him. "After everything we've been through together. After I stayed, after I helped your family, after I—" He stopped, running a hand through his dark hair. "But have it your way."

The hurt in his voice raked through her like claws. She

wanted to reach for him, to take back the doubt and fear, but the words stuck in her throat.

"I'll see you later," he said, heading for the door.

"Liam, wait—"

But he was gone, the door closing behind him with a quiet finality that somehow hurt more than if he'd slammed it.

Sienna sank onto the edge of the four-poster bed and buried her face in her hands, guilt and longing warring in her chest. He'd offered her everything—love, acceptance, a future—and she'd thrown it back in his face.

Deep down, in the place where old wounds lived, she still couldn't believe she deserved it.

The next morning, Sienna woke alone in the four-poster bed, the space beside her cold and undisturbed. After their argument the night before, she hadn't expected Liam to return, but the empty room still left her aching with disappointment.

She found him in the castle's breakfast room with her family, looking like he'd slept poorly. His hair stuck up in untidy tufts, and dark circles shadowed his eyes, clear signs he'd likely spent the night on a library couch instead of a proper bed.

"Sleep well?" he asked as she joined them, his tone cool and distant.

"Fine, thank you." The lie came easily, though from the look he gave her, she doubted he believed it any more than she believed his casual front.

Her family seemed oblivious to the tension between them,

chattering excitedly about the castle and their comfortable night's sleep. Mrs. Fraser bustled around them with her usual efficiency, but Sienna caught the housekeeper's sharp glance between her and Liam, as if she sensed something amiss.

Angus appeared in the doorway with his usual impeccable timing. "Saber Mitchell is available for a video call this morning."

An hour later, they assembled in Niall's office, where the large table accommodated the entire family, plus their hosts. The video screen flickered to life, and Sienna's stomach tightened. She didn't know what to expect.

"Good morning, Saber. London," Niall said, his voice steady. "This is the Teague family."

Saber was tall, with black hair, broad shoulders, and striking green eyes that immediately locked on Liam—sharp, assessing, and faintly worried.

London, a curvy, brown-haired woman, clutched Saber's arm. Her concern softened into a broad smile. "Liam! It's so good to see you. We've been so worried."

"Liam," Saber said. "How are you?"

Sienna caught the flicker of emotion across Liam's face, the slight glitter in his gaze as he murmured, "I'm okay." He cleared his throat and ran through quick introductions, starting with her parents.

"Good morning, everyone," Saber said, his warm smile now directed at the group. "I've brought some friends who wanted to meet you. This is Marcus, a wolf shifter, and his mate, Ria."

Sienna's breath caught as the camera panned to a woman with distinctive cat ears that didn't quite fold back properly and hair streaked like a calico's. Ria stood close to Marcus's side, offering a tentative smile, but obviously uneasy in the spotlight.

"Hello," Ria said, her golden-brown eyes flicking nervously between the camera and Marcus.

Calan shifted his hair to reveal his pointed black ears, and Kitto's tail flicked into view. "We're like you," Calan said, understanding her shyness.

Relief flooded Ria's features, and she nodded, some of the tension leaving her shoulders. Marcus's protective stance relaxed as he saw her comfort level increase.

"Ria's been the only one in our community with unique traits," Marcus said. "She's been looking forward to meeting others, but she's not much for big groups."

"We understand," Hedrek said.

Sienna felt her heart sink. "We don't have passports. None of us do. Papa and the boys don't exactly blend for official photos and interviews."

"That's not as big a problem as you might think," Saber said. "I have contacts who specialize in helping shifter families with unique circumstances. People who understand the challenges of documentation for those who don't fit the standard mold."

"Is that legal?" Tamsin asked.

Saber smiled. "It's more about knowing which forms to fill out, which officials to speak with, and how to handle the photography discreetly. These contacts have helped other families in similar situations."

"But surely the photos—" Jago began.

"We can handle those with proper lighting and angles," London finished. "It's not about deception, it's about presentation. Official documents need clear identification photos, and there are ways to achieve that."

Hedrek and Tamsin exchanged a look of amazement.

"Would you really arrange this for people you don't know?" Hedrek asked.

"You're family now," Saber said, consulting his notes. "Liam's family, which means you're ours too. Hedrek, you're potters, yes?"

"We are. It's been our family trade for generations."

"Perfect." London pulled out a tablet. "I've been researching local clay sources. There's a farmer about twenty minutes from town with excellent deposits who's looking for a partner. He'd provide the raw materials, and you'd bring the expertise. He takes a percentage of sales; you get access to quality clay."

Tamsin leaned forward, interest sparking in her expression. "That sounds ideal. Working with local materials."

"There's more," London said. "We have two empty retail premises in town. One would be perfect for a pottery studio and shop. The tourist season brings thousands of visitors looking for authentic handmade goods."

Kitto had been unusually quiet, but now he spoke up. "What about other opportunities? I mean, besides pottery?"

London's face lit up. "I've seen some of your work. Niall showed us photos of the hearts you painted. Have you ever considered digital art?"

"Digital?" Kitto's ears pricked forward with interest.

"Online commission work. Fantasy art, character designs, illustrations for books and games. The market is enormous, and you could work from anywhere with an internet connection. I could introduce you to some contacts."

"Really?" Kitto bounced in his chair, his cat ears twitching with barely contained excitement.

London grinned. "Yes."

Sienna leaned forward despite her earlier reservations. "What about housing?"

Saber nodded. "I know of a cottage available that's fully furnished. You could stay there while you get established. No charge for the first three months, then we'll work out something reasonable."

"That's incredibly generous," Tamsin said, tears brightening her eyes.

"It's practical." Saber's expression seemed genuine. "Close families build resilient communities. We want you to succeed."

Niall cleared his throat. "I had a thought last night. Hedrek, you mentioned your land in Cornwall."

"Yes, it's family land passed down for generations. I hate to abandon it, but the taxes..."

"I've been looking to expand my honey operations. Your property has excellent potential for hives, and its isolation is perfect for what I need. I'd like to lease the land—enough to cover taxes and provide you with a small income. You'd keep ownership, and perhaps I could use your cottage when I visit." Niall smiled, his enthusiasm shining through.

Hedrek's jaw dropped. "You'd do that?"

"Good business for both of us. Your land gets maintained, my bees get new territory, and you have a safety net if New Zealand doesn't work out."

The silence that followed was heavy with possibility. Sienna watched her parents' faces, seeing hope warring with caution in their expressions.

"This is overwhelming," Hedrek said. "Good overwhelming, but..."

"You don't need to decide today," Saber said. "Discuss it as a family. Isabella and I can start the preliminary paperwork whenever you're ready, but there's no pressure."

"How long would that take?" Sienna asked.

"About four weeks for documentation, then travel arrangements. My contacts are efficient, and they understand the urgency that sometimes comes with shifter relocations. Enough time for you to tie up loose ends and plan properly."

Marcus leaned into the camera. "Ria wanted me to tell you she's looking forward to meeting you all in person, if you decide to come."

Ria nodded shyly, offering another small smile. Despite her reserve, the hope in her golden eyes was unmistakable.

Despite everything, Sienna smiled back. Leaving Cornwall had meant mere survival—now there was the chance of belonging.

"We'll discuss this as a family," Hedrek said, glancing around the table. "But thank you. All of you. This is more than we dared hope for."

"You deserve a chance to flourish," Saber said. "We'll be here when you're ready to decide."

As the call ended and the screen went dark, the Teague family sat in contemplative silence. Finally, Jamie spoke up.

"It sounds too good to be true."

"The best things usually do," Tamsin murmured, reaching for her husband's hand. "But sometimes, if we're lucky, they turn out to be real."

Sienna glanced at Liam, who had remained unusually

quiet throughout the call, responding only when directly addressed. The careful distance he maintained—physical and emotional—was a stark reminder of the wall she'd built between them the night before.

Despite everything, she found herself drawn to the possibilities Saber had outlined—a place where her family wouldn't have to hide, where Kitto could pursue his art, and where her parents and brothers might finally find peace.

If only she could believe she deserved it.

The video call had ended with promises to stay in touch, but as her family dispersed to explore the castle grounds, Sienna found herself alone with Liam. A tense quiet lingered, carrying unspoken words and the memory of their argument the previous night.

"That went well," she said, breaking the silence.

"Your family seems excited about the possibilities." Liam's voice was level as he gathered papers from the table.

"It's more than we ever hoped for." She hesitated before adding, "Thank you for arranging this. For everything."

He looked up at that, a flicker passing through his eyes—more blue today than green. "No need to thank me, Sienna."

His voice, distant and formal, drove a sharp ache through her heart. She wanted to bridge the gap between them, to take back the words that had driven him away, but fear held her tongue.

"I want to go home," Liam said, his words cutting through the silence, raw and urgent.

Sienna's heart stopped. "Of course. You must miss it terribly."

"I do." He set down the papers and faced her fully. "But I don't wish to go alone."

Confusion swirled through her. "Suzie and Niall could visit—"

"That's not what I mean." His voice was quiet but firm. "I want you to come with me. You and your family. I want all of you to come to Middlemarch."

She stared at him, searching his face for some sign that he was joking, but his expression was deadly serious. "That's what Saber was offering."

"Yes, but I'm not Saber." Liam stepped closer, his familiar scent washing over her. "I'm not offering out of charity or community spirit. I want you there because I want a future with you."

"Liam..." She backed away instinctively, her shoulders hitting the wall behind her and rattling a framed certificate. "You don't understand. Can't possibly want—"

"You?" His gaze flashed with a combo of hurt and anger. "Why is it so impossible to believe I might care about you?"

"Because no one does!" The words burst free, raw and desperate. "Because I'm damaged goods. Because any man who gets involved with me is signing up for a lifetime of stares and whispers."

"Stop." His voice cut through her spiral like a whip crack.

"You don't know what it's like," she pressed on, as if he hadn't spoken. "You have no idea what it means to be part of this family. The genetic lottery we lost. The chance that any children we had might—"

"Might what?" Liam snapped. "Have ears like Kitto? A tail like your father? Be different?"

"Yes! Who wants that burden? Who wants to explain to their kids why people cross the street to avoid them? Why they can't have normal jobs or lives?"

"I would." His voice was steady, certain. "I'd want that, Sienna. I'd be proud to call them mine."

She shook her head. "You say that now, but when reality hits—"

"When it hits, I'll love them as fiercely as I love your brothers. Just as I love you."

The world tilted under her feet. "You don't love me," she whispered.

"Don't I?" His laugh was bitter. "What do you think the past few months were about? Last night?"

"Guilt," she said. "Obligation. Stockholm syndrome. I kidnapped you, Liam. I ruined your life. You're just—"

"Confused? Delusional?" His voice rose, control slipping. "Give me some credit, Sienna. I know the difference between obligation and love."

"But we're not mates," she said, clinging to the one argument that still made sense. "We don't have that connection. That instant recognition."

"So what? Not every couple has fireworks and destiny. Some of us have something quieter. Something that grows over time, built on trust and respect and shared experiences."

"Like what we have?" The question came out smaller than intended.

"Like what we could have, if you'd let yourself believe in it." He took another step closer, and she could see the frustration in every line of his body. "If you'd stop punishing yourself for something that wasn't entirely your fault."

Sienna laughed, the sound harsh and full of judgment. "I drugged you. I kidnapped you and stole months of your life."

"And gave me the best family I've ever known in return," Liam said. "You think I had something wonderful waiting for me in New Zealand? That people who loved me unconditionally surrounded me?"

The pain in his voice made her flinch. "You had friends. Saber and London and—"

"I had colleagues and friends. Good people who cared about me, yes, but not family. Not the acceptance your father showed me from the first day. Not the way your mother fussed over me when I was sick, or the way your brothers included me in everything without question."

"But your job—"

Liam tugged at his hair, frustration clear in every movement. "A good job, yes, but replaceable. What you gave me—what your family gave me—that's precious."

Sienna blinked hard as tears threatened to fall. "So this is about gratitude. About what we gave you."

"This is about love. About wanting to build a life with someone who challenges me and frustrates me and makes me want to be a better man."

"I'm a mess. I'm broken and guilty."

"You're the most courageous person I know, willing to risk everything for your family. You faced down hunters and bullies and your own fears to keep the people you love safe. And you came to the castle alone to confess what you'd done, knowing you might face consequences."

"That isn't strength. It was desperation."

"Sometimes they're the same thing." Liam's voice gentled.

"Sometimes the bravest thing you can do is trust someone else with your heart."

Silence settled over them, weighted with potential and fear. Sienna wanted to believe him, to take the leap he was offering, but the voices in her head, years of rejection and whispered warnings about Teague genetics, were too loud.

"I can't," she whispered. "I can't risk you waking up one day and realizing what you've gotten yourself into."

Something died in Liam's expression. The hope that had been flickering there despite everything guttered out, leaving behind resignation.

"Then we have nothing more to talk about," he said.

"Liam, please—"

But he was already leaving, his controlled movements hurting more than anger ever could. The door closed behind him with quiet finality, and Sienna sank into a chair, her body shaking.

She'd done it again—pushed away the one person who saw past her family's differences.

And this time, she wasn't sure he'd come back.

CHAPTER 22

LIAM FOUND NIALL IN his office, surrounded by maps and what appeared to be correspondence about honey suppliers. The older man looked up as Liam entered, taking in his expression with a single sharp glance.

"That bad?" Niall asked, setting down his pen.

"I need to book a flight home. As soon as possible."

Niall tilted back in his chair, studying him. "What happened?"

"Nothing. That's the problem." Liam strode to the window, staring out at the loch, where he could see the Teague brothers in their leopard forms, playing near the water's edge. Even from this distance, their joy was evident. "Sienna can't see past her guilt. She doesn't believe that anyone would want her."

"And you've tried talking to her?"

"I've tried everything." His laugh held every scrap of the bitterness he felt. "I told her I loved her. That I wanted a future with her, children, whatever they might look like."

"But?"

"But she's convinced it's guilt or obligation. Or that I've somehow confused trauma with affection."

Liam turned from the window, his jaw tight. "She thinks I'm with her because I owe her family for taking me in."

Niall was silent for a long moment. "Do you?"

"What?"

"Are you with her because they gave you something you were missing?"

"No." The denial came fast and fierce. "At least... I don't think so." But even as the words left his mouth, doubt slithered in. "God, what if she's right? What if I can't tell the difference anymore?"

"Liam," Niall said, "I've seen the way you look at her. The way she looks back. That's not duty."

"Then why won't she believe me?"

"Because she's scared." Niall stood, moving to the decanter on his desk and pouring two glasses of whisky. "Because accepting what you're offering means risking everything. And for someone who has suffered like she has, it's easier to push love away than to lose it later."

Liam accepted the glass but didn't drink. "So what am I supposed to do—keep beating my head against the wall until she believes me?"

"You could give her time."

"Time to come up with more reasons we can't be together?" Liam drained the whisky in one burning gulp. "I'm tired of battling for someone who doesn't want to be fought for."

Niall nodded. "And the family? They're good people, and they care about you."

"Yeah. They are. The best I've ever known." Liam's voice softened. "But I can't stay unless she accepts me. It's not fair to anyone, and it's only going to get more painful."

"Have you told them you're leaving?"

"I will. But I need to ask them not to tell Sienna until after I'm gone."

Niall's brows rose. "Why?"

"Because if she knows, she'll either try to stop me out of guilt or be relieved I'm going. Either way, it makes it harder."

Niall pulled out his phone, already scrolling through airline websites. "There's a red-eye flight tonight that connects through London. Gets you to Auckland tomorrow evening, local time."

"Perfect. Book it."

"Done." Niall looked up from his phone. "Suzie and I will drive you to the airport."

"Thank you for everything." Liam headed for the door. "And Niall? Help them take Saber's offer when they're ready. They deserve a fresh start."

"Of course. But you could still change your mind."

"No. I couldn't survive going through this again."

For the next few hours, Liam sought each family member individually. He found Hedrek first, walking alone in the rose garden, his leonine features serene in the afternoon light.

"Hedrek, could I have a word?"

The older man turned, and his expression immediately grew concerned. "Of course, lad. What's troubling you?"

"I'm leaving tonight. Going back to New Zealand."

Hedrek's face went blank. "I see. And Sienna?"

"Doesn't know. Please don't tell her until after I'm gone."

"Lad—"

"Please." Liam swallowed hard. "She's made it clear she doesn't want what I'm offering. If she knows I'm leaving, she'll either feel guilty or relieved, and I can't handle either reaction."

After a long assessing look, Hedrek finally nodded. "If that's what you need."

"It is. But I wanted to thank you for welcoming me and treating me like family, for showing me what that even means."

Hedrek's gaze brightened with emotion. "You'll always be family to us, lad. Distance doesn't change that."

They embraced briefly, and Liam had to swallow hard against the lump in his throat.

He found Tamsin in the kitchen, helping Mrs. Fraser with dinner preparations. When he asked for a private word, she followed him to the small pantry, her brow furrowed.

"You're leaving," she said before he could speak. It wasn't a question.

"How did you—"

"You have the same look Sienna had when she came back from the gathering. Like someone who'd made a hard decision they didn't want to make. Does she know?"

"No. And I need you to promise not to tell her."

"Oh, Liam." Tamsin reached up to cup his face. "What happened between you?"

"She can't trust that I want her. And I can't keep struggling to change her mind." He covered her hands with his. "Take Saber's offer. Go to New Zealand. You'll be happy there."

"Will you be happy there? Without us?"

"I'll manage."

Tamsin pulled him into a fierce hug. "You're a good man,

Liam. Don't let anyone tell you different."

Finding the boys required more strategy. He caught them one by one as they returned from their various activities.

Jago was easiest with his direct manner. "You're leaving because of Sienna."

"Yes."

"She's an idiot."

"She's scared."

"Same thing, sometimes." Jago gripped his shoulder. "Take care of yourself. And if she comes to her senses and follows you to New Zealand…"

"She won't."

"If she does, don't make it easy for her. Make her work for it."

Calan was harder. The quiet brother had always been more sensitive to emotional undercurrents. "You love her."

"I do."

"And she loves you too. She's too stubborn to admit it."

"Maybe. But I can't wait forever for her to figure that out."

Calan nodded sadly. "I understand. But I'll miss you."

"I'll miss you too."

Kitto was the hardest of all. When Liam found him in the art room, sketching, the youngest brother took one look at his face and his shoulders slumped.

"When?" Kitto asked.

"Tonight."

"Because of Sienna."

"I can't stay where I'm not wanted."

"But we want you here."

"I know. And that makes this so hard." Liam settled beside

231

him. "If she doesn't want me in this family, I can't force my way in. None of us would benefit from that."

Kitto looked stricken. "Will we see you again?"

"If you come to New Zealand, yes. I hope you will. What about your art opportunities with London?"

"I'll still take them. No matter where I am." Kitto managed a watery smile. "Maybe I can visit you sometime."

"I'd like that."

He found Jamie sitting alone by the loch, skipping stones across the dark water.

"Leaving again?" Jamie asked without looking up.

Liam sat beside him. "How did you know?"

"Seen that look before. My dad had it every time he walked out." Jamie's voice was carefully neutral. "Difference is, you're saying goodbye."

"I'm not your father, Jamie. This isn't about not caring."

"I know." Jamie looked at him. "Doesn't make it hurt less."

"I'm sorry."

"Are you coming back?"

"Probably not."

Jamie nodded and went back to throwing stones. "Thanks for not lying about it."

At nine-thirty, Liam slipped out of the castle through the servants' entrance, his single bag slung over his shoulder. The car was waiting, engine running quietly in the darkness.

As they pulled away, he caught one last glimpse of the castle's lit windows. Somewhere inside, Sienna was probably still looking for him, wondering where he'd gone.

By morning, she'd have her answer.

And he'd be nothing but a memory.

CHAPTER 23

"GONE?" SIENNA STARED AT Niall and Suzie, a cold weight sinking to the pit of her stomach. "What do you mean, gone?"

"Liam flew home last night," Niall said.

Denial rose sharp in her, hurt and pride warring within. "He didn't...he didn't say goodbye."

"Liam asked us not to wake you," Suzie said, her earlier hostility replaced by something that might have been sympathy. "He thought it would be easier."

Easier for whom? Sienna's hands trembled as she processed this. After everything they'd been through together, he'd left without a word.

"Do you have his number? I need to—"

"He specifically asked us not to give it to you," Niall said, his expression telling her he wouldn't break his word to Liam.

Sienna turned and walked outside, needing air and space to think. Her brothers were sitting by the fountain, and from their neutral expressions, it was clear they'd heard the news.

"You knew he was leaving." It wasn't a question.

"He came to say goodbye," Jago confirmed. "He asked us to thank Ma and Pa for their kindness."

"But not me." The words came out smaller than she'd intended.

Kitto eyed her with an expression far too mature for his years. "What did you expect, Sienna? You've been pushing him away since we left Cornwall."

"I have not."

"You moved out of the tent you were sharing and started sleeping separately. Some days you barely spoke to him unless it was about practical things," Calan said.

"You blamed him for getting sick and slowing us down," Jago added. "We could see it in your face every time you looked at him."

Sienna wanted to protest, but they weren't wrong. She had pulled away, blamed him—not in words, but in attitude. Her guilt over what she'd done to him had been so all-consuming that she never considered the harm she was still causing.

"I thought I was giving him space," she said, the words thin and uncertain. "After what I did to him..."

"What you did was wrong," Kitto said bluntly. "But what you've been doing since is worse. At least the kidnapping had a purpose. This was cruel."

The word landed like a slap. *Cruel.* Is that what she'd become?

"Sienna?" Her mother's voice came from behind her. "What's wrong?"

"Liam left," Jago said when Sienna struggled to find her voice. "Sienna's upset he didn't say goodbye."

Her parents exchanged one of their wordless conversations before her mother sat beside her on the fountain's edge.

"Oh, sweetheart," Tamsin said. "What did you expect him to do?"

"I thought we had time to resolve things."

"Did you tell him that?" her father asked. "Because from where we stood, it looked like you wanted nothing to do with the poor lad."

"That's not true."

"Isn't it?" Her mother's brown gaze was sad but direct. "Sienna, we've watched you pull away from him bit by bit. Every time he tried to get close, you found a reason to step back."

"Because I felt guilty! Because I ruined his life."

"So you kept upending it?" Calan asked with devastating logic.

Sienna stared at her brother, who rarely spoke up, and felt something crumble inside her chest. He was right. She had been so absorbed in self-recrimination she'd never truly tried to set things right.

"I didn't know how," she whispered. "How do you apologize for something like that? How do you make it up to someone when you've stolen months of their life?"

"You start with the truth," her father said. "You tell them why you did it, and you let them decide if they can forgive you. But you don't get to make that decision for them by pushing them away."

"And you shouldn't use your guilt as an excuse to keep hurting them," her mother added.

Sienna leaned forward, letting her palms cover her face.

They were right. All of them. She'd been so focused on guarding herself against his potential rejection that she'd pushed him away first. Over and over again.

"I've made such a mess of everything," Sienna said.

"Yeah," Jago said with typical bluntness. "You have."

"But you can clean up a mess," their mother said. "If you're willing to do the work."

Sienna scanned her family. They weren't angry. Frustrated, maybe, but also hopeful. They still believed in her. "How? He's gone. He doesn't want to talk to me."

"Then find another way," Kitto said. "Write him a letter. Suzie can send it for you."

"And then what? He's building a new life. Why would he want me in it?"

"Because maybe," her mother murmured, "if you're honest about your feelings instead of hiding behind your guilt, you might discover you have more to offer than you think."

Sienna sat in the garden long after her family had gone inside, watching the stars emerge one by one. She allowed herself to think about what she actually wanted, rather than what she thought she deserved.

She wanted Liam. Not because her family needed him, and not because he was convenient or kind or helpful. She wanted him because somewhere between Cornwall and Scotland, between camping and crisis and quiet moments stolen together, she'd fallen in love with him.

And she'd been too afraid to admit it, even to herself.

By the time she went inside, she knew what she had to do. It might be too late, but she had to try. She owed him the truth, and herself the courage to deliver it.

She found Suzie in the kitchen, making tea.

"I need to ask you for a favor," Sienna said.

Suzie glanced up, studying her face in the dim light. Whatever she saw there made her nod.

"All right," she said. "I'm listening."

CHAPTER 24

THE FLIGHT FROM SCOTLAND seemed endless. Three connections, cramped seats, and too much time to think. By the time Liam stumbled off the Air New Zealand domestic flight in Dunedin, his shoulders ached and his head throbbed with that familiar dull pain that had become his unwelcome companion.

"Liam!" Scott's voice cut through the terminal noise, and seconds later, he enveloped Liam in a crushing hug. "Christ, mate, you look like hell."

"Feel like it too," Liam managed, surprised by how good it was to see a familiar face. Behind Scott, Saber approached with a more measured but equally warm embrace.

"Welcome home," Saber said, but his sharp gaze was cataloging everything—Liam's weight loss, the tension around his eyes, and the careful way he held himself.

"Good to be back." The words came automatically, and they weren't entirely untrue. The familiar accents, the cooler air, the rolling hills of Otago stretching into the distance—it all felt like coming back to himself after months of being someone else.

But something was missing. The anticipation he'd expected, the pure relief of being home, seemed muted.

During the drive to Middlemarch, Liam answered their questions about Scotland and the castle, keeping the conversation at a surface level. Yes, it had been great to see Niall and Suzie. Yes, the gathering was interesting—until everything went sideways. No, he was fine, just tired from the travel.

Scott filled the silence with town gossip—who was dating whom, upcoming events. The everyday things that should've comforted him but faded into background noise.

"Your old room's ready," Saber said as they pulled into his driveway. "Emily's made enough food to feed a rugby team. She's been cooking nonstop since I told her you were coming home. The twins are looking forward to seeing you."

Liam nodded his thanks. As they unloaded his meager belongings, he caught Saber and Scott exchanging one of those looks. The kind that said they were worried, but trying not to show it.

He spent the next two days going through the motions of being back. Emily fussed over him with home-cooked meals. Scott dropped by each evening with updates on mutual friends, trying to coax him out for a beer. Saber offered practical help—a place to stay, job contacts, and the use of his truck.

Everyone was kind. Welcoming, and careful not to ask the obvious questions about those missing months.

Liam was grateful for their restraint. He wasn't ready

to explain. How did you tell people you'd fallen for your kidnapper? That you'd found a family who accepted you, then walked away because you couldn't handle the uncertainty?

On his third morning, he sat at Saber's kitchen table, staring into a cup of coffee that had gone cold as he lost himself in thought.

"Rough night?" Saber asked, settling across from him with his own mug.

"Couldn't sleep." It was becoming a pattern. He'd lie in bed, exhausted but wired, his mind cycling through memories he couldn't shake. Hedrek's laugh. Tamsin checking his fever, her expression pensive and troubled. The boys' excitement over pottery sales. Sienna's face in firelight.

"Want to talk about it?"

"Not really." His reply emerged sharper than he'd intended, and he saw Saber's eyebrows rise. "Sorry. Everything still feels weird."

"Makes sense," Saber said. "If you're restless, I've got a suggestion for you."

Despite himself, Liam experienced a hint of interest. "Yeah?"

"Cam Sinclair runs a sheep and cattle station up in Mackenzie country. It's remote—wide open land where you won't see another soul for miles." Saber leaned back in his chair. "His regular hand broke his leg and won't be fit for three months. Cam's looking for someone experienced with livestock, someone who can handle the solitude."

"All human crew?"

"Shifter. Cam is particular about that. Says it's the only way to run a proper station when you're dealing with the country he works." Saber studied Liam's face. "It's remote. No cell signal, just radio. Supplies come in every couple of weeks. Some find it tough being that cut off."

It sounded perfect. "When would he need someone?"

"Lambing season's coming up, and Cam's already short-handed," Saber said. "It's hard work, basic accommodation, and, yeah, it's in the middle of nowhere. But the food's good, and it might give you the space to think."

"I'll take it."

The speed of his response surprised them both. Saber set down his coffee cup. "You sure? You haven't even heard about the pay."

"I'm positive." The weight lifted off Liam's chest, a first since his arrival home. Breathing room. Distance. The chance to lose himself in physical work and wide-open country. "When can I leave?"

"I'll call Cam today, but probably within the week." Saber was still watching him with a careful expression. "Liam, you don't have to run from whatever happened over there."

"I'm not running." The denial came too quickly, and they both knew it. Liam rubbed the back of his neck. "I need time to figure things out."

"Fair enough." Saber's tone was neutral, but his expression was kind. "We'll be here when you return."

That afternoon, Scott found him packing his few belongings into the same pack he'd brought from Scotland.

"So it's true? You're heading for the high country?"

"Saber told you."

"Course he did. We're worried about you, mate." Scott leaned against the doorframe, arms crossed. "This isn't like you. The Liam I know doesn't just disappear."

"Maybe the Liam you knew changed." The words tasted bitter, but they were true. The man who'd attended the gathering, eager and adventurous, was a stranger now.

"Bullshit." Scott's voice was flat. "Whatever happened over there, whatever's eating at you—disappearing into the mountains won't fix it."

"I'm not hiding. It's work. Routine."

"It's both, and you know it." Scott stepped into the room, his expression serious. "I don't know what went wrong, and I won't push. But don't kid yourself—three months of sheep and silence won't make this disappear."

Liam stopped packing and looked at his friend, *really* looked. Scott's concern was real, his frustration born of caring. But he didn't—*couldn't*—understand.

"Maybe not," Liam said. "But it's what I can handle right now."

Scott studied him, then nodded. "All right. But promise me this—don't make any big decisions while you're up there. Give it the full three months before you decide what's next."

"Deal."

They shook on it, and Liam felt a flicker of the friendship that had sustained him through his early days in Middlemarch. Whatever else had changed, Scott was still in his corner.

Two days later, Saber drove him to the edge of the Mackenzie Basin, where Cam Sinclair waited with a dusty Land Cruiser and a firm handshake.

"You'll do," Cam said after a brief assessment. He was a weathered man in his fifties, with a steady presence that spoke of decades of dealing with unpredictable animals and unforgiving country. "Saber says you know your way around livestock."

"I do."

"Good. We'll work you hard, feed you well, and leave you alone when you need it. Sound fair?"

Liam gave a brief nod. "Fair."

He shouldered his pack and climbed into the passenger seat. As they left the main road and entered the vast golden grassland of the high country, he experienced something he hadn't in weeks.

Peace—or at least the possibility of it.

Behind them, his life in Middlemarch faded into the hills. Ahead lay three months of weathered mountains, snow-dusted peaks, and paddocks that rolled on for miles. A place ruled by seasons and stock, where the rest of the world was far away.

And for now, that was exactly what he needed.

Chapter 25

Dear Liam,

I wish to formally apologize for my actions during—

Sienna crumpled the paper and tossed it toward the fireplace in her guest room. Too stiff. Too formal. It was like drafting a council report.

She pulled out another sheet from the stationery Suzie had provided and tried again.

Liam, I can't stop thinking about how sorry I am and how much I miss you, and I know I don't deserve forgiveness, but please—

Another crumpled ball joined the first. Too desperate. Too much.

With a frustrated sigh, she set the pen down and walked to the window. The Scottish countryside stretched out below, green and peaceful in the afternoon light. Somewhere far away, Liam was tending sheep along the river flats of Middlemarch. Did he think about her at all, or had he put those months in Cornwall behind him?

A soft knock at the door interrupted her brooding. "Come in."

Suzie entered, carrying a tea tray. "Thought you might need fortification for your letter writing."

"I can't seem to find the right words." Sienna gestured at the fireplace, where her failed attempts had landed. "Everything sounds either too cold or too pathetic."

"Maybe because you're thinking too hard about what you should say instead of what you want to say." Suzie set the tray down and poured two cups of tea. "What would you tell him if he were standing right here?"

Sienna accepted the tea gratefully. "That I was an idiot. That I was so hung up on what I'd done wrong, I couldn't see what felt right."

"Acknowledging that is a start." Suzie settled into the window seat. "You know, Niall has been muttering about a business problem for weeks. I think you might be the solution he needs."

"Pardon?"

"Honey." Suzie's gaze lit with amusement. "My parents started keeping bees—Niall helped them set up during our last visit because they wanted to diversify the farm. He got completely obsessed, designed better hives, improved extraction methods, the works. Now their honey production is booming, but they just want to tend the bees. They hate the idea of retail."

Sienna experienced a hint of curiosity. "Selling honey?"

"Yes, in a proper shop. Different varieties from local producers, maybe some pottery to display them in. Niall's been looking for someone who understands both sides—the product and the selling." Suzie paused. "You managed the market stall with your mother. You know how to talk to customers, how to present goods attractively."

"But I know nothing about honey."

"Niall could teach you everything in his sleep. He's obsessed." Suzie grinned. "Bear shifter, remember? It's practically genetic."

Despite her worry about the letter, Sienna smiled. "Where would this shop be?"

"Middlemarch. There's a perfect spot on the main street, and the town gets plenty of tourists during the season." Suzie's tone grew serious. "But it would mean leaving your family. Would you do that?"

The question hit deeper than Sienna expected. Parting from her family had always seemed impossible, but sitting here in Scotland, she realized something had already shifted. Her parents and brothers had been right—she couldn't live her whole life protecting them from a world that might reject them.

"I think I might be. What about Kitto's art? London mentioned some online opportunities, but it might be better in person."

"She did. Kitto could do custom illustrations, caricatures, maybe even design work. The internet makes location less important for that kind of thing." Suzie studied Sienna's face. "This isn't charity, you know. Niall genuinely needs someone reliable, and from what I've seen, you're exactly that."

And it would put me in the same country as Liam, Sienna thought but didn't say it aloud.

"Let me talk to Kitto," she said instead. "See what he thinks."

That evening, she found her youngest brother in the garden, sketching the castle's silhouette against the sunset.

"Kitto? Can I ask you something?"

He looked up, pencil still poised. "If it's about Liam, I told you—"

"It's about New Zealand. London mentioned some art opportunities there. Would you be interested in going to Middlemarch?"

Kitto's ears perked up—literally. "You mean doing commissions in person? Custom portraits, caricatures, that kind of thing?"

She nodded and told him about the honey shop. As she spoke, she watched his expression shift from hopeful curiosity to genuine excitement.

"I could do portraits, logos, maybe even book illustrations," he said, already sketching absently as ideas sparked. "But if I'm working face-to-face, I'll have to be careful. You know, with people noticing the ears and tail."

"What about Ma and Pa? The others?" she asked.

Kitto's ears flattened. "I've been thinking about that since we arrived at the castle. They're happy, Sienna. Really happy. Pa's already talking about collaborating with Niall on pottery containers for honey. Jamie's settled in like he belongs. And Jago and Calan..." He shrugged. "They love helping with the estate work. For the first time, they're not looking over their shoulders, waiting for someone to stare or whisper."

"So you think they'll stay?"

"I think for as long as Niall and Suzie want them. And from what I can see, that could be indefinite." He set down his pencil and looked at her seriously. "The question is, what do *you* want?"

That night, Sienna sat at the desk again, but this time the words came more easily.

Dear Liam,

I've written this letter a dozen times, and nothing feels like enough for what I need to say. But Suzie told me to stop overthinking and be honest. So here goes.

I'm sorry. Not just for taking you from the gathering—that was unforgivable—but for every moment after when I was scared or too proud to be honest about what was happening between us. I was so caught up in my guilt, I couldn't see past it to what we might have.

You once asked if I was sure we weren't mates. I said no, but I think I was wrong—not about the instant recognition some couples have, but about the quieter bond that grows slowly. The kind that makes you miss someone's voice when they're not there. One that makes you look for them in every room.

I miss you, Liam. Your laugh and how you made my brothers feel normal. Watching you with my parents, seeing the respect you showed them. I miss the way you kissed me and made me feel like maybe I deserved something good.

Niall has offered me a job in Middlemarch—running a honey shop for Suzie's family. Kitto wants to come too, for the art opportunities London mentioned. We'd be leaving our family for the first time, which terrifies me. But not as much as the thought of never seeing you again.

I know I have no right to ask for your forgiveness, let alone anything more. But if you think there's still something worth exploring between us, I'll be in Middlemarch by the end of the month.

With love and hope,
Sienna

She read it through twice, her heart hammering. It was honest—maybe too honest—but it felt right. Before she could second-guess herself, she folded it and slipped it into an envelope.

"Saber Mitchell, Middlemarch, New Zealand," she wrote on the front, then added a note asking him to forward it to Liam wherever he might be working.

Three weeks later, Scott met Liam at Lake Tekapo. They'd driven from opposite directions—Scott from Middlemarch, Liam from Cam's high country station—meeting halfway on one of Liam's rare days off. The autumn air was crisp, the lake a startling blue under the clear sky, and the mountains stood sharp and snow-dusted in the distance.

"You know," Scott said, settling beside him on a rocky outcrop, "for someone hiding out from civilization, you look like hell."

Liam wiped sweat from his brow with the back of his glove. "Thanks. Real morale booster."

"Just calling it." Scott pulled a thermos from his pack and poured two cups of coffee. "When's the last time you slept properly?"

"I sleep fine." Mostly true. The farm work knocked him out most nights—*it was the dreams that messed with him.*

"Uh-huh." Scott handed him a cup. "So. Interesting news from home. Saber says we've got some new arrivals from Scotland."

Liam stilled. "Scotland?"

"Yep. A young woman and her brother. Something about a honey shop venture with Niall." He shot Liam a look. "That'd be your Sienna, then."

The coffee sat heavy in his stomach. "She's in Middlemarch?"

"They've been there a couple of weeks. Her and the artistic brother—Kitto? He's doing caricatures at the weekend market and is a huge hit with the tourists." Scott kept his tone light. "Saber says she seems determined. And a bit lost. You planning to do anything about that?"

"Like what?" The words came out sharper than he meant. "She made her choice. She wanted to stay with her family."

Scott took a sip of coffee. "Funny thing about choices," he said. "Sometimes people change their minds."

They sat in comfortable silence for a while, watching the light change across the lake. Eventually, Scott checked his watch.

"I should head back," he said. "Early start tomorrow. But Liam? Don't write her off completely. From what Saber says, she's taking an enormous risk coming to New Zealand. That's got to mean something."

After Scott left, Liam drove back to the station alone, their conversation echoing in his head. When he pulled up at the homestead, Cam emerged from the office with an envelope in his hand.

"Mail came while you were out," Cam said, handing it over. "This came for you via Saber Mitchell."

Liam's heart stopped. There was only one person who would write to him through Saber.

With shaking hands, he opened the envelope and read.

By the time he finished, the afternoon light was fading. The tightness in his chest had loosened, breaking the weeks-long grip.

Cam appeared in the doorway, took one look at Liam's face, and grinned. "Good news, I take it?"

"Yeah." Liam folded the letter carefully. "Cam, I need to ask a favor. Could you post a letter for me on the next supply run?"

"Course. Taking your time to think it through, eh? Smart man."

Liam nodded, already composing his reply in his head. He had two months left on his contract, and Sienna was building a new life in Middlemarch. Maybe slow was precisely what they both needed. Time to get to know each other properly, without a crisis or guilt clouding everything between them.

He had so much he wanted to tell her—about the mountains, about the work, about how he'd figured out what home meant to him. And if her letter was anything to go by, she had things to tell him too.

For the first time since leaving Scotland, Liam felt like they were moving in the right direction—together, even if they were taking the long way around.

CHAPTER 26

THE SHOP DOOR STOOD ajar.

Sienna's keys dangled from her fingers as she stared at the gap where wood should've met the frame. She always locked up—Emily had drilled that in after the third time burglars struck Middlemarch this winter.

The deadbolt hung uselessly, the brass bright where someone had forced it from the wood.

After a long hesitation, she pushed the door open with a trembling hand.

Inside, she gaped at the overturned displays, sticky puddles spreading across the floorboards, and the empty shelves where their premium spring honey should have gleamed in the morning light.

"No, no, no." She barely heard herself over the rush of blood in her ears.

For long seconds, she stood paralyzed in the doorway, her mind skittering. Call Saber. Call Emily. Call Niall in Scotland because he'd know what to do. Someone older, wiser, more experienced. Someone who could fix this.

Her fingers were already scrolling through her contacts when she stopped. Liam's last letter crinkled in her jacket pocket. *I want the woman who figured out how to save Sophie, not the one consumed by guilt and constantly apologizing.*

Her panic eased. She found the number for Laura Adams, one of Middlemarch's two policemen, and made the call.

"Laura? It's Sienna from the honey shop. We've had a break-in." She stepped around the shards of glass. "I need to file a report, but I can't wait long before I clean up. Today was meant to be a busy day."

Laura arrived within ten minutes, with Charlie, her fellow cop, close behind. Sienna had heard about the local constables—both human and both mated to shifters. According to Saber, they juggled the unique challenges of Middlemarch's mixed community without missing a beat.

"Professionals." Laura surveyed the scene, her expression grim. "They knew exactly what to target." She gestured at the untouched jars of basic clover honey while the premium shelves stood empty. "Do you have any idea who might target your high-end stock specifically?"

"Could be anyone," Charlie said, taking photos of the forced lock. "Manuka honey is expensive. It'd be easy enough to on-sell."

Sienna did a quick inventory while they worked. The thieves had taken every jar of the premium spring wildflower, the entire batch of rare manuka, and the Taieri Gold limited-edition blend, which sold for forty dollars a jar.

"I'll need a list so I can give you a report for your insurance company," Laura said, "but Charlie's right—this was planned. Someone who knows the business."

Yeah. Three hours until the Saturday market opened, and half her stock was gone.

"We'll canvas the area, check with other shop owners," Charlie promised. "But don't get your hopes up—this feels like professionals passing through."

Right. So she was on her own. Time to fix this.

Kitto arrived as Laura and Charlie were leaving, art supplies slung over his shoulder for the Saturday market.

He took one look at the chaos and dropped his bag. "What the hell happened?"

"Professional thieves with expensive taste," Sienna said, grabbing her car keys from behind the counter. "I need you to clean this up and open the shop. Tell anyone who asks that we'll have stock by noon."

"But where are you going?"

"To find honey."

She was already heading for the door, running through every farm contact she'd made over the past month, every favor she might call in.

"Can you handle things here?"

Kitto nodded, his ears perking up under his hat. "Course I can. Go fix this."

"Make signs," she called over her shoulder. "Local Artisan Emergency Collection. Make it sound exclusive, not desperate. And Kitto? If anyone asks about the break-in, tell them we're sorting it."

"Got it." He was already rolling up his sleeves. "Sienna? Kick their arses."

The first farm was twenty minutes out of town, run by old Tom Brennan, who'd doubted *some young girl from overseas* when she'd first introduced herself. Now she prayed that skepticism hadn't extended to helping her in a crisis.

Her phone rang as she pulled into his drive. Kitto.

"The shop's clean, the sign is up, and I've already had three people asking about the emergency collection," he reported. "Whatever you're planning, they're buying it."

"Good. I'll be back in two hours."

"Better make it ninety minutes. Mrs. Patterson's coming in specifically for the manuka honey. She's bringing her book club."

Sienna rubbed the back of her neck. Mrs. Patterson was their best customer, and the precious manuka stock was sitting in some thief's car, not on her shelves. "I'll find some," she promised, and hung up before Kitto could ask her how.

Tom Brennan emerged from his barn, wiping his hands on a rag, his weathered face guarded until Sienna explained her situation.

"Professional job, eh?" He scratched his chin. "Heard there's been a spate of them up north. I've got some wildflower honey, but it doesn't have pretty labels."

"I'll take whatever you have available."

Twenty minutes later, her car boot held twelve jars of excellent honey in plain mason jars. The second farm—Sarah Mitchell's organic operation—yielded eight jars of premium clover and a stroke of luck.

"I've got three jars of manuka I was saving for a special order that fell through," Sarah said. "Forty-five each?"

"Sold." By eleven-thirty, Sienna had loaded her car with

thirty-two jars of honey from four different farms. Not quite her original stock, but enough. Her phone buzzed as she pulled back into town.

Kitto's text read: **Queue forming outside. Whatever your plan is, it's working.**

By noon, Sienna's hastily arranged display looked better than it had before the theft. Kitto's hand-lettered signs—Emergency Local Artisan Collection, Limited Spring Harvest, and Exclusive Farm-Direct Selection—made the mismatched jars look intentional rather than last-ditch.

Mrs. Patterson arrived with her book club as promised, eyeing the manuka honey with approval. "Oh, how lovely! You've sourced from Sarah Mitchell's farm. I've heard wonderful things about her organic methods."

"We like to support local producers," Sienna said, amazed at how easily the words came.

By two o'clock, she'd sold more stock than on any Saturday since opening. The emergency collection had become a selling point, with customers drawn to the story of exclusive farm partnerships and limited batches.

"Bloody brilliant," Kitto said as they counted the till receipts. "You've turned a disaster into our best day ever."

Sienna stared at the empty shelves—bare because they'd sold out, not because they'd been robbed. "We did," she said with a wide smile.

Dear Liam,

Someone broke into the shop last night and stole half of our premium stock. Six months ago, I would've panicked, called everyone I knew, and probably closed for the day.Instead, I spent the morning driving to every farm within fifty kilometers, negotiating emergency supplies, and somehow turning a theft into our best sales day ever.

I impressed myself today.

For the first time, I really understand what you meant about being partners, not just surviving side by side.

I don't need rescuing anymore, Liam.

But I'd still like to share the wins with someone.

Love,
Sienna

P.S. Kitto says to tell you his Emergency Collection signs were the real genius behind today's success. He's not wrong.

"A letter arrived for you," Emily said as Sienna walked in from the shop.

"Sienna has a secret admirer." Kitto snatched the envelope from Emily before she could hand it over. He flipped it over to check the return address. "It's from Liam. Read it—what does he say?"

"I will if you give it back," Sienna snapped.

"They argue like us," one of Emily's twin girls said.

"They do." Emily's eyes sparkled as if she were trying not to laugh. "And they're old enough to know better. Siblings shouldn't tease each other. Arguing disturbs the peace. Keep it up, and I'll assign extra chores."

"Does that mean I don't have to do the dishes tonight?" the girl asked hopefully.

"There's always plenty of chores," Emily said. "Off you go—homework first."

"Open the letter," Kitto said.

Sienna scowled at him. "It's private."

"Kitto," Emily warned, now laughing openly. "Sienna's allowed her privacy. I'm sure she'll share if she wants to. And there's nothing stopping you from writing to Liam."

"I'm not good at writing," Kitto muttered.

"Draw him pictures," Emily said, nudging him toward Saber's office. "I'll help you."

Grateful for the distraction, Sienna tore open the envelope and pulled out two sheets of paper.

Dear Sienna,

I had to read your letter twice before I believed it. Not because I doubted you could handle a crisis—I've seen you in action—but because the woman who wrote about impressing herself doesn't sound like the one who used to carry the weight of her whole family on her shoulders.

You turned a theft into your best sales day. That's not luck. That's bloody brilliant business sense. I'm proud of you, but more importantly, you should be proud of your achievements.

Speaking of pride, I showed your letter to Cam (my boss). He laughed and said he needs to hire you for marketing.

Things are good here. The work's hard but satisfying, and the mountains have a way of clearing your head. I've been thinking a lot about the future and about sharing victories, like you said.

Scott tells me there's a Singles Ball coming up in Middlemarch—late November, I think. I could get the weekend off if I had a good reason to attend.

So, tell me: do you want to test this new, confident version of yourself on the dance floor?

But I have to ask—are you talking about shared victories because you want me, or because I'm familiar and safe?

I hope it's the first one.
Liam

P.S. Tell Kitto I noted his artistic genius and appreciated it. And yes, I may have included something for him that's not sheep droppings. Don't let the twins get to it first.

Dear Liam,

You asked if I'm choosing you because I want you, or because you're safe.

Emily has introduced me to half a dozen eligible bachelors in Middlemarch. They were all nice and untouched by my disasters. None of them has seen me fall apart or had their lives upended by my terrible choices.

Safe would be easier.

But I don't want simple. I want the man who stayed, even when I gave him every reason to walk, the man who didn't think twice about helping to rescue Sophie. The man who saw potential in my brothers when everyone else saw freaks.

I want you.

Not because you're familiar, but because you're you.

And yes, I'll go to the ball with you. Fair warning, though—I've never been to a proper dance. Kitto has been trying to teach me to waltz in Emily's kitchen. The twins think we're both hopeless.

I can't wait to see you again.

Love,
Sienna

P.S. Whatever you sent made Kitto turn three shades of red and mutter something about mountain men and their bloody sense of humor. The twins are now demanding that you send them something equally mysterious. You've started something.

The marquee glowed against the November twilight, strings of lights woven through the surrounding trees like captured stars. Music drifted across the paddock—softer, more elegant than the raucous rock from Sienna's memory of Stoneford town dances.

"I can't believe we're actually here," Kitto murmured, adjusting his collar. In his dark suit with his hair styled to hide his ears, he looked every inch the dapper young gentleman. Only Sienna could see the slight bulge where he'd tucked his tail away.

"You look perfect," she assured him, smoothing her own nerves as much as the red silk of Emily's dress. The fabric caught the fairy lights as they approached the entrance, and she felt transformed—not into a princess, but into a woman who made her own rules.

Saber and Emily flanked them like proud parents, but when Saber looked at the dress, something deeper flickered across his face. His gaze met Emily's, and the smile they shared recalled their first dance, the night everything began between them.

"That dress," Emily whispered, "brings back some wonderful memories."

"Best decision I ever made, asking the woman in red to dance," Saber said.

They joined the queue at the entrance, Sienna's pulse racing. The scent of crushed grass mingled with perfume and aftershave. Somewhere inside that glowing tent, Liam was waiting.

"There!" Kitto pointed ahead in the line. "I can see him."

Sienna followed his gaze, and the world tilted. Liam stood near the entrance in a dark suit, scanning the crowd. Even from this distance, she saw how he held himself: confident and alert, as if bracing for something important.

Then his gaze found hers—and the crowd, the music, the lights—all of it faded away.

"Liam," she whispered.

CHAPTER 27

Wow. The red dress. It clung to her curves, impossible to ignore, but when Liam's gaze lifted to her face, everything else fell away.

Sienna was the scarlet woman, and in that moment, every thought in his head sharpened into one.

He wanted her.

Sienna.

The woman in red.

He grinned and closed the distance with long, ground-eating strides. The dress had caught his eye, but when their gazes locked, nothing else mattered.

"Hi," he said when he reached them, his voice soft and wondering.

"Hi," she whispered.

"Are they gonna stare at each other all night?" Kitto asked, his tone more fond than impatient.

Sienna blinked, suddenly aware they had an audience. Saber

and Emily stood nearby, wearing identical grins, and several other guests had turned to watch.

"Forgive me." Liam didn't look sorry at all. "I didn't notice anyone but her." He nodded toward Sienna. "You all look great, truly—but *her*..." He trailed off, his expression saying what words couldn't.

"It's the dress," Emily said to Saber, sounding smug. "It's magical."

"True, kitten. Dance? For old time's sake?" Saber extended his arm.

"Nothing I'd like better," Emily replied, and together they drifted toward the dance floor, hands entwined.

Liam smiled at Sienna, then turned to her brother. "First things first—let me introduce Kitto to my friends. I want everyone to meet the artist who's taken Middlemarch by storm."

He led them toward a group of young shifters that included Scott. The introductions flowed, and Liam felt a flicker of pride as Kitto straightened under their welcome and the eager questions about his artwork and market stall.

Once Kitto was deep in animated conversation, Liam turned back to Sienna. "May I have this dance, Ms. Teague?"

"I'm not—I haven't danced much," she admitted, biting her bottom lip and brushing a finger against the edge of her red lipstick. The subtle gesture caught his attention.

"Neither have I. We can figure it out together," he said. "Besides, I'd rather talk than dance. Want to find a quiet corner?"

He took her hand and led her onto the dance floor. The marquee buzzed with conversation, warm air carrying the scent of decorative flowers, sizzling sausage rolls from the nearby barbecues, and the faint sweetness of spilled wine. A band played cover songs from the corner stage, their melodies weaving through the hum of the crowd. When she melted into his arms, tension drained from her body, and he guided them to a quieter spot near the edge. They swayed together, bodies close, her warmth pressing against him as the music threaded through the crowded marquee.

"I've missed you," he murmured.

"Every day," she said when they drew apart. "More than I thought possible."

They drifted in comfortable silence, simply enjoying being close again. Then Sienna spoke.

"You said in your letter that the mountains taught you things."

"Yeah...I was so caught up in trying to have the perfect job, the perfect life, I didn't see what mattered." His hand pressed against her back. "It wasn't the work at the station that made me happy. It was hearing from you, knowing you were here."

"Liam—"

"Let me finish." His voice was gentle but sure. "It wasn't safety or familiarity that pulled me back here. It was *you*. Starting over in a new country? That takes guts. The way you handle everything...it makes me want to improve myself."

Tears pricked her eyes. "I feel the same way. I didn't dare say it out loud, afraid you'd think it was guilt or gratitude. But it's not. It's more than that."

He stopped dancing right there on the floor and kissed her. It was sweet and passionate and full of promise, and when they broke apart, several couples nearby were smiling.

"I have something to tell you about Mama and Papa."

"They've decided about New Zealand?"

"Yes. They're staying in Scotland. Turns out they really love it there. Niall and Suzie have become like family, and Papa is even teaming up with Niall on some pottery designs. Mama helps with the castle, and I've never seen Jago and Calan so happy. They enjoy helping on the estate and do a little pottery on the side."

Liam squeezed her waist, enjoying the quiet closeness between them. "And you're okay with them staying?"

She leaned into him, the faint scent of wine and flowers drifting between them. "They're happy—that's all I ever wanted. The move to New Zealand works for Kitto and me, but I understand that the change might've been too much for Mama, Papa, and my older brothers. They're more cautious than I am. I came here because it felt right for me—because you're here."

Liam brushed a strand of hair from her face, warmed by the honesty in her voice.

"Liam!" Saber's shout cut through the music as he approached with Emily in tow. "Sorry to interrupt, but I needed to catch you before the evening got away from us."

They stopped dancing, though Liam kept his arm around Sienna's waist, as the band launched into a rocking fifties number.

Saber said, "I've been asking around about jobs. Nothing local, I'm afraid. But what if you set yourself up as a general contractor? Farm work, maintenance, maybe some construction. You'd learn new skills while waiting for the right opportunity."

Liam paused, shoulders tight. Six months ago, this would have crushed him. Now, he considered it.

"Honestly," he said, "I'd rather stay in Middlemarch than chase some perfect farm job elsewhere. It's not the work—it's being here, with the people I care about."

Saber raised an eyebrow. "Good to hear. You remember Henry Anderson? He and Maia are here tonight. Henry said he and Gerard might have some work for you."

He nodded toward the refreshment table. Henry stood with his usual frown, though a little softer tonight. Maia was mid-story, hands moving as she talked.

"Henry runs a security business," Saber added to Sienna as they walked over. "They're expanding. Part-time work. Not farming, but worth a look."

"Henry, Maia," Saber called. "You remember Liam? This is his girlfriend, Sienna Teague."

The introductions were warm and immediate. Henry had a firm handshake and a direct gaze, while Maia's sunshiny enthusiasm was infectious.

"Saber mentioned you're looking for work," Henry said. "Security isn't for everyone, but if you're interested in learning something new, Gerard and I could use someone reliable."

"What kind of security?" Liam asked.

"Mostly residential and small business. Some event work during the tourist season. It's part-time to start, but there's room to grow if you like it."

"I'm interested," Liam said after a glance at Sienna.

"Excellent. Actually," Henry continued, "Saber also mentioned you two might be looking for accommodation?"

"Possibly," Liam said, his hand tightening around Sienna's.

Maia jumped in. "I have a house to rent—three bedrooms, fully furnished, great location. I've had some interest, though."

"Could we see it?" Sienna asked, eagerness lighting her smile.

"How about tomorrow morning? Does that work for you? Fair warning—we have another couple viewing it in the afternoon, and the housing market in Middlemarch is pretty tight right now. Good places don't stay available for long."

Liam and Sienna exchanged a look, and he saw her excitement reflected in her eyes.

"We'd love to see it," Liam said. "What time works for you?"

"How about ten?" Henry suggested. "I'll give you the address."

As Henry scribbled down the details, excitement surged through Liam. A house. A proper home. Together.

They spoke with Henry and Maia for a few more minutes before the couple excused themselves to mingle with other guests.

"Actually," Liam said once they were alone, "I booked a room at the new motel in town. I was hoping we'd have something to celebrate tonight."

Sienna's cheeks warmed, and he caught the spark in her features. He let his hand brush hers, just enough to make the contact linger.

"That was optimistic of you."

"I prefer hopeful," he said, grinning.

He pulled her closer, and the music faded behind them. Every brush of her hand, every sway of her body against his, carried a new weight, a promise that made his pulse quicken.

"One more dance?" he asked.

"One more," she said.

They moved together, feeling the rhythm in their own bodies rather than the band. He thought of the motel, of having her to himself, of the heat between them that made the world shrink to just this floor, this moment.

"Ready to get out of here?" he murmured in her ear.

"More than ready," she replied, and he felt it, a pull that was impossible to resist.

They found Kitto holding court with Scott's group, sketching caricatures on napkins as his audience laughed appreciatively.

"We're heading out," Sienna said. "Will you be all right getting home?"

"Scott said he'd give me a lift," Kitto replied with a wink. "Have fun."

"Thanks for trusting me with your sister," Liam said.

Kitto's grin widened. "Just don't mess it up."

"I won't."

They said quick goodbyes to Saber and Emily, who sent them off with knowing smiles and waves. Then they walked across the paddock toward the car park, Liam's hand warm in hers.

"The motel's on the other side of town," Liam said as they reached his borrowed truck.

"I know where it is." Sienna's voice was steady, but he heard the excitement beneath.

"Liam?"

"Yeah?"

"I'm nervous."

He stopped walking and turned to face her, his hands rising to cup her face. "We don't have to do anything. We can talk, or sleep, or—"

She silenced him with a kiss, pouring all her feelings into it, and he tasted love, desire, hope, and absolute certainty.

"I'm ready," she said when they stepped apart. "I've been ready for months, but I'm nervous."

"Me too," he said, smiling. "Because it matters."

They drove through Middlemarch's quiet streets, hands linked across the console. Liam parked outside unit seven and came around to open her door.

"Still nervous?" he asked.

"Yeah," she admitted. "But excited too."

He unlocked the door and held it open. Mussed hair, a red dress glowing in the corridor light—she stole his breath all over again. Her gaze met his, full of trust and anticipation, and for a moment he forgot everything else.

CHAPTER 28

THE DOOR CLICKED SHUT behind them with a finality that sent heat coursing through Sienna's veins. The room wasn't fancy—beige walls, a queen bed with a floral comforter, and a small table by the window overlooking the car park. But the lamp cast everything in warm, golden light, and a bottle of champagne waited in an ice bucket on the dresser.

"You planned this." She took in the champagne and the rose petals scattered across the bedspread.

Her throat tightened. No one had ever done something so deliberately romantic for her before—silly, over-the-top, and perfect.

"I booked it this morning and asked the desk for a few extras." His gaze caught hers, dark and intent. "I didn't want tonight to be ordinary."

They stood facing each other in the soft lamplight, the weight of months apart and exchanged letters settling between them. The air crackled with possibility.

"Second thoughts?" Liam's voice dropped lower than usual, rough with want.

"About you? Never." She stepped closer, her hands finding the lapels of his jacket, his heart hammering beneath her palms. "About taking so long to get here? Definitely."

His laugh rumbled low and warm. "We made it tonight."

"We did." She pushed his jacket off his shoulders, letting it fall to the floor. "And I've been dreaming about this for months. Every night. Every morning. Sometimes in the middle of the day when I should've been working and thinking about honey."

"Only dreaming?" His hands settled on her waist, thumbs brushing over the silk of her red dress, the heat of his touch burning through the thin fabric.

She tugged at his tie, fingers fumbling with the knot. "God, Liam, do you know what you've done to me? I've never wanted anyone the way I want you."

"Sienna." Her name came out as a growl. He backed her against the door, caging her with his arms. "You think you're the only one who's been going crazy? I've jerked off to your letters so many times the pages have become worn."

Heat pooled low in her belly at his confession. "Show me. Show me what you imagined."

He kissed her then, with nothing gentle about it. The kiss was teeth and tongue and raw hunger. She moaned into his mouth, her hips pressing forward, seeking friction. When he lifted her against the door, her legs wrapped around his waist instinctively, her dress riding up her thighs.

"Fuck," he ground out against her mouth. Even through their clothes, his hardness pressed insistently against her.

SHELLEY MUNRO

"You're perfect. I've been fantasizing about this, about you."

"The bed." Sienna tilted her head, and his mouth found her throat, sucking hard enough to mark. "Please, I need—"

"Tell me exactly what you need." He carried her across the room, still kissing her neck, her jaw, anywhere he could reach.

"You, inside me. Filling me. Making me forget my name."

He set her on the edge of the bed, standing between her spread thighs. His hands slid to the zipper of her dress, but he paused, gaze meeting hers.

"I've missed you." His voice broke with emotion. "Not only this. You. Hearing your voice in the morning. Your laugh when one of your brothers is being an idiot. The way you bite your lip when you're thinking."

"I've missed your hands." She guided them to her breasts. "The way you touch me...like I matter. Like I'm precious." She sighed. "Like I'm yours."

"You are mine." His thumbs circled her nipples through the silk. "And I'm going to spend all night proving it."

The zipper whispered down, and he peeled the red silk away slowly, revealing the black lace beneath. His sharp intake of breath made her shiver.

"Christ, Sienna." His hands skimmed over the delicate fabric, fingers tracing the edge where lace met skin. "You wore this for me?"

"I bought it thinking of you." She arched into his touch. "And I imagined you taking it off me with your teeth."

He dropped to his knees between her thighs, pressing his face to her stomach, breathing her in. "I've been thinking about tasting you for months. Some mornings I woke up with your scent in my memory, and it drove me insane."

274

His mouth moved lower, teeth catching the edge of her panties, and she whimpered. But instead of removing them, he pressed his mouth against her through the lace, his tongue finding her clit with unerring accuracy.

"Oh God." Her fingers tangled in his hair. "Liam, please—"

"Please what?" He looked up at her, gaze dark with lust. "Tell me. I want to hear you say it."

"Lick me. Taste me. Make me come."

He tore her panties aside, not bothering to remove them properly. The first sweep of his tongue had her crying out, hips bucking against his face. He held her steady, one arm across her hips while his other hand slid two fingers inside her, curling perfectly.

"So wet." His words vibrated against her. "Is this all for me?"

"Keep touching me and find out."

He worked her with lips and tongue and fingers, alternating between gentle teasing and intense pressure, reading her body like a map he'd memorized. When her thighs began to shake, when she teetered on the edge, he pulled back.

"No, don't stop—"

"I want you to come around my cock the first time." He stood, yanking his shirt off, buttons scattering. "Need to be inside you when you fall apart."

She sat up, reaching for his belt. "My turn."

Her hands shook as she undid his pants, pushing them down along with his boxers. His cock sprang free, thick and hard, a bead of pre-cum at the tip. She leaned forward, catching it with her tongue, and his entire body shuddered.

"Sienna—"

She took him deep, relaxing her throat, swallowing around

him. His hands fisted in her hair, not pushing, holding on like she was anchoring him to earth.

"So hot. I'm not going to last if you keep—"

She pulled off with a wet pop, looking up at him through her lashes. "Then take me. Now. I can't wait anymore."

He reached for the drawer, tearing open a condom packet with unsteady hands. She helped him roll it on, their fingers tangling together, both frantic with need.

When he pushed inside her, they both stilled, breath caught in their throats. The connection was electric—every nerve ending in her body alive, every inch of contact perfect. He stretched her, filling her, and his body vibrated with the effort of holding still.

"You're..." He buried his face in her neck, breathing raggedly. "Sienna. You're home."

She rolled her hips, taking him deeper and urgently seeking more. "Then come home. Hard. Don't hold back."

Liam snapped. His control shattered as he drove into her, setting a rhythm that had her crying out with each thrust. She met him stroke for stroke, nails raking down his back, marking him as hers.

"Harder." Her voice broke on the word. "I want to remember this tomorrow. I want the ache to remind me."

He flipped her onto her stomach, pulling her hips up, and thrust back in from behind. The angle was devastating, hitting spots that made her see stars. She groaned.

"Like this?" He punctuated the question with a deep thrust.

"Yes! God, yes, right there—"

One hand slid around to her clit, rubbing in tight circles while he pounded into her. The dual sensation overwhelmed her, and she came with a scream, her body clenching around his length, waves of pleasure so intense they bordered on pain.

Two strokes later, he followed her over, her name torn from his throat as he pulsed inside her, his body shaking with release.

They collapsed together, sweaty and breathless. But even as they recovered, his hands kept moving over her skin, relearning every curve.

"I love you." His voice came out hoarse. "Should've told you months ago."

She turned to face him. "You're everything to me, Liam. Everything I never thought I could have."

They kissed, slow and deep, and he hardened against her thigh again.

"Again?" But she was already spreading her legs, inviting him in.

"I've got months to make up for." He slid down her body. "And I plan to be thorough."

He took his time, mapping every inch of her with his mouth. He found spots she didn't know were sensitive—the inside of her elbow, the dip of her waist, the back of her knee. By the time he settled between her thighs again, she writhed beneath him, incoherent with need.

"Please," she begged. "I need—"

"Shhh, I've got you." He licked into her slowly, savoring, while his fingers worked her open. When he added a third finger, stretching her, she keened.

"You're so responsive. So perfect. I could do this for hours."

"I'll die. You're going to kill me."

"No, you won't." He sucked her clit into his mouth, lashing it with his tongue. "You're going to come for me again. And again. Until you can't remember anything but my name."

He was true to his word. He brought her to the edge and back, over and over, until tears streamed down her face and she sobbed with need. Only then did he grab a condom and slide back up her body, entering her in one smooth thrust.

"Look at me. I want to see your beautiful eyes when you come."

She forced her eyes open, meeting his intense gaze. He moved slowly, deliberately, each thrust measured to hit exactly where she needed. When he reached between them to touch her clit, her orgasm crashed through her in pulsating waves.

He kissed her through it, swallowing her cries, his own release following moments later.

Later, she straddled him, riding him slow and deep, her breasts bouncing with each movement. His hands gripped her hips hard enough to bruise, and she loved it, loved the evidence of his desire.

"You're beautiful." His voice sounded wrecked. "Look at you, taking me so well. Made for me."

She leaned down, changing the angle, and they both made broken sounds. "Made for each other." She bit his shoulder hard enough to leave a red mark.

He shuddered hard and then flipped them, driving into her with renewed vigor. "Mine," he punctuated each thrust. "Mine, mine, mine."

"Yours." She grinned wickedly. "And you're mine. My captive, remember?"

He laughed, breathless. "Always."

They lost count of how many times they came together that night, exploring every position, every fantasy they'd harbored during their separation. When dawn finally broke through the curtains, their limbs tangled together, both thoroughly debauched and deliriously happy.

"Morning, beautiful." His voice was rough from sleep and overuse.

"Morning yourself." She stretched, delicious aches blooming in muscles she'd forgotten she had. Between her thighs, heat swelled and sensitivity lingered, evidence of their night together.

"Sore?"

"Mmm, the best kind." She traced the scratch marks on his back. "You?"

"Battle scars. I'll wear them with honor."

They ordered coffee and pastries from the motel's continental breakfast service, eating in bed with Liam wearing only his boxer shorts and Sienna wrapped in his dress shirt from the night before. She kept shifting her weight, hyperaware of how the fabric brushed against her sensitive skin.

"I texted Kitto earlier." She glanced at her phone. "He's dropping off some clothes for me—jeans and a sweater. Can't exactly view a house in a ball gown. Not unless we're buying a castle."

"Shame." Liam's hand slid up her bare thigh under the shirt. "You look good in my clothes. We might need to make that a habit."

His fingers found her still-wet center, and her breath hitched, immediately ready again despite the soreness.

"We have to meet Henry and Maia," she protested weakly.

"We have twenty minutes." He pulled her onto his lap. "I

279

can do a lot in twenty minutes."

He proved it too, bringing her to a swift, intense orgasm with his fingers alone while she muffled her cries against his shoulder.

When Kitto knocked on the door with her clothes, she answered it on shaky legs, her face flushed and her lips swollen.

"Not one word," she warned as she took the bag.

"Wouldn't dream of it." His knowing smirk said everything. "Good luck house hunting."

Once dressed in her own clothes again—denim snug on her hips, sweater soft and familiar—she steadied herself, though every step reminded her of the night before, a secret thrill that made her press her thighs together.

"Ready to go look at our potential home?" Liam's hand rested possessively on her lower back.

Our home. The words sent a different heat through her, warm and lasting. "Let's do it."

Henry and Maia were waiting on the verandah when they arrived, warm smiles and coffee cups in hand.

The little house stood bathed in sunlight, cheerful orange marigolds edging the path that led to the front steps. Painted white with pale green accents, it wasn't grand, but it had soul. A broad verandah curved around two sides, inviting lazy mornings, evening drinks, and everything in between.

"I loved sitting out here with my morning coffee when I lived here," Maia said, catching Sienna's lingering gaze.

Sienna felt Liam's fingers brush hers before sliding into a steady grip, their hands interlocking like it was second nature.

"We're looking forward to seeing the interior," he said.

The home was light and welcoming. The kitchen gleamed

with whitewashed cupboards and a deep farmhouse sink, the scent of lemon polish lingering in the air. A sturdy wooden table sat beneath the window, perfectly positioned for family breakfasts or lingering over coffee. From the main hallway, a sun-drenched room caught Sienna's attention. Large windows framed the rolling hills dotted with ancient schist rock outcrops, the rugged landscape typical of Middlemarch. Clusters of native trees stood scattered against the distant mountains, their silhouettes sharp against the sky.

She ran her hand along the windowsill. "Look at all this light."

Liam came up behind her. "This would be perfect for Kitto," he said. "If he wants to live with us."

She turned toward him, surprised—and deeply touched.

"You think he'd want to?" she asked.

"He's your family. And I'd like him around. It already feels like he's part of the package."

Emotion swelled in her chest. She pursed her lips, nodded once, then looked back out at the view, blinking fast.

The bedrooms were simple but spacious. Sienna could already picture one with Kitto's paint-streaked jeans draped over a chair and canvases stacked against the wall.

Beyond the house, an expansive lawn unfurled toward paddocks, where a handful of alpacas grazed in the distance.

"Felix Mitchell rents the land," Henry explained. "Quiet neighbors, unless it's shearing day."

Sienna smiled. "This lawn could become a veggie garden. Fresh herbs, tomatoes, beans."

"The soil's excellent," Maia said. "I always meant to plant one, but playing rugby doesn't leave me much time."

Henry gave Liam a knowing look. "Sounds like a job for you. Speaking of which, have you thought any more about that part-time role? Gerard and I need someone reliable, and the hours leave room for you to explore other options."

Liam didn't answer right away. He glanced at Sienna, and she saw the shift in his expression—something steady and sure.

"I have," he said. "And I'm interested."

They stepped back inside for one last look while Henry and Maia settled on the verandah with their refreshed coffees.

"What do you think?" Liam asked, though she could hear it in his voice. He'd already decided this opportunity would work for him. For them both.

"I think six months ago, you would've said no to any job that didn't involve farming," she said. "And I would've panicked if you did."

"And now?"

"Now I believe in us and in taking risks."

He laced his fingers through hers. "I used to think that work was everything. But it's not." His gaze swept the little house before returning to her. "This is what matters. A new job, new skills. None of it means anything if we're apart. I want to stay here with you."

Sienna smiled, feeling peace settle inside her. This wasn't just a house. It was the beginning of home.

They looked at each other for a long beat. Then, in perfect unison, they said, "We'll take it."

Henry grinned. "Excellent! I was hoping you'd say that. Maia never admits it, but she's been rooting for you two since she heard your story."

"What story?" Sienna asked, instantly on alert.

"Nothing dramatic," Maia said. "Just that you're new to Middlemarch and seem like lovely people. Local gossip."

The paperwork was surprisingly straightforward—first month's rent, a security deposit, and a simple lease agreement. When Maia mentioned they could move in within the week, a sharp flicker of excitement shot through Sienna.

"I'll need to finish my contract with Cam first," Liam said. "Two more months in the Mackenzie country."

"I'll start moving our things in," Sienna replied. "Get it ready for when you return."

Liam tapped on the doorway of the sunroom. "The office room will be perfect for Kitto's studio. He deserves a space of his own."

"He'd love that," Sienna said. "Emily and Saber have been amazing, but I think he's ready for a fresh start." She paused. "I know I am."

As they walked back to the car, the keys to their new place jingling in Sienna's pocket, Liam halted and held her close.

She laughed. "What?"

He spun her once, grinning. "Just realizing we're really doing this. House, jobs, figuring out a life."

"Scared?" she asked once he set her down.

"Terrified. And positive it's what I want."

"Good." She rose on her toes to kiss him. "Because you're stuck with me now."

"Forever?"

She winked. "If fortune favors you."

"I'm the luckiest man alive," he said, his gaze glinting with sincerity.

As they drove back toward town, the hills swallowed the

view of their new home. Sienna shifted in her seat, aware of the pleasant ache between her thighs, the tender spots where Liam had marked her.

"You okay?" Liam noticed her subtle movement.

"Perfect." She caught his hand and brought it to her lips.

His eyes darkened. "Wait until we have our own place. Our own bed. No more months apart."

"Promises, promises," she teased, but her body already responded to the heat in his voice.

Home wasn't a place. It was this: the man beside her who'd worshipped her body all night, the road ahead full of possibility, and the certainty that whatever came next, they'd face it together—preferably naked and tangled in their own sheets.

Chapter 29

Two months later.

Liam had called once he reached Tekapo, promising to be in Middlemarch by early evening.

"Stop fussing," Kitto said, watching Sienna rearrange the roses again. "He's coming here for you, not your flower arrangements. Though, okay, they look beautiful—please don't throw a cushion at me."

Sienna smiled despite herself until she noticed the bag slung over Kitto's shoulder. "Where are you going?"

"Emily and Saber's. I'm babysitting the twins while they sneak off for a romantic weekend. Very strategic, if you ask me." His ears twitched with mischief. "Emily said you and Liam might want the house to yourselves."

"Oh." Hard to argue, considering everything Emily and Saber had done for them.

"I'm heading to the shop first to frame some prints. See you tomorrow." Kitto grinned, pausing at the door.

"Middlemarch feels like home, but I miss Ma and Pa. Jago and Calan too, even if they are bossy pains."

"We see their ugly mugs once a week on video."

"Not the same. I miss the in-person chaos."

"Mama and Papa are happy in Scotland, and like keeping tabs on Stoneford through Niall. But Jago and Calan might visit."

"They're jealous," Kitto said, smug now. "Especially since I showed them my new commission and shiny red motorcycle."

After he left, the day dragged. Sienna checked the crockpot three times, rearranged the cushions twice, and paced from kitchen to front window more than she cared to admit. This felt like the beginning of everything she wanted, so naturally, her brain tried to sabotage it.

A knock came two hours earlier than expected.

Her stomach flipped. Her feline senses stretched, and her heart leaped.

"Liam!"

"I didn't stop for a break, and traffic was light," he said, gaze sweeping her from head to toe with a heat that made her shiver. "I couldn't wait."

His honesty and the blazing love in his expression dissolved her anxiety. She launched herself into his arms, and he caught her, embracing her tightly. Their kiss felt like home and the start of an adventure, and they didn't come up for air for a long time.

"I'm so glad to see you," Liam murmured, voice thick with emotion. "The mountains were stunning, but I kept wishing you were there."

"I missed you too," she laughed. "Kitto was ready to lock me outside for excessive pacing."

"Where is he?"

"Babysitting Emily and Saber's twins."

"Those two are pint-sized chaos. Saber and I used to barricade ourselves in the office."

"Kitto handles them like a pro. Emily calls him her secret weapon." She threaded her fingers through his. "Come inside. I want to hear everything and show you what we've done to make this place homey."

He didn't follow.

Instead, Liam scooped her into his arms.

"Liam!"

He grinned, boyish and bright. "I like traditions, so I'm carrying you over the threshold."

"We've already been here together."

"Not like this. The first time as..." He hesitated. "Partners—no, more than that."

Her heart melted, and she kissed his cheek. "Definitely more. And I love that you wanted to mark the occasion."

He carried her into the kitchen. Sunshine bathed the space, the rich scent of beef stew wafting from the crock pot and enveloping them.

"Smells amazing," he said, cupping her face and kissing her slowly. When they parted, both were breathless. "I love you, Sienna."

"And I am so in love with you. Even when you're early and mess with my perfectly timed dinner."

Peace settled over her. This was right.

"Now," she said, stepping back reluctantly, "tell me about the mountains while I finish dinner."

Liam leaned against the counter, words tumbling out as he described Cam's station—the endless views, the braided silver rivers, and the sunrise over snow-dusted peaks.

"Some mornings, I'd shift and run the ridgelines. You can see for miles. Cam wants to meet you. He says any woman who can survive a kidnapping and still land on her feet is welcome at his table."

"You told him about that?"

"I talked about you all the time. All the men know how incredible you are. How you saved a child from hunters, built a life here, and run a business. You're a legend."

Warmth bloomed in her chest. "I'm not the same woman who went to the Scottish gathering."

"No, you're stronger. You know who you are now."

"So do you. You're not lost anymore."

He smiled, brushing a thumb across her hand. "I'm exactly where I belong. With you."

The crock pot chimed, and they laughed softly together.

"Perfect timing," she said, leaning into him.

"There's one more thing," he murmured, voice thick with desire. "What happens tonight?"

"Dinner and wine," she teased, eyes sparkling. "Then I'll show you what Kitto and I did to the house. And after that..."

"After that," he whispered, closing the space between them, "I'll take you to our room and show you how much I missed you."

Her breath caught. A flush crept over her skin, heat coiling low in her belly. "Sounds perfect."

"I have long-term plans, sweetheart."

"Oh?"

"The kind where I mark you, so every shifter in three provinces knows you're mine. And you do the same to me."

She trembled, slick heat coiling at his words. *"Liam."*

He stepped back with effort. "But first, dinner. I want to do this right. Tonight should be perfect."

"It already is. We're together."

They moved around the kitchen in sync, Liam pouring wine while she served their beef stew and mashed potatoes. It was a domestic rhythm that seemed instantly natural.

"To new beginnings," Liam said, raising his glass.

"To finding our way home," Sienna replied.

Later, they washed dishes side by side, hips bumping, laughter soft and warm.

"Ready to see what we've done?" she asked.

She showed him the living room with Kitto's painted Cornish border, framed photos from Cornwall, Scotland, and Middlemarch, and two of her father's signature blue-and-white pottery pieces.

"It feels like us," Liam said, running a hand over the mantel. "Like our story."

"That was the goal. So you'd know you belong here too."

In the spare room, she showed him Kitto's desk by the north-facing window.

"He's finding his place," Liam said.

"He talks about moving out eventually, but for now we're family."

"And families give each other space to grow."

She stopped at their bedroom door. "Ready to see our room?"

His response was to kiss the spot just below her ear.

She pushed open the door to a softly lit room. Tamsin's Cornish blue and cream quilt lay on the bed, sheer curtains glowing silver with moonlight. The air held a faint trace of lavender and beeswax, and from outside came the distant rustle of wind through the trees.

"Perfect," Liam murmured, though his focus had already shifted to her.

"I was nervous," she admitted. "About living together, about whether we'd—"

He silenced her with a kiss, passionate and consuming. "I was too. But I want this. You. All of it."

"Then what are we waiting for?"

This time, their kiss held nothing back. It was deep, hungry, and laced with months of built-up need. Every letter he'd written, every restless night she'd endured, every fantasy neither had dared say aloud—they all poured into the collision of their mouths and bodies. His leopard prowled beneath his skin, and hers rose to meet it, their beasts recognizing what their human sides had fought for so long.

Clothes disappeared in a frenzy, fabric tearing under fingers that shifted between human and claw. When her bare skin met his, the contact sent shockwaves through them both.

"God, Sienna," Liam groaned against her throat, his voice caught between man and beast. "Your scent is driving me wild."

She arched into him, her leopard purring audibly. "I missed you, and it was even worse once we'd made love. I understood exactly what I was missing."

He backed her toward the bed, worshipping every curve—cupping her breasts, stroking down her back, and coming to rest on her backside. His touch left a trail of fire on her skin. She could see his control fraying in the tremor of his fingers, in the way his eyes flickered between human blue-green and leopard intensity.

"Mine," he growled, and the word vibrated through her bones.

"Prove it," she challenged, nipping at his jaw hard enough to leave a mark.

He scooped her up and deposited her on the bed, the quilt cover cool against her overheated back. His mouth found her breast, teeth grazing the peak before soothing with his tongue. The dual sensation made her cry out, her nails—half-shifted to claws—raked down his shoulders.

"Please," she panted, rolling her hips against him. "I need—"

"I know what you need." His hand slipped between them, fingers finding her slick and ready. "So wet for me, sweetheart. Your body knows who it belongs to."

She keened at his touch, her inner muscles clenching around his fingers as he worked her. "Liam, I can't—I need you inside me now."

He grabbed a condom, and when he sank into her at last, they both went still. Gazes locked. Breathing ragged. The connection between them snapped taut, binding them beyond the physical. Their leopards recognized their mates, and the recognition sang through their blood.

"Finally," she breathed.

Then they moved, finding a rhythm that spoke of desperation and a homecoming. She met him thrust for thrust, her body welcoming him deeper with each roll of her hips. The air grew thick with sweat and breathy moans, with the sound of skin against skin and whispered endearments that turned filthy and sweet by turns.

He changed angles, hitting a spot that made her see stars. "There," she gasped, her legs tightening around him. "Right there, don't stop."

"Never stopping," he promised, his control fraying. "I intend to fill you up, mark you inside and out. Everyone will know you're mine."

The possessive words sent her higher. Her climax built like a storm in her bones. His mouth found her throat, tongue tracing where her pulse hammered.

"Do it," she whispered. "I want to wear your mark where everyone can see."

He froze above her, his blue-green eyes glowing with gold tinges. "Sienna, sweetheart. It'll hurt."

"Good," she said, clenching around him and watching his control shatter. "I want the pain. The proof. I need you to claim me."

His breath caught, then he growled—a guttural sound that resonated in her core. He pressed her wrists to the bed, pinning her beneath him, and licked the spot he planned to bite. The gesture was pure leopard, and it made her inner cat purr.

"Together," he said, voice gravel. "We claim each other."

"Together," she echoed, baring her neck even as she prepared to mark him in return.

Their bites came at the same time—his canines piercing her skin as hers sank into the corded muscle where his neck met his shoulder. The pain was white-hot, catapulting them both over the edge. Sienna screamed her release, her body seizing around him as waves of pleasure crashed through her. He pulsed inside her, his climax triggered by hers, filling her with heat as he shuddered above her.

They clung to each other, gasping and trembling as pain blurred into ecstasy. Sex and satisfaction saturated the air, the coppery tang of blood coated their tongues, and the musk of a successful mating swirled around them.

He licked the mark he'd left, soothing the sting. The gesture sent aftershocks through her, making her whimper and clutch at him.

"Mine," he whispered, voice wrecked.

"Yours," she said, lips brushing the mark she'd given him. "And you're mine. Forever."

They weren't done. Their leopards demanded more, and their human sides were greedy. He was already hardening inside her again, and she rolled them over, straddling him with a wicked smile.

"My turn," she purred, and began to move.

Later—much later—Sienna lay curled against his chest, her body satiated and tingling. She traced the fresh mark on Liam's neck—warm, swollen, and pulsing with their bond. The moment her fingertips brushed the bite, a ragged breath escaped him, his body responding to her touch.

"Careful," he warned, voice rough. "Keep that up, and we won't sleep at all tonight."

"Promise?" she teased, but let her hand fall to his chest.

She traced patterns on his skin, marveling that he was here and was hers. When she touched her own mark, sharp pain mixed with an echo of pleasure made her breath catch. The bond between them thrummed, connecting them in ways she'd never imagined.

"How do you feel?" she asked into the darkness.

His arms tightened around her. "Complete. Like everything before this was waiting for you."

She smiled, eyes closing, until he kissed her temple.

"Sienna? Will you marry me?"

"Are you asking because we're mated now?"

"No." His hand smoothed over her ribs. "Because I want the universe to know you chose me. Human law, shifter law, every law that exists. I've had the ring in my bag since before I left. I bought it in Tekapo after you wrote me that letter about the break-in, when you said you impressed yourself with your own strength."

Her throat tightened. "That long?"

"That's when I knew. You weren't merely surviving anymore. You were thriving and ready for the next step. We were both ready."

Emotion clawed up her throat, sharp and hot. "Yes! Yes, I'll marry you."

His grin was everything—joyful and disbelieving and stunned. "Good. Because I had no backup plan if you said no."

She laughed. "The ring can wait until tomorrow. I'm not letting you out of this bed."

"We have forever," he said, pulling her closer beneath the quilt. "And I plan to spend every minute showing you how much you mean to me."

As they drifted toward sleep, wrapped in love and moonlight and the scent of each other, Sienna knew whatever came next—weddings, land, building their life together—they'd face it side by side.

They had found their way home to each other. And they

weren't going anywhere.

Their leopards purred in agreement, at peace. Sienna pressed closer, breathing Liam in, and smiled against his chest as his arms tightened around her one last time before sleep claimed them both.

About Author

USA Today bestselling author Shelley Munro lives in Auckland, the City of Sails, with her husband and a cheeky Jack Russell/mystery breed dog.

Typical New Zealanders, Shelley and her husband left home for their big OE soon after they married (translation of New Zealand speak - big overseas experience). A twelve-month-long adventure lengthened to six years of roaming the world. Enduring memories include being almost sat on by a mountain gorilla in Rwanda, lazing on white sandy beaches in India, whale watching in Alaska, searching for leprechauns in Ireland, and dealing with ghosts in an English pub.

While travel is still a big attraction, these days Shelley is most likely found in front of her computer following another love - that of writing stories of contemporary and paranormal romance and adventure. Other interests include watching rugby (strictly for research purposes), cycling, playing croquet and the ukelele, and curling up with an enjoyable book.

Visit Shelley at her website.
https://shelleymunro.com/

Sign Up for Shelley's Newsletter
https://shelleymunro.com/newsletter/

ALSO BY SHELLEY

Paranormal

Middlemarch Shifters
My Scarlet Woman
My Younger Lover
My Peeping Tom
My Assassin
My Estranged Lover
My Feline Protector
My Determined Suitor
My Cat Burglar
My Stray Cat
My Second Chance
My Plan B
My Cat Nap
My Romantic Tangle
My Blue Lady

My Twin Trouble
My Precious Gift
My Grumpy Wolf

Middlemarch Gathering
My Highland Mate
My Highland Fling
My Elusive Mate
My Valiant Princess
My Highland Wedding
My Highland Billionaire

Dragon Investigators
Blue Moon Dragon
Blood Moon Dragon
Black Moon Dragon
Snow Moon Dragon

Dragon Isles
Liza
Cherry
Rena
Sasha